Eldene Ana McGrady

Tragedy, Adventure, and a New Beginning

Melvin L. Edwards

ISBN 978-1-63844-782-5 (paperback)
ISBN 978-1-63844-784-9 (hardcover)
ISBN 978-1-63844-783-2 (digital)

Christian Faith Publishing, Inc.
832 Park Avenue
Meadville, PA 16335
www.christianfaithpublishing.com

Printed in the United States of America

Chapter 1

Tragedy Strikes

It was a typical January morning in Baltimore, Maryland. The year is 1848, and Baltimore is the largest seaport south of New York. The sun was barely peaking over the horizon, and fog was hanging over the harbor. It was cold and damp. The moisture was freezing on the trees and shrubs, and there were glassy puddles of frozen water, formed from rain the evening before. From the incline that the McGrady's property is located on above the harbor, you can see the rows of sails from the many cargo ships anchored in Chesapeake Bay, peeking through the fog, waiting for their turn to off-load or load their shipments.

Jake and Eldene McGrady live about a mile from the docks where he is a partner in a company that furnishes labor and equipment to load and unload barges and ships.

They grew up together near the town of Frederick, where Eldene's dad owns a lumber mill. There were from sixteen to twenty children, from first to twelfth grade, in the small school that they attended. There was just a one-year difference in their ages, and by the time they were ready to go on to college, they were inseparable. Eldene knew that she wanted to spend the rest of her life as Jake's wife.

Jake McGrady got up early, as usual, to go to work.

"Breakfast is ready, dear," called Eldene.

"Good morning, beautiful," he said as he gave her a loving good morning kiss.

"Good morning, you smell good this morning." She loved the musky scent of the cologne he used after shaving. Jake is a tall handsome man. Eldene loved his muscular six-foot-two-inch frame and the way his reddish-brown hair makes his appealing blue eyes sparkle with life. She loved to put her arms around him and snuggle as she enjoyed his aroma.

Jake smiled and sat down at the table and started drinking his nice hot cup of coffee as Eldene set the table. This morning she had fixed his favorite breakfast, eggs and biscuits covered with a layer of thick sausage gravy. Jake loves the way that Eldene makes biscuits. They were always so fluffy and light and browned to perfection. The gravy is creamy and thick, and the sausage is just spicy enough to make it tasty and fulfilling. He likes his eggs over medium with a little extra pepper. Jake looked at Eldene and realized how much he admires and loves her. She is the love of his life, and he adores her sparkly, bubbly personality. Her gorgeous long soft auburn, hair hangs down over her perfectly rounded shoulders and frames her beautiful face, causing her hazel eyes to capture your attention. Her smile is enhanced by a line of gorgeous white teeth. Eldene is beautiful, feisty, and sassy, with an Irish temper that flares when provoked. She is five feet six inches tall, and her perfect figure makes her a very attractive woman. She has an outgoing positive attitude and loves adventure and the outdoors. She likes to explore and relishes a good challenge.

"Wear your heavier coat today, dear," she said as he walked over to the coatrack near the front door.

"Okay, Mother," Jake said jokingly. "What would I do without you?" He chuckled.

Eldene walked over to him and put her arms around his neck and gave him a long sensual kiss on the lips and said, "You would be lost, my dear. You would be lost."

"You're absolutely right, sweetheart," he said as he finished putting on his warmer coat.

Jake waved as he walked out of the front door into a very cold crisp morning. "Goodbye, my love, I'll see you after work."

The fog laid over the harbor like a flannel blanket covering a feather bed. Jake doesn't live to far from the docks, so he likes to walk to work. He could see his breath as he walked along the street toward the harbor. Jake heard a commotion behind him and turned to see what was going on. He saw a large freight wagon coming straight for him. It was out of control and moving too fast. Jake tried to jump out of the way, but his feet slipped on the ice, and he fell in front of the wagon. He was trampled by the horses and ran over by the wagon. Jake never felt them hit him; he was killed almost instantly. By the time the driver got the wagon stopped and the horses under control, it was too late to do anything.

Eldene heard the ruckus and knew that something bad had happened. She grabbed her coat and bolted out of the door with her mind in a panic. She ran down the street, trying not to slip on the icy road, when she saw the dark figure lying on the street. A lump formed in her throat as she approached the lifeless figure.

"Jake, oh my god, Jake!" she yelled as she ran toward him. She fell to her knees beside the figure. She could tell it was Jake by the smell of his cologne. "Please, God, please let him be alive!" He was lying in a pool of blood and barely recognizable. She put her ear near his nose and mouth and tried to hear his breathing, but there was nothing. She couldn't see his breath or feel any signs of life. She knew that Jake was dead. She was still kneeling beside him, in a trance, as help finally came. They had to physically remove her so that they could get to Jake.

Eldene heard someone say, "It's Jake McGrady! He's dead!"

Jake's lifeless body was lifted onto a buckboard while Eldene watched, in disbelief, as they drove off with his battered body.

Eldene walked home, in a daze, and sat on the porch, staring at the street. She knew that Taylor and Patty would be coming down the stairs, ready for breakfast, and she would have to tell them that their father had just been killed. She mustered up all of the strength that she could and went into the house. She poured herself a cup of coffee and sat down to wait for the kids.

As Taylor and Patty came down the stairs, they were laughing and joking with each other as usual.

"Come on, slowpoke, we're going to be late for school," Taylor said as he hurried Patty down the stairs.

Taylor James McGrady, at fifteen and a half years old, stands six feet tall and is muscular, like his father. He has reddish-brown hair and blue eyes that sparkle with mischief. He is handsome, happy, rugged, and confident with an outgoing positive personality.

"It's your fault, you big dummy," answered Patty. "You took so long in the privy." She stuck out her tongue and hurried down behind him.

They saw Eldene sitting at the table. Tears were running down her cheeks.

"What's the matter, Mom?"

Eldene looked up and burst out crying uncontrollably.

"Mommy, Mommy, what's wrong? Did something happen?" They sat down at the table, wondering what was going on.

Taylor reached over and cupped his mom's hands in his and asked again, "Mom, what is it? What's wrong? Has something happened to Daddo or Nana?"

Eldene finally began collecting her senses, and after a few minutes, she was able to tell them what had happened. Taylor just sat there with a look of disbelief on his face.

Patty began sobbing and saying, "No, it's not possible. He can't be dead! Please, God, he can't be dead. What will I do without my Daddy? He just can't be dead."

Fourteen-and-a-half-year-old Patricia Ana McGrady, born just eleven months after Taylor, is pretty and feisty, like her mother. She has auburn hair and hazel eyes that sparkle with life. She is a shapely beautiful young lady with a great sense of humor and is well liked by her family and friends.

Taylor, not knowing what else to do, hugged both his mom and sister while trying to be strong.

He said, "We'll get through this." But his heart was aching, and he couldn't hold back the tears. They stood there in a huddle for a while, sobbing and trying to console one another.

The next few days were difficult to get through. Eldene had to make all of the funeral arrangements and notify family and their many friends. It was very difficult for her to explain each time without tearing up.

"I have such an empty lost feeling, like a piece of my heart has been torn from my chest," she said, talking to herself and pacing the floor. "I just wish this whole week would be over with so that I can figure out just what I am going to do without Jake. Oh, dear god, what am I going to do?"

She began thinking about them growing up together. "I am going to be so lost without him." She put her head in her hands and began sobbing. "Jake, oh Jake, my dear sweet Jake, I miss you so much. You were my rock, how can I possibly go on without you?"

Not long after they were married, they were expecting their first child. Jake continued on and finished college with a degree in business.

"Thanks to you, Mom, and CJ, I have been able to keep myself together and get through it all in one piece. I feel very blessed to have such a caring mom and sister."

Taylor was being very brave and took charge whenever he could.

Patty was doing her best to keep herself calm and help out. She was missing her daddy very much and was having a hard time keeping her emotions from taking over. She walked around in a daze most of the time.

"I feel like I'm going to fall apart," she talked to herself as she felt tears welling up. "If it wasn't for Mommy and Taylor, I would fall to pieces."

She also had a very special relationship with her aunt CJ and her nana and daddo. Everyone was being supportive and compassionate.

The next few days after the funeral were a little hectic as Eldene started getting her affairs in order. Taylor and Patty were back in school, and she kept herself as busy as possible so she wouldn't have to think too much. She would break out in tears several times during the day, so to keep herself busy, she was doing a lot of things that she really didn't need to do. It was very hard for her to imagine being without Jake. He was a great dad and a very devoted loving husband.

It was the middle of January, and Eldene was sitting in her dress shop, staring out of the window and feeling that she didn't want to be there anymore. After Taylor was born, she borrowed money from her dad and mom to open a fabric and dress shop. She has been very successful, but she was getting burned out.

Talking to herself, she said, "I have no regrets over buying the dress shop, but I don't want to be here any longer."

I have to make a decision about my half of the labor business that I've inherited, thought Eldene. *I was never a part of the business, and I know very little about it. I have to decide if I want to try and sell my half to Jake's longtime partner or try to learn the business and run my part.*

Jake was responsible for the equipment and loading of delivery wagons, while Dan, Jake's partner, is responsible for the labor to load and unload ships and barges.

Sometimes their employees were as many as two hundred people. The employees were mostly immigrants from Ireland, Germany, and Italy. Although there was a mix of nationalities, everyone worked well together for the most part. Jake and Dan were very fair with their workers. They received the best pay on the docks and were treated with respect. They all liked Jake and Dan.

"What in the world am I going to do with the dress shop if I decide to run Jake's business?" she pondered. "I wouldn't last a month on the docks. At least with the dress shop, I know what I'm doing. The dock business makes more money than I could ever make in the dress shop, but I am afraid that it will be too much to handle. I'm going to go talk to Dad and Mom. Oh my god, I'm talking to myself," she said, putting her hands on her cheeks. "I had better wake up and get busy."

After she closed the shop, she went home and told Taylor and Patty that she was going to see her dad and mom.

"What's going on?" Taylor asked. "Can we go with you?"

"No," explained Eldene, "I don't want you to miss school. I'll be back in a couple of days. I just need to talk to Daddo and Nana about some things that are bothering me. I'll explain everything when I return."

"Mommy," exclaimed Patty, "you shouldn't be traveling alone that far! We should go with you."

"I'll be just fine, honey, don't be such a worrywart."

"I just don't want anything to happen to you, Mommy. I couldn't live without you."

Eldene realized that Patty was still grieving, as she was. She put her arms around her and said, "I love you, sweetheart, and I'll never leave you. You can stay with Aunt CJ while I'm gone. CJ only lives a few houses away, and you won't have to miss any school."

"What about me?" asked Taylor. "I'll be here all alone?"

"You're a big boy, and someone has to feed the livestock and gather the eggs," she commented as she made a gesture toward the small barn behind the house. "I want you to tell Joe, the milkman, to cut the milk order in half and be sure to be here when Billy delivers the ice for the icebox tomorrow, after school. We should keep the stove burning so the house won't be so cold. If you stoke it with coal and turn the damper down, it should last until you get home from school," she said as she pointed toward the large wood heater in the living room.

"Okay, Mom, you can count on me to take care of things." He felt proud that his mom trusts him. "I won't let you down."

The next morning, Taylor got up early, went to the barn, harnessed the horse, and hooked up the buckboard.

When Eldene got up, the buckboard was parked in front of the house, and the horse was tethered to the hitching rail. Taylor was cooking bacon and eggs and setting the table for breakfast.

"Good morning, Mom," he said as he set a cup of coffee down on the table. "Breakfast is almost ready."

"My goodness, you're up early this morning," she said as she put sugar and cream in her coffee.

"Yep," he exclaimed, "I want you to get an early start."

Patty came down the stairs, rubbing her eyes and yawning.

"Are you leaving already?" she said as she stretched her arms and continued yawning.

Yes, honey, I'm on my way. Be sure and help Aunt CJ and get to school on time. I'll be back the day after tomorrow."

She hugged both of them and gave them each a good-bye kiss. She put on her coat and grabbed the lunch that Taylor had made for her, and walked out of the door toward the waiting buckboard.

Big Jim and Patricia, Eldene's father and mother, lived west of Baltimore, about twenty-five miles toward Frederick. It isn't a very difficult trip due to the well-traveled road. All of the freight wagons and stage coaches travel this route to deliver their goods and passengers to various locations between Cumberland and Baltimore.

It was a nice clear morning, and Eldene figured that she would be at her folks' place by sundown. Normally she would take the stagecoach, but she felt like taking her own rig this time.

As she traveled along, she started thinking about Jake and the fun they used to have together. They would sometimes go to visit Big Jim and Patricia and camp overnight on the way.

"Taylor and Patty used to love camping and sitting by the fire at night," she said to herself. "They used to love to listen while Jake told stories around the campfire. I miss him so much. What am I going to do without him?" Tears welled up inside her.

She met a stagecoach and was startled into reality. "I had better pay attention," she said aloud as she snapped the reins and yelled, "Heeya, giddyap, Penny."

It was early evening when she arrived at her folks' place. She had made good time, but it felt good to be done with the trip. She tied Penny up to the hitching rail and walked toward the house.

Big Jim was just getting home from work. He was on the front porch, taking off his boots, when he noticed Eldene walking toward the house.

"Well, hello, lass!" he yelled. "What brings you up here, where are the kids?" he inquired as he ran over to put his arms around her. They gave each other a big hug.

Big Jim's six-foot-four-inch frame towered over her. His dark wavy hair was a little mussed from removing his hat. He had a dark mustache and blue eyes. He was in excellent shape from working in the sawmill that he owned. He spoke with a quite noticeable Irish accent.

"Taylor is taking care of things at home, and Patty is with CJ. I came up for some good old fatherly advice," she added.

"Well, let's put your horse away and get your buggy taken care of, and we'll have some of your mommy's good cooking while we talk." He rattled on while heading for the barn.

"Okay," Eldene said, "I am kind of hungry."

Patricia was surprised to see Eldene and started to cry as she hugged her. "Hi, honey," she said as she wiped the tears away with her apron. "How are you doing, dear? We've been worried about you."

Patricia was in good shape for her age. She had long auburn hair that she kept tied back with a ribbon, and round hazel eyes. She is very beautiful and full of vim and vigor.

"I'm okay, Mom, I just needed to come and talk to you and Daddy," she said, wiping her own tears away.

"Let's have some supper and relax a little," Patricia said as she started setting the table. "How are those two grand-kids of mine?" she asked.

"They're fine, Mom. Taylor is taking care of things at home, and Patty is staying with CJ."

As they ate, Eldene explained her predicament. They finished supper, cleaned up the dishes, and retired to the living room to talk things over.

"Talking to you and Mom always helps. I'm feeling a little lost without Jake."

"What do you want to do, Deeny?" Big Jim asked. "Don't you think that the dock business would be a lit-tle too much to handle?" he said hesitantly. "I mean, the workers are all rough-talking and ill-mannered, and it doesn't seem like a very fitting place for a woman to be. I'm not sure that they would even take orders from a woman, Deeny," he said with a measure of caution so as not to be insulting. "I know how capable you are and all, but this would be biting off a big chunk, and you have the dress shop to think about. You could have quite a nest egg by selling Jake's half of the business and have a pretty good livelihood," he continued.

"I know, Dad," she replied. "I realize the problem, but the dress shop bores me to death. I've gotten all I can get out of it, and I have no more interest in trying to make it anything else. Frankly I'm tired of listening to the gossip and the chatter of all those women," she griped. "I've had enough, and I don't think I want to do it anymore," she said in exasperation. "I thought that maybe Taylor could help with the dock business, but he's only fifteen, and it will be another five or six years before he will be ready. I don't think I want to try and supervise a bunch of rude dirty-talking men either," she said in a stern manner. "As a matter of fact, I have been thinking about selling every-thing and going out West and starting all over again."

Patricia had been relatively quiet up to this point, but that remark broke her silence.

"You what?" she exclaimed in a sharp tone. "Are you crazy? You would be giving up so much, and we would probably never get to see you again. I couldn't bear the thought of you going so far away," she said as tears welled up in her eyes.

"I'm sorry if I upset you, Mommy, but it wouldn't be as bad as it seems. They have started construction on the railroad from Cumberland, and they plan on having it through to the West Coast in a couple of years," she said with excitement. "We would be able to travel back and forth in just a few days."

Patricia didn't like this idea at all and said, "The thought of riding several thousand miles on a train does not sound appealing to me."

Big Jim sat quiet for a moment and then said, "Of course we don't want you to go out West, and I want you to think long and hard about this. I want you to pray about things and trust the Lord in making your decision. Go and talk to the pastor of your church. We'll certainly be praying about it too. This is a major decision and should be thought out thoroughly," he said with conviction. "We love you, and we don't want anything to happen to you. Have you mentioned anything about this to your sister yet?"

"I love you too, Dad and Mom, and I would miss you terribly," she said as she went over and hugged them both. "You both have always been there for me, and I could never forget that. I haven't spoken to anyone else about it yet, but I plan on talking to CJ as soon as I get back to Baltimore."

Eldene slept well that night. She had finally gotten some peace of mind. Talking to her parents always helped when she was about to do something new and adventurous. She knew that going out West was a big challenge, but the excitement she was feeling, and the thought of the adventure was exhilarating. The more she thought about it, the more excited she became.

Eldene was up early the next morning. She hitched Penny up to the buckboard while her mom made breakfast. She was anxious to get back home.

Big Jim could tell that she had made a decision, and he expressed his concern once again. They were sitting around the breakfast table, talking, and he and Patricia both offered more advice.

Big Jim pleaded adamantly, "Think long and carefully before you make a decision to do what's running around in your pretty little head. Going out West with two children is a big undertaking, and it is also very dangerous."

"I know, Dad," she said, "I will talk to the pastor." She started to clean the table.

"No, that's okay, honey," Patricia said. "You had better get started back so you can get home before dark."

Eldene stepped up into the buckboard and made a clicking noise with her tongue. Penny understood and started prancing toward the road.

"Goodbye, Mom, goodbye, Dad!" she yelled as she snapped the reins, sending Penny into a trot.

"Goodbye, Deeny, please be careful!" yelled Big Jim and Patricia simultaneously.

"I will and I'll pray about things." Her head was spinning a mile a minute as she jostled down the road. She looked up to toward heaven and said, "Please, dear God, let this be the right decision. You know, Lord, that I have made up my mind, and I need your help. I'm asking you to bless me and help me as I try to make everyone understand. Thank you, Father, for listening. Amen."

She arrived home just before dark. Taylor was doing the chores when she pulled up in front of the barn.

"You're home." He ran over to give her a hand with Penny and the buckboard. Eldene gave him a big hug.

"Be sure and give Penny some oats, honey. I'll go over to CJ's and get Patty."

"Okay, Mom, I will," he said as he led Penny into the barn.

Eldene returned home with her arm around Patty's shoulder. They were chatting as they walked toward the house.

After they had some supper, Eldene said excitedly, "Let's go sit by the fireplace, I have something I want to discuss with you both." They followed her into the living room with puzzled looks.

Taylor looked at Patty and shrugged his shoulders. "Sure, Mom, what's going on?"

Taylor and Patty sat on the couch. Eldene stoked the fire and sat on the armchair facing them. The flames from the fire were dancing back and forth, changing shapes and colors from transparent blues, oranges, and reds. The flames were reflecting on the faces of Taylor and Patty, and you could see the puzzled look on their faces in the dim light.

Eldene cleared her throat and said, "I'm going to sell your dad's half of the business to Dan. I don't know anything about running it, and being a woman doesn't help matters any."

Patty comments with exuberance, "That sounds like a good idea. I can help you in the dress shop! We can expa—"

"Whoa there, honey," Eldene interrupted, "I have some more to say. I am thinking about selling the dress shop too. I'm thinking of something new and more exciting," she added.

Patty loved the dress shop and couldn't imagine anything more exciting.

Taylor, being adventurous like his mom, replied, "Oh yeah, Mom, what is it?"

"*Well*," she said, "I've been thinking about selling everything, including the property, and the three of us going out West to California or Oregon and starting over with a new life."

Taylor's eyes opened wide, and you could see the excitement in his face. "Wow, Mom, are you serious? Do you think we could do that?"

"Sure, honey," she replied, "why not?"

"Gosh, Mom, you know that Dad wanted me to go to college and join him in the dock business. I—I have to admit that I am not too excited about it. Without Dad, it just wouldn't be the same. Going out West sounds like a good idea to me."

"I understand how you feel," responded Eldene. "I feel that without Jake, what's the point?"

Patty was still dazed and just sat there, staring into space. She was not adventurous, and she liked it here in Baltimore. This news was not at all what she wanted to hear. She could barely hear Eldene and Taylor talking. It seemed that they were miles away and that she was dreaming.

"Mommy!" she said as she snapped out of her trance. "We can't do that!" she exclaimed "What about school and my friends? I can't leave them."

"Listen, honey." She saw the desperation in Patty's eyes. "I'm sure they have schools in the West"—trying to calm Patty—"and we will make new friends." Patty started crying and ran upstairs.

Eldene realized that this wasn't going to be easy. She looked at Taylor and said, "We'll talk some more tomorrow. "I need to try and calm Patty down."

Patty was lying across her bed, sobbing.

"Sweetheart," she said sympathetically, "I understand how you must feel. Please listen to what I have to say. I've just lost the love of my life, and you have lost your daddy. I feel like I have a hole in me, as big as a well, that I will never be able to fill, and I know that you are feeling an emptiness also. This would be a new start for us, and it would help us to move on with our lives. We would stay busy getting ready, and it would keep our minds occupied. I believe that as long as we are together and staying busy and doing something with our lives, we will get through this terrible tragedy."

"It's, it's so sudden, Mommy, I—I—I can't just leave my friends."

"I love you more than life itself, sweetheart, and I don't want to hurt you. I know that you will be able to adjust, and we will have a great new life ahead of us."

Patty wiped the tears from her eyes and said, "Mommy, I'm so scared. I'm not sure I can do this. I love my friends, and I'm afraid I'll never get to see them again."

"You'll make new friends sooner than you think, and besides, you will be coming back here to go to college before you know it. You're a strong young girl, and I know we can do this as long as we are together. We need this change, and as long as we have each other, we can do anything. You can do this, sweetheart, I know you can."

Somehow Patty felt a little better and said, as she put her arms around Eldene, "I love you, Mommy, and I'll do my best."

"Get some sleep, and we'll talk more tomorrow," said Eldene as she kissed her good night.

The next morning, Eldene was sitting at the table, drinking a cup of coffee, when Taylor and Patty came down for breakfast. Their breakfast and school lunches were waiting for them.

Taylor noticed that Eldene was writing some things down on a piece of paper and asked, "What are you writing, Mam?"

"I'm just doing some figuring. I'm figuring out the cost of putting together a covered wagon and everything that goes with it."

"We'll see you after school, Mom."

"Okay, kids. Don't worry, okay?"

"I'll try, Mommy," answered Patty.

"I love you, sweetheart, I know you will." She hugged and kissed them, and they left for school.

Eldene decided to go talk to CJ about the dress shop. CJ had always been interested in the shop.

"Hi, Deeny," called CJ as she opened the front door. "You've just made my day," she said as they hugged each other. "What brings you here so early?" She was thinking that Eldene would be at the dress shop. CJ was two years younger than Eldene and had always looked up to her. She is a very pretty young woman with reddish hair and green eyes. Her five-foot-five-inch frame is shapely, and she always looks adorable!

"I want to talk to you about the dress shop," she said without hesitation. "You've always liked the shop, and I want to sell it to you."

Taken aback, CJ said, "You want to do wha—"

"I want to sell you the dress shop," she interrupted, "lock, stock, and barrel! My mind is made up, and that's what I want to do."

"Why, Deeny?" she asked. "What's going on?"

"I've decided to sell everything, including the house and property, and the kids and I are going out West and starting a whole new life."

CJ just stood there for a minute with a look of disbelief. After she got over the initial shock, she said with a raised voice, "You can't be serious! You're a woman with two kids with solid roots here in Baltimore. This is where your family is! This is where your friends are! What are you thinking?" she continued.

Eldene, trying to calm CJ down, grabbed her by the shoulders and, with a stern look, explained, "CJ, honey, I just don't want to continue on here without Jake. What we built together is gone, and I'm ready to try something new and different."

"Yeah, Deeny, but going out West?"

"It just sounds so exciting to me. I know it has its dangers with me being a widow with two youngsters, but I intend on being totally prepared. I have to move on with my life, and I want to do this. Taylor and Patty are young and strong, and together we will be able to build a new life together."

"What about Dad and Mom, what will they think about you going across the country in a covered wagon wi—"

"I've already talked to them, and they expressed their concerns. Of course they don't want us to go, but I know I'll have their blessings. The first six or seven hundred miles will be on the National Road. It goes all the way to the west border of Illinois."

"What about the next two thousand miles? They will be going through the wilderness. Who knows what you will be running into out there? Wild animal, Indians, deserts, mountains, tornadoes, and God only knows what else."

"We will be with a large wagon train, and we'll be just fine."

"Have you talked to the pastor?"

"Yes, and he thinks I have to follow my heart, and this is what my heart tells me to do. I've thought about it and prayed about it, and my mind is made up."

"Oh, Deeny." CJ wept "I think I understand, but I will miss you so terribly much."

"I know, CJ," Eldene said as she put her arms around her. "I will miss you too." They stood there, embracing for a few minutes. "We'll write often," whispered Eldene. "I'll make sure that you know where we are and what we are doing. Besides I can hardly wait until you can come out West, on the train, to visit us. We'll have so much to tell each other," Eldene expressed with excitement. "I have to go now, but I'll be back tomorrow for your answer." She waved as she walked out the door.

Eldene headed down to the docks to talk to Dan about the business.

Dan, a man with a five-foot-eight-inch stocky build, was a very friendly outgoing person that wears his heart on his sleeve. He saw Eldene and greeted her with a big hug.

"Hi, Deeny, I've been expecting you. Have a seat, we have a lot to talk about."

"Listen, Dan, I've done a lot of thinking, and I believe that it would be better for you and me if I sold you Jake's, that is, my half of the business. I'm just not up to running it."

Dan thought for a minute and said, "I have to say that I'm not surprised, and I've been thinking about how to approach you. I will give you a fair price for your half of the business if that's what you want to do."

"That's what I want to do. I know that you will give me a fair deal."

"I'll have the papers drawn up and give you the money in a couple of days. I want to wish you and the children the best, and if you need anything, don't hesitate to contact me."

Feeling relieved, Eldene nodded with a smile and said, "Thank you, Dan. You're a good person, and I appreciate you very much. I'll never forget your family and all the good times we've had over the years. God bless you," she said as she walked out of Dan's office.

Eldene was starting to get very excited about everything. She walked to the dress shop and actually started whistling as she made plans in her mind.

*****

The next few weeks were busy. CJ decided to buy the dress shop, and Dan bought the dock business and, to her good fortune, the house and property. He said he would need it for his new ramrod and his family.

Eldene's head was spinning. Since both the business and the property were now taken care of, she decided that they would move to her folks' place to finish preparing for the journey West. She was glad that Baltimore was the first place to have telegraph service, so she was able to communicate with Big Jim through the wire and save a lot of traveling time. She knew that her parents would be trying to change her mind, but she was determined, and once she made up her mind, nothing was going to stop her.

She waited until she heard back from Big Jim and Patricia. The message read, "Concerned about decision. Stop. Come when ready. Stop. Love, Dad."

She read the wire and said, "Thanks, Tipsy." She walked out with a smile on her face.

She started back home knowing that she was going to have trouble when she explained to Patty that they were leaving Baltimore right away. She hadn't told the kids of her decision to finish their moving preparations at their grandparents' home. The kids were already home from school when she arrived. She put away the buckboard and took care of Penny before she went into the house.

Later that night, she told Taylor and Patty what was going to happen. Taylor was excited and happy. Patty just sat there and started to cry.

"Mom, we can't go yet. I have too much to do, and I ca—"

"Look, honey," Eldene interrupted, "we've been through all of this, and it really doesn't matter when we go at this point. What I mean is," she continued, "that you are leaving school for a while, and we will be keeping up with your studies as much as possible while we are traveling. You will be able to start school again when we get settled. We will get as much material from your teacher as we can, and with Taylor's and my help, we will be able to keep up with your studies. You'll feel better tomorrow."

Patty wiped the tears from her face and said, "It's not the same, Mom, it's just not the same." Knowing that she might as well make the best of things, she said, "I'll try my best to make things work."

The next few days were hectic as they tied up loose ends and packed. Taylor began loading the wagon and buckboard. The furniture was staying with the house, so they were packing mostly clothes and cooking gear and bedding, etc. Eldene decided that she and Patty would be wearing men's clothing. She purchased several pairs of pants and shirts and altered them to fit Patty and herself. She bought long underwear and both men's and women's undergarments that would fit under men's clothing.

Patty had a regular temper tantrum when she realized that she wouldn't be taking or wearing her dresses. "Mommy, I can't wear just men's cloths all of the time. I have to look like a girl."

"Look, sweetheart, the way I have altered the clothes, a man wouldn't be caught dead in them, you'll see."

"Me either," Patty mumbled under her breath.

"We will be going through mountains and valleys and crossing rivers and deserts. Dresses would be too cumbersome and impractical. You can pick out your favorite dress and petticoat, and we will pack it in the trunk to wear when we get to where we are going."

Patty sighed. "I guess I don't have a chance of winning." She reluctantly went back to work. She waited until Eldene was out of the room and chose her favorite high-button shoes and packed them underneath her favorite dress and undergarments. She also packed her favorite ribbons and bows. She looked up to see if her mom was looking, and after neatly packing her men's clothing on top, except the ones she had chosen to wear, she closed the lid on the trunk. She felt like she was getting away with something, and somehow that made her feel better. Patty was hardly ever defiant, she just felt exasperated.

Patty looked at the shirt and pants for a moment and said aloud, "I may as well try them on to see how ridiculous I'm going to look."

She put on the clothes and looked in the mirror. Turning this way and that way and looking at herself, she said, "I guess mom knows what she is doing. I don't look as bad as I thought I would."

Eldene had purchased three of the recently manufactured Sharps rifles and three thousand rounds of ammunition. She also purchased two more revolvers with holsters and belts. She also had Jake's old revolver. She bought one thousand .45 caliber lead balls with enough caps, flints, and wading for all three pistols. She had purchased Taylor and herself each a good-quality skinning knife, with leather belt sheaves also.

They finished loading the wagon and buckboard. They then spent the afternoon riding the saddle horses around, saying goodbye to their neighbors and friends.

They went over to CJ's to say goodbye to her and Uncle Bill and their children. Everyone was hugging and kissing and crying. Eldene, Taylor, and Patty waved as they left for the journey to their grandparents' home.

"We will be safe, and we'll send word as we go through places with postal service!" yelled Eldene.

"God bless and keep you!" yelled CJ as she waved goodbye.

Chapter 2

The New Beginning

The next morning, everyone was up early and scampering around, getting the final few things loaded. They had breakfast, and while Patty cleaned up and packed the dishes, Taylor hooked up the team to the freight wagon as Eldene hooked Penny to the buckboard.

Patty saddled her mare, named Socks because of the white running up the lower part of her legs, a beautiful spirited roan filly. She tethered the other three riding horses to the wagon and buckboard.

Eldene decided to keep all of the horses until they were ready to leave for Illinois to catch the wagon train. She had been accepted to join the train in Springfield, Illinois, on the first of June.

The wagons were loaded, hooked up, and ready to go. They made one more look around the house and grounds and decided that they were ready to hit the road. Eldene locked the doors, put the key in a predetermined place, for Dan, and walked to the buckboard. As she lifted herself up, she looked over her shoulder and sighed.

"Goodbye, old house, we will always remember you." A tear ran down her cheek as she looked at the beautiful two-story Victorian. She thought about the fun they had building the wraparound porch. "We'll have another home someday. Thank you for being so comfortable and keeping us warm for so many years."

Taylor was in the wagon, ready to go. Patty was in her saddle and waiting for her mom to lead the way.

"Let's go, everyone," said Eldene as she snapped the reins and made a clicking sound with her tongue. Penny started forward, and everyone followed.

Taylor went behind Eldene, and Patty fell in behind Taylor.

"Patty, you sure look good in those man pants," Taylor joked.

"Shut up!" Patty yelled, shaking her fist at him.

Taylor laughed and snapped the reins. "Giddyap, there giddyap."

The air was crisp and clean with a bit of a chill. The sky was blue and clear. The snow birds were chirping, pecking at the ground, and the squirrels were chattering at one another as if they were wondering what's happening. There was frozen dew on the trees and grass that sparkled in the morning sun, like thousands of little crystals, and made things look so serene and peaceful.

Eldene looked toward the cemetery where Jake is buried, and with tears trickling down her cheeks, she said sadly, "Goodbye, my love, I'll see you when God calls me."

She said a silent prayer and wiped the tears away. "Sometimes I miss you so much that it is hard to move forward. I know I have to be strong for the kids and move on with life. I know that you are proud of me, and you will always be a part of me. I know that you are watching over us." She shook her head to clear her mind and snapped the reins. She clicked her tongue and said, "Giddyap there, Penny, giddyap."

She figured that they may not make the whole twenty-five miles to her parents' home in one day, so she was planning on camping along the way. There were a few stagecoaches and freight wagons on the road, slowing them down, but they seemed to be making pretty good time.

Patty isn't as cheerful as Taylor. She was missing her friends and school already. She was hoping that her mom will change her mind and turn around. As they continued on, she realized that it was not likely. After a few miles, she started getting restless.

"Mom!" she yelled. "My feet are cold."

"Get off of your horse and walk for a while, honey," Eldene yelled back. "They will warm up when they get some circulation."

Patty waved and dismounted. She started walking and leading her horse.

"I would rather be home," she mumbled as she stumbled a little. Patty walked for about a mile and decided to ride Socks again. She barely got into the saddle when she heard a commotion up the hill to her right. She looked up just in time to see a white-tailed deer running down the hill at full speed. The poor deer's tongue was hanging out, and she could tell that the poor thing was near exhaustion.

There was a coyote chasing the deer, and he was right on her heels. They both ran between Pattie's horse and Taylor's wagon.

Taylor had heard the noise also. He stopped his rig and jumped off, grabbed a rock, and hurled it toward the coyote while screaming, "Get out of here, and leave that deer alone, you mangy critter."

He barely missed the coyote with the rock, but it was enough to startle him. The coyote came to a skidding halt, turned suddenly, and started to run back up the hill. He had turned so quickly that he didn't see Patty's horse and almost ran into her. Socks whinnied, reared up on her back legs, began flailing her front legs in the air, and nearly dumped Patty.

"Whoa there, Socks," she said as she leaned forward and tightened the reins. "Settle down, girl." Patty was a good rider and quickly got the filly under control.

Taylor calmed the horse that was tied behind his wagon. The coyote ran up the hill, stopped, turned around and yelped at Taylor and Patty, as if he was cussing them out for robbing him and his family of their supper. He then turned and ran into the woods.

Patty looked to see that the deer had stopped running and was trying to get her strength back. She was happy for the poor doe.

Patty wiped her brow and said, "Wow, that was a little exciting. I thought for sure that poor doe was a goner."

"Yeah," answered Taylor, "she was on her last leg."

Eldene stopped and tied her rig to a tree and ran back to see that no one was hurt.

Relieved, she said, "Wow, that's a once-in-a-lifetime happening. I've never seen anything like that before," she quipped. That was really something."

They stopped more than usual to rest and water the horses. They were pulling a pretty good load, and Eldene didn't want to overdo it. They had traveled about fifteen miles, and Taylor was starting to feel a little fatigued from handling the reins for so many hours.

"Hey, Mom, let's find a nice spot and camp for the night. My arms are tired, and Patty is getting worn out."

"Yeah, Mom, let's stop." Patty joined in. "Let's build a nice fire and warm up a little."

"I'm getting a little tired too. Let's find a spot." They spotted a wide grassy spot about a hundred feet off the road and decided that it would be a good place to camp for the night.

They pulled the wagons in line and unhooked the team and Penny.

Taylor took the six horses over to a nearby creek and let them drink their fill. Afterward he tethered them to a rope strung between two trees and made sure that they had some hay from the bale that they had brought with them.

He had no more than finished when Eldene yelled, "Okay, you guys, supper in ten minutes."

"Wow!" yelled Taylor, suddenly realizing that almost an hour had passed while he was tending to the horses. They gathered around the campfire, and Eldene dished up some camp-style potatoes and beans with a slice of ham that she had cooked before they left home. They ate their supper and talked and laughed about the coyote incident and other things they saw on the road.

"I'm glad to warm my cold feet and rest my tired sore butt," said Patty.

"Can you imagine how sore your butt would be if you were wearing a long dress and a petticoat?" Laughed Taylor.

Taylor rolled his bed out under the buckboard, and Eldene and Patty rolled theirs out under the larger wagon. They made sure that the wheels were well blocked so that the wagons wouldn't roll, and they all went to bed for the night.

The next morning, Taylor got up first and built a fire and put the coffeepot on.

Eldene woke up and exclaimed, "Oh my, that coffee smells so good."

She got out of bed, and Taylor handed her a cup of coffee. She took a sip and said, "This is just what the doctor ordered. Get up, Patty," she called, "it's time to get back on the road."

"It's too cold," groaned Patty.

Taylor took some cold water over and threatened to pour it on her.

Patty screamed, "Don't you dare, you big brat,"

"You've got about two minutes, and then you're going to get wet," teased Taylor.

"Okay, okay!" exclaimed Patty. "I'm up."

Taylor giggled. "It's a good thing," he said as he walked over to the fire and poured her a cup of coffee. They ate some oatmeal, washed the dishes, and rolled up their bedding. Taylor harnessed the horses and saddled Patty's filly. He was hooking the team to the wagon when he heard a loud echoing whistling sound followed by a sort of braying noise. He recognized the whistle immediately. He looked up and saw a huge bull elk bugling, no more than a hundred feet away.

The majestic animal had a rack with about ten points and was strutting through the tall grass like he ruled the world. His bugling was answered by another elk in the distance.

"Mom, Patty," he said in a loud whisper, "look at the huge bull elk over there."

"Wow, he's really close," Patty whispered back. "What if he comes after us?"

"He won't," Eldene added as the elk strutted off into the woods.

"That was really great." Gasped Taylor.

"Yeah," said Patty, "and scary."

Eldene finished hooking Penny to the buckboard and said, "Okay, you kids, let's get going."

Taylor was already in the wagon, and Patty was in the saddle, ready to go. Eldene clicked her tongue at Penny, and they headed up the road toward Sweeny's Mill.

The rest of the trip was less eventful. They met a couple of freight wagons and a stagecoach, but there weren't any more mishaps. They arrived at Daddo and Nana's place at just about noon. Patricia came running out to meet them.

"Hello, kids. Hello, Deeny!" she yelled as they dismounted.

"Hi, Nana," Taylor and Patty said in unison as they rushed over to give her a big hug.

"Howdy, Mom," said Eldene as she hugged her.

"Was the trip okay?"

"Oh goodness, Nana," Patty said excitedly, "you should have seen what happened on the way here".

"Yeah," Taylor added mischievously. "A coyote almost ran over Patty."

"Well, not quite," interrupted Eldene. "We'll tell you all about it after we put the wagons in the barn and take care of the animals," she said as she led Penny toward the barn. "Come on, kids, let's take care of the horses."

Taylor followed, laughing and teasing Patty as she led Socks.

"You think you're *so* darned cute, don't you, smarty-pants?"

Taylor continued laughing as Patty waved her fist with a playful smirk on her face. They put the horses away and made sure they were fed and watered. After they finished with the animals, they went into the house where Patricia had made some sandwiches and set the table for lunch.

"You all must be famished after that long trip," she said as she poured each of them some fresh milk.

"We are a little hungry," answered Eldene.

"Yes, 'um," said both Taylor and Patty as they took turns washing up.

"That oatmeal we had at daybreak didn't last long enough," quipped Taylor. "It looks really good, Nana, my stomach is beginning to growl a little."

"Mine too, Nana," said Patty. "I could eat a cow."

"Me too," said Taylor as he smacked his lips.

Patricia said grace, and they enjoyed their lunch while they told her about their exciting eventful trip.

"I've noticed that you and Patty are wearing trousers and men's shirts. What's that all about?" asked Patricia.

Eldene explained her reason for the clothing.

Patricia just shrugged and said, "I guess it does make sense."

They whiled away the afternoon resting and talking as they waited for Big Jim to get home from the mill.

Taylor and Patty were playing checkers while Eldene and Patricia were discussing their upcoming adventure to the wild, wild West. Patricia was trying to convince Eldene to reconsider. Eldene was trying to convince Patricia that they were going to be perfectly safe.

Big Jim rode in just before dark. He put his horse away and came into the house with his famous grin on his face. Taylor and Patty jumped up and greeted him with hugs and kisses.

"Hi, Grandpa," they said as he returned their affection.

Eldene walked over to him and gave him big hug and kissed him on the cheek. "Hi, Dad, did you have a good day?"

"Yep, I sure did," he answered.

Big Jim held Eldene at arm's length, and looking her in the eye, he said firmly, "So you are bound and determined to do this foolish thing, aren't you?"

"Yes, Dad," she replied, "we have it all planned, and we are ready to start putting things together."

"Is there anything we can do to change your mind? Can't you start over here instead of traipsing off to the far reaches of the world where we have no way of keeping in touch, and we may never see each other again?" he added sharply.

Eldene looked up at Big Jim and said, "Dad, the decision has been made, we've made our commitment, and that's the way it's going to be. The railroad will be through to the West Coast in two or three years, and we'll be able to see each other almost as often as we do now. Besides,

Dad," she added with excitement, "the timber stands out West are massive, and people are moving out there by the droves. You might even want to consider moving your mill out there."

Big Jim raised his eyebrows. You could see the wheels turning in his head. "Hmm, I never thought about that."

"Just think, Dad, Mom," Eldene said with a new enthusiasm, "a sawmill and furniture construction operation in Oregon. I understand that Portland is beginning to grow, and that's only one place."

Big Jim just stood sort of in a trance. You could tell that he was daydreaming. After a moment or two, he shook his head and said, "Okay, back to reality. I need to wash up and have some of that pot roast that I smell cooking. He took off his coat and went over to the basin to wash up. "We'll talk about this problem some later."

"Problem, what problem? I don't see a problem." Laughed Eldene as she and Patty started setting the table.

Patricia was quiet as she started dishing up the food, but you could tell that she too was thinking about what Eldene had said.

Oh, dear god, she thought, *what am I thinking?*

Big Jim looked up from his plate with a knife in one hand and a fork in the other, and said, pointing the knife and shaking it gently, "Since your mind is made up, I'm going to make damned sure that you are completely equipped with the best wagon and team that money can buy. I want Taylor, Patty, and you, my dear crazy daughter, to be as comfortable and trouble-free as possible. He then looked over at Patty and said, "And you, young lady,"— noticing her man clothes—"I don't cotton to a girl or a woman wearing men's clothing, but I have to admit that it makes better sense than a dress in this situation," he said with a grin. "With your mom being a seamstress and all, you don't look half-bad. You look downright pretty."

"Thank you, Daddo, I think," Patty said, wrinkling her mouth to one side. "I don't like them much either."

Taylor was just sitting there, grinning. He wanted to say something but decided not to.

"I think she's beautiful," said Eldene.

Patty tried to smile.

That night Big Jim had a hard time sleeping. His mind churned most of the night about what Eldene had said about building a milling operation in Oregon.

Patricia found herself tossing and turning also. The thought of another operation on the West Coast was intriguing. They have been in the same spot for years, and although successful, they often thought of expanding. They had never given the West a thought, and it was very exuberating.

Big Jim must have drifted off to sleep sometime during the night because he felt good when he awoke the next morning. His eyes flew open at the crack of dawn, as usual.

Patricia was stirring. "I had a terrible time sleeping last night." She yawned. "I just kept thinking about what Eldene said about Oregon.

"Me too," said Big Jim, I couldn't think of anything else. Maybe she's got something there? "Maybe we'll have to start checking things out?"

"I'm going to go make some coffee and start breakfast," said Patricia as she washed up, combed her hair, and brushed her teeth. "That daughter of ours has my mind going in circles."

"I know what you mean," said Big Jim. "Mine's spinning pretty fast too. By the way, honey, I'll be back early from the mill. I'm just going in to get things started this morning, then I'm coming back home to help Eldene and the kids start getting things together."

"Okey dokey, dear," said Patricia as she kissed him on the cheek.

Eldene and Taylor hooked up the two wagons that their belongings were in and pulled them around to the back of the house. They unloaded everything onto the porch. The porch was enclosed, and everything was protected from the weather. They set several mouse and rat traps around to keep the varmints from getting into their stuff while they were getting their covered wagon ready for the trip. They had no more than finished when Big Jim came home driving a brand-new freight wagon hooked to two large great-looking mules. His horse that he always rode to work was tied behind.

"Whoa, Jack. Whoa, Jenny," he yelled as he pulled back on the reins. Big Jim jumped down from the wagon and tethered the mules to a hitching rail. "Come over and take a look at what I've got for you!" he yelled.

"Wow, Dad, that's a nice-looking rig. Where did you get that from?"

"Well," said Big Jim, "we just bought four new freight wagons, so I've decided to let you have one of them to fix up for you trip out West. I was thinking about things, and what could be better that a freight wagon for such a trip. They have the room you need for your belongings and the strength for the weight. The sides are high enough to strap water barrels, a cooking grate, and other equipment too, and we will be able to fit a heavy canvas over it to convert it into a covered wagon. The wheel bearings are made for heavy loads, and the brakes are oversized and on all four wheels instead of just two. We will be able to make it virtually weatherproof. So what do you think?"

"Holy cow!" yelled Taylor. "It sure is big!"

They looked the new rig over, and Eldene gave Big Jim a big hug.

"Thanks, Dad, this is exactly what we need, it's beautiful. Thank you, thank you, thank you," she repeated, as she bounced around the wagon again, looking it over once more.

"Why mules and not horses, Daddo?" asked Taylor.

Big Jim looked at Taylor and said, "They are strong, they can go farther than horses without water, they work for hours without rest, they don't reproduce, and they are easy to take care of. A good team of mules like these—young, strong, and well trained—will take you all the way to the West Coast," he added. "Using the mules, you will be able to get along with only two riding horses."

"It sounds right to me." Nodded Eldene.

"Yep, me too," Taylor added.

"All righty then," said Big Jim, "let's get these mules put away and start designing the cover for the wagon."

They were able to get canvas from the mill. They used it to cover the lumber and furniture during delivery runs. Eldene figured that because of the size of the wagon, they would need eight ribs to hold the canvas in place over the wagon. She knew that most covered wagons had from four to six ribs.

"Where can we get the ribs made for the canvas?" she asked.

"Well, just so you know, lass, they are called bows, not ribs, and as you know, we have our own blacksmith at the mill, so instead of using wood, we will make them out of spring steel," answered Big Jim. "We can make them thin enough so they won't be too heavy, and they will be strong enough to withstand the rough terrain and weather."

Eldene was always amazed at Big Jim's wisdom. She never doubted anything he said or did.

Taylor liked being with his grandpa. He learned something new daily.

Eldene, Patricia, and Patty laid the canvas out in the barn and started stitching it together. They folded the seams for strength and waterproofing. They also double-stitched every joint.

Big Jim and Taylor worked on the wagon, while the blacksmith was making the steel bows. They mounted two ten-gallon water barrels on each side of the wagon. There was a cooking grate mounted to the rear of the wagon bed just behind the wheel. They made the tailgate to fold down into a table. They had mounted brackets along the sides to hang pots and pans and extra gear. Big Jim mounted brackets to hang their rifles on the back of the seat so they would be easy to reach. By the time the canvas and bows were ready, they had a place for everything.

Because of the high sides on the wagon, they were able to make fold-up beds on the sides, with storage space underneath. There was room for their clothing trunks and water-tight food-storage bins along the sides and under the beds so they would have an aisle down the middle to get through the wagon from front to back.

Patty's hands started to ache from sewing the heavy canvas material. She held her hands up and showed Eldene the blisters and complained.

"Mom, look at my poor hands, I can hardly move my fingers. We've been at this for four days, are we ever going to finish?"

Eldene and Patricia looked at their own hands and realized that they too had blisters and sores.

"We are almost done stitching, honey," said Eldene. "We'll have to doctor our hands and sore backs afterward."

"Thanks, Grandma," quipped Patty. "We have to stick together."

That night everyone was sitting around the fire, talking about the day's accomplishments. Big Jim told them that the canvas bows and mounting brackets are ready to install on the wagon.

"So soon?" asked Eldene? "That didn't take very long."

"Nope," answered Big Jim, "Pete's the best blacksmith east of the Mississippi."

"I've got a great idea." Patty offered. "Let's take a couple of days off and let our hands heal a little before we try to mount that heavy canvas."

"I'll tell you what," said Big Jim, "you ladies can rest. I will get three or four guys from the mill to help us mount the canvas."

Patty jumped up and hugged Big Jim. "I love you, Daddo, thank you."

"Well, that's okay, sweetheart. We can't have you falling apart on us now, can we?" teased Big Jim.

"Yeah, Patty." Smirked Taylor. "You have to stay pretty for those good-looking cowboys out West!"

"You had better work on yourself, you big poop head," Patty kidded. "I'm sure they have pretty cowgirls out there, and you've got a lot of handsoming up to do."

Taylor jumped up and chased Patty upstairs, yelling, "Okay, smarty-pants, I'll get you for that."

Patty ran into her room, giggling. It felt good to get the best of her brother once in a while.

The next day was Saturday, and Big Jim went to the mill and brought back three strong-looking men to help mount the canvas. Taylor was busy installing the mounting brackets onto the sides of the wagon. The canvas wasn't extremely heavy, but it was too much for the girls to handle, and they had plenty of other stuff to do. The men secured the bows to the wagon by bolting the ends to the brackets that Taylor had mounted. They stretched the canvas over the bows and secured it to the wagon bed. They made sure that it was far enough down over the bed to help make it weatherproof. Taylor mistakenly called the bows, ribs, and one of the mill workers said, "Listen, young feller, them there things y'all call ribs is really bows because on account of how they are bent."

"Bows, huh," said Taylor, scratching his head, pretending that he didn't know. "All right then, from now on they're bows."

They finished stretching the canvas and stood back, admiring their work.

Big Jim said proudly, "That is a hell of a good-looking rig. That's a hell of a bonnet."

"It sure is, Daddo," added Taylor.

Eldene, Patty, and Patricia came running toward the barn, yelling all at the same time.

"Oh my god, Dad, it's absolutely perfect," Eldene said excitedly as she walked around the wagon, admiring the work. "It's just perfect. All we have to do to finish up is sew the drawstrings in the front and back," she added.

"Yep, that's about it," Big Jim said, puffing out his chest.

Everyone was talking and gabbing at the same time when Big Jim yelled, "Hey, you know what? This calls for a celebration. I just happen to have some homemade beer in the cellar, and I think it's time to open a few of them."

Everyone yelled their approvals, and they went toward the house, talking and laughing. The men had beer, while Taylor and the girls drank some hot cocoa. They all talked about the day's activities and laughed and joked.

Taylor wanted to have a beer with his daddo but decided not to ask for one since he had never had one before, and he wasn't sure how it would make him feel. He had seen a few drunken people, and he didn't like the way they acted and sure didn't want to embarrass himself in front of his family.

Everyone celebrated for a while, and then Big Jim took the men back to the mill. It turned out to be a very satisfying productive day.

The next morning, Eldene was up early. Patricia and Big Jim were already eating their breakfast.

"Good morning, dear," Patricia said cheerfully.

Eldene poured herself a cup of coffee and sat down at the table.

"Good morning, Mom, Dad," she responded. "Well, Dad, what's next?" she asked.

"Well, let's look at the list," he said, pulling a piece of paper out of his bib pocket. "We have the water barrels mounted, the jockey box is mounted, the gun racks are mounted, the cooking grate is done, the chicken coop is mounted, water bag hooks are installed." As he read down the list, he checked things off. Rubbing his chin, he said, "Everything seems to be in order."

"I'm going to go down the road to the Hannery's ranch today and see if I can get a good cow and a couple of chick—" Eldene started to say.

"Just a minute, honey," Big Jim interrupted. "I've given this some thought, and I think that you would be better off with a couple of milking goats."

"Goats?" questioned Eldene in a slightly raised voice. "Goats?" she repeated! Why goats?"

"Well, in the first place, they will eat almost anything, they're easier to take care of than a dumb cow, and they're easy to milk," continued Big Jim. "You will be much happier with goats."

"Goats, huh?" said Eldene, sipping her coffee. "I never thought of goats. All righty then, goats it will be." Eldene laughed. "Mr. Hannery will have to teach me how to milk them. I don't even know which end to milk!" Everyone laughed.

Later that morning, after Taylor and Patty got up and around, they hitched up the buckboard and headed down the road to the Hannery's ranch. It was only about three or four miles, so it wouldn't be a hard trip. The Hannerys were an older couple, but they were very spry for a couple in their sixties. As they approached the ranch, they could see the beautiful pastures stretching out for thousands of yards.

Four horses started running toward them with their manes flying and their tails up. Beautiful well-bred Arabians running over to the fence to check them out. They ran up to the fence and neighed at Penny. Penny whinnied back, and the Arabians followed along the fence as far as they could, neighing and kicking up their hind quarters.

"What beautiful animals," commented Eldene.

There was another pasture in the distance with a couple hundred head of cows. A smaller area had a couple of Hereford bulls roaming around.

Mr. and Mrs. Hannery met them as they pulled up to the hitching rail in front of the house.

"Hello, Mr. and Mrs. Hannery."

"Hello, folks," said Mr. Hannery. "What brings you here to this neck of the woods today?"

Eldene jumped down from the buckboard and explained everything to the Hannerys.

"That's mighty ambitious for a young woman with a couple of youngsters," said Mrs. Hannery.

"Yes, ma'am," answered Eldene, "I guess it is."

Taylor and Patty ran over to the corral where there were a few goats roaming around.

Patty pointed at one of the goats and said, "Look, Taylor, that one looks a lot like you." She laughed and added, "As a matter of fact, he could be your twin."

"Oh yeah, smarty-pants! I see his sister right over there." He laughed. "Only, she's better-looking than you."

Eldene walked up and said, "All right you two, we've got to pick out a couple of good-looking female goats to become part of our family."

"Oh no!" yelled Taylor. "I can't handle two more sisters."

He jumped over the fence, laughing as Patty waved her fist at him.

"I'll get you, wait and see!" Patty yelled.

Taylor was laughing so hard that he almost tripped over a goat.

They picked out a couple of nice-looking nannies and tethered them to the wagon. They walked over to the chicken house and picked out three good-looking young Rhode Island Reds.

Patty pointed at a big rooster and joked, "Look, Taylor, there's a big dumb cluck like you."

"Funny," Taylor said snidely as he stuffed his hands in his armpits and strutted around, making clucking sounds like a rooster. Everyone started laughing.

They put the chickens in a wire coop that Mr. Hannery loaned them, and loaded them into the wagon. After Mr. Hannery taught them how to milk the goats, they headed back to the Sweeny place. Eldene was beginning to feel ready to start out on their huge adventure. There were times when she felt afraid, but she figured it was just nerves. The challenges that she could imagine were very exciting to her, and she felt ready for the trip.

Eldene had a list of her own that she went to work on. She made sure that they had two axes, a double blade and a single blade. She rounded up a couple of shovels, a pitchfork, a splitting wedge, and a splitting mall that could double for a sledgehammer.

As she collected the items, Taylor made sure that they were secured to the wagon.

"Don't forget to get a couple of good files for sharpening the tools," said Taylor. "Oh yeah, and a whetstone for the knives," he added.

"Let's not forget an extra flint or two to light our fires with," said Eldene.

Big Jim rode into the barn.

"I didn't realize it was so late," said Eldene. "Time seems to be flying by."

"I see you've been busy today," said Big Jim. "You've got a couple of good-looking goats there."

"Yep, and we know how to milk 'um too," quipped Eldene proudly.

"Yep, that's right," added Taylor.

"That's great, lad," said Big Jim as he looked the animals over. "Now you'll have fresh milk for your big adventure. Fresh milk and fresh eggs, we just have to add some cracked corn for the hens and some cured smoked beef to your store," he added. "It's beginning to look like you are ready to start out on the road to the West. By the way," he added with some excitement in his voice, "you're mom and I, *well*, we've been talking things over and have decided to consider opening an operation out there. We'll wait until you have looked things over and picked out the best place for us to set the whole thing up," he continued.

"That's wonderful," Eldene said as she hugged Big Jim. "I'm more excited than ever, that's just wonderful."

They checked over their lists one more time and decided that the only thing left to do was organize the clothing trunks under Taylor's and Patty's folding bunks. Eldene and Patricia had sewn canvas flaps over the front and rear openings that could be rolled up and tied so they would have light inside the wagon during the day. The canvas was made from a medium-weight white material so that it would reflect the heat from the sun and let in as much light as possible.

"The wagon is ready to christen and be given a name," Taylor joked.

"That's a good idea," echoed Big Jim and Eldene.

"Let's think of a good one that pertains to the journey," Eldene said with excitement. "Let's include Patty and Nana when we decide."

"Let's all go in and wash up for supper, and we can ponder over it while we eat," said Big Jim.

Taylor started toward the house the minute he heard the word *supper*. "Yippy!" he yelled. "I'm hungry as a horse."

"I'll swear," Eldene said while scratching her head, "that lad is always hungry. How am I ever going to keep him fed for two thousand miles?"

"Just be thankful he is healthy and full of vim and vigor." Laughed Big Jim. "He's a fine strong young man, and he is still growing."

Patricia had the table all set for supper when they entered the dining room.

"Oh boy, fried chicken, mashed potatoes, gravy, corn on the cob, and Nana's yummy biscuits," said Taylor, licking his lips.

They all sat around the table. Big Jim said grace, and they began. Eldene explained that they were going to name the covered wagon and asked everyone to offer their suggestions.

"How about the Adventurer." Taylor offered.

"How about Homeward Bound, like back to Baltimore," said Patty as she did her funny little lip wrinkle.

Everyone chuckled.

"That's a good idea," Patricia joked.

"All right, let's get serious," said Eldene, "let's name it, the Journey," she added.

"Um," said Big Jim, rubbing his chin, "how about the Bounder since you are westward bound, it sort of fits."

Everyone liked the sound of that one. They all gave their verbal stamp of approval.

"Then it's settled, we will call the wagon, Bounder," Eldene agreed. "It has a nice ring to it. "Bounder, Bounder," she said, raising her eyebrows as she pictured it in her head. "That's it!"

"We have checked and double-checked our lists and the Bounder," she said again, raising her eyebrows, "is ready, except for the clothing trunks and the food. We will be leaving the day after tomorrow. The sooner we get on the way, the sooner we will get to the place where we have to join the wagon train."

The next morning, Eldene and Taylor were up early. They were both excited about getting started.

"One more day, and we will begin a whole new way of life," said Eldene.

"Yep," answered Taylor. "It looks like we are going to be pioneers."

Big Jim entered the room and joined in.

Pouring a cup of coffee, he said, "I am staying home today and helping you finish things up. I want to make sure that you don't miss anything."

"Thanks, Dad, I can't express how much we appreciate the things you do for us."

"Well, you know, Deeny, how I feel about my family," added Big Jim. "Family always comes first."

"I know, Daddy, and we all love you very much," said Eldene as she gave him a hug and a kiss on the cheek.

They spent the day loading the clothing trunks and putting the food in the proper storage bins. They made sure that they had rice, sugar, coffee, and beans. Although Jake and Eldene had always grown their own vegetables and fruit, they did occasionally use them from a tin can. Eldene packed several tin cans of peas, corn, tomatoes, and green beans. She made sure they had some salt pork and *ch'arki* made from mutton, pork, and beef.

They made sure that their guns were loaded, and ammo was secure. They picked the two youngest saddle horses, Patty's filly, Socks, and Taylor's sorrel, a young spirited gelding named Barney, to accompany them. They laid out all of their tack and checked it over to make sure there were no loose, damaged, or missing parts. Everything seemed to be in good shape and ready for tomorrow.

Big Jim made sure that they had axle grease, and he double-checked the toolbox to make sure it was in order.

They finished out the day discussing dos and don'ts with Big Jim and Patricia.

Patty was not as cheerful as Eldene and Taylor. She was missing her daddy and school friends. She just sat quietly and drifted in and out of deep thought.

Everyone talked for a while and decided it was getting late and time to turn in for the night.

Eldene was lying in bed, thinking about Jake. She realized that it was going on three months since his death. She had been too busy thinking about other things the last few weeks. Tears welled up as she thought about the life they had together, and she quietly sobbed herself to sleep.

Chapter 3

The Journey Begins

Big Jim and Taylor harnessed the mules and made sure the chickens were in their cage, and goats were tethered to the rear of the Bounder. They had decided that Taylor and Patty would start out riding their horses, with Eldene driving the Bounder. They were, at last, ready to head into something new and different. Eldene and Taylor were excited and anxious. Patty was worried and sad about her friends and school. She was thinking about how much she didn't like wearing man pants, and she didn't like the idea of traveling for six or seven months, in a wagon or on a horse, to a place she knew nothing about. All she knew was she had made a promise to her mom, and she would do her best to keep it. She knew that she could be strong when she set her mind to it.

"I could probably have stayed with Aunt CJ," she mumbled to herself, "but then I would probably never see Mom and Taylor ever again." She let out a big sigh and stepped up into her stirrup and swung into the saddle. Eldene was ready to go, and so was Taylor. They had said their goodbyes and given their hugs and kisses to everyone.

Eldene snapped the reins and whistled to Jack and Jenny. "Heeya, heeya," she yelled as the mules leaned forward and headed toward the road to Cumberland. Jack and Jenny were large strong mules and had no trouble pulling the Bounder.

Taylor and Patty waved to Big Jim and Patricia, yelling, "Goodbye, Daddo and Nana," simultaneously.

"Goodbye," answered Big Jim and Patricia. "Keep in touch, and we'll see you soon."

They headed west on the well-traveled Cumberland road. Cumberland Road, or National Road as it is sometimes referred to, is the first road funded and built by the federal government. It accommodates large freight wagons and stagecoaches as well as covered wagons. Several miles of the sixty feet wide road is macadamized with flat shale rock. Their load, being much heavier than it was on the Baltimore trip to the Sweeny's, would make traveling a little slower. *But on a road as well traveled as this one*, thought Eldene, *we should be able to go twenty miles in a day*. That would take them to Frederick. She figured they could make it to Cumberland in five to six days.

The morning air was cold and crisp. They could see the breath trailing out of the animals' nostrils as they snorted, bleated, and whinnied into action. The chickens were clucking and trying to get out of their cages. The goats didn't like being tied to the Bounder, and they were straining against their lead ropes. For a while, it was pandemonium!

Eldene realized that the weather was about to change. She looked up at the sky and saw the dark billowing clouds moving in a westerly direction. The wind was blowing, and the temperature seemed to be dropping. She felt the cold air touching her skin and knew that soon there would be either rain or snow. She pulled her collar up and shivered a little at the thought as she prompted Jenny and Jack to pick up the pace a little.

Taylor and Patty were chatting back and forth as they rode up the road, side by side.

"It seems to be getting a little colder," commented Patty as she adjusted herself in the saddle.

"Yeah," said Taylor, "I think so too." He looked up, scanning the sky.

Eldene noticed a couple of Conestogas on the road ahead of them. She wondered what part of the West they might be going to. She was caught up in her thoughts when she noticed that it had started to snow.

She decided to pull over and get the slickers out for Taylor and Patty. "It looks like we are going to have some wet stuff for a while," she said as she handed them their slickers. "We could be in for a pretty wet ride."

"Yeah," answered Patty as she put her slicker on, "my feet are beginning to feel a little cold."

"You can ride in the Bounder with me if you want to. I could use some company," she added.

"All right," Patty said without hesitation. She dismounted and tied Socks to the Bounder with a lead rope.

Eldene decided to put her slicker on also. The snow was turning into a rain-snow mixture, and it was coming down a little harder. She had noticed that she could no longer see the wagons up ahead. Things were getting more and more difficult as the rain and snow came down together, as if it was angry at them for being out there.

"Okay, God," said Taylor, "we've had enough." Taylor's slicker was keeping him dry for the most part, but the wet slushy stuff hitting his face was hard to deal with. He was glad the wide brim of his hat (his dad's favorite hat) kept the water from running down his neck, but it seemed as though there was a waterfall cascading down the front of his hat and splashing off his slicker, onto the ground.

"Wow, we have only covered about five or six miles, and we're getting our first hardship lesson. It can't get much worse than this," he commented.

The rain and snow mixture continued for a couple more hours, and as the day warmed a little, it then turned into a cold rain. They had met several freight wagons and a couple of stagecoaches and also had to move over a couple of times to let a couple of stagecoaches pass from behind.

Patty was inside the Bounder, drying her face and hair. She was thankful that they had done a good job on the canopy. There weren't any leaks that she could see, she thought, so things weren't so bad. She was thinking about the life they had left behind when suddenly, there was a loud commotion coming from behind them.

Patty jumped up and went to the rear of the Bounder to see what was going on. When she opened the flap, she saw a large freight wagon pulled by a four-horse team coming upon them. The driver was yelling and snapping the reins to get the teams to move faster. Taylor's horse spooked, and he was having a hard time controlling him. "Whoa, boy, settle down, Barney," he said as he tightened up on the reins.

The driver was heeing and hawing as he snapped his whip at the horses. The horses were snorting and wheezing as they followed the commands of the crazed driver.

Eldene, realizing the dangerous situation that they were in, pulled to the right as far as she possibly could.

Patty started yelling at the driver of the freight wagon, "Hey, mister, are you trying to kill us all!"

The driver ignored her and continued cracking his whip. Patty's temper started to flare, and she screamed as loud as she could, "Hey, mister, slow down, you're coming too close to our wagon!"

The driver snapped the whip and yelled in a louder, angrier voice, "Heeya, heeya, giddyap, you mangy critters."

Patty's face and hair got splashed with cold muddy slush. The side of the Bounder was also splashed with muck and slush as the speeding wagon tried to pass.

The goats and chickens were going crazy, and Socks started rearing and tugging at her towrope.

By now the freight wagon was beside them. The wagon wheels were so close to the Bounder's that they were almost touching.

Taylor was behind the freight wagon, trying to calm Barney down.

Patty wiped her face and rushed to the front of the Bounder to see if she could help Eldene. She opened the weather flap to see the mules balking from fear and Eldene tugging at the reins.

"Whoa, Jack, whoa Jenny," she was screaming as she tried to control them.

"Get those long-eared jackasses out of my way!" the driver yelled as he cracked his whip and spurted obscenities as the freight wagon passed.

Jack and Jenny began settling down. Eldene guided the Bounder off the road and halted the mules.

"That was to close for comfort," she said as she got down and began tending to the other animals. "What was that idiot thinking, he could have killed us!"

Taylor was able to get Barney calmed down. He rushed to the Bounder and asked anxiously, "Is everyone all right? Is Patty okay?" he asked as he dismounted to help Eldene with the animals. "I hope we don't ever see that guy again."

"That makes two of us," answered Eldene. "It might not be too good for him if we do."

Patty exclaimed angrily, "That fool almost ran us over. I think he was trying to kill us." Her hair was dripping from the slush that splashed, and her Irish temper was flaring. "I wish I could get my hands on that—that—that—" She ended in frustration.

The rain had stopped, and the sun was peeking through the clouds, as if to say, "I'm still here."

Eldene decided that they'd had enough for one day. They pulled off the road at the next opportunity and started to set up camp for the night. They unhooked the Bounder and made sure all the animals were fed, watered, and taken care of for the night.

Taylor fetched some wood and started a fire while Patty fetched some water for cooking and coffee. Taylor had a little trouble with the fire at first, but then he was able to find some dry stuff next to a downed tree.

They were enjoying a hot cup of coffee and talking about the crazy freight wagon driver and the bad weather. As they were talking about the weather, Taylor came up with an idea to attach a rollup canvas to the sides of the Bounder's canopy.

"We could make them about eight feet wide and have a pole at each end to hold them up in the shape of a lean-to."

"That's a great idea," said Eldene, raising her eyebrows. That way we would have shade and a shelter for cooking and resting whenever we need it. Good thinking, young man, that's just what we are going to do when we reach Frederick."

Taylor grinned, puffed out his chest, and patted himself on the back.

Patty looked at Taylor and rolled her eyes. "Oh, *brother*, don't let your head get so big that Dad's hat won't fit!" Everyone laughed, and Patty felt good for getting one over on Taylor.

As they approached Frederick, they could see covered wagons and freight wagons lined along the road. They found a place to park their rig and tied the mules to a tree beside the road. They decided to walk the rest of the way into town. Not wanting to leave the Bounder unattended, she was about to ask Taylor to stay with it when she recognized a familiar face a couple of wagons ahead.

"Look, kids, isn't that one of the men that helped us put the canopy on the Bounder?"

"Yep, it sure is," answered Taylor "He's the one that says y'all a lot."

Eldene thought about it for a minute and decided to ask him to watch the Bounder for them.

"Well, I'll be hornswoggled. Howdy, ma'am, how y'all doing?"

"I'm doing fine, mister—mister—"

"Just call me Bill."

"Okay, Bill, I see you have a load of lumber to deliver.'"

"Yes, ma'am, I shore enough do, but I have to wait for four more hours before I can git my danged turn to unload."

"I'm sorry that you have to wait, but since you do, you think you could watch the Bounder for us?"

"The Bounder?" he asked, scratching his head. "Oh, I git it, y'all done went and named y'all's riggen'. That's purty danged good." He chuckled. "Shore, I'll keep my eye peeled fer y'all. I can't go nowhere, nohow."

"Thank you, we'll be back as soon as possible."

"Hi, Bill," said Taylor.

"Howdy there, young feller, and you too, young missy. Y'all don't worry now, ya hear?"

As they walked, passing the other wagons, Eldene noticed the people were looking at her and Patty and whispering to one another.

"Mom, those people are talking about us."

"I think they are talking about the way we are dressed," said Eldene. "Just keep walking and smiling and not let it bother us."

"Okay, but I don't have to like it," answered Patty.

"They think that you're a boy," Taylor joked.

"Thanks, brother dear. That really helps a lot."

"All right you two. Get going and let's get things done."

Patty stuck her tongue out at Taylor and bopped him on the shoulder.

Their first stop in town was the telegraph office. Eldene sent a message to her folks. She also wired CJ. After they finished at the telegraph office, they located a mercantile and found canvas for the weather flaps on the sides of the Bounder. Eldene bought Patty and herself each a wide-brim hat.

Patty put her hat on and tipped it to one side, turned slightly, shrugged, and winked at Taylor.

"You look like a regular cowgirl there, Ms. Prissy," he joked. "All you need now is some little doggies." Patty winked again and sashayed toward the door.

"Come on, children, let's go have some lunch and get back on the road. We're burning up a lot of daylight here."

"I sure could use a nice hot bath after that wild trip," Patty commented.

"Yeah, Mom," added Taylor, "I saw a bathhouse up the street aways."

As they walked down the street, they saw a sign on a building across the street that read "Hot bath and a towel Fifty cents. Soap and wash cloth ten cents extra."

They crossed the street and entered the bathhouse. They decided that it looked clean and well kept, so Eldene paid the attendant for the baths, towels, soap, and wash-cloths for each of them. Eldene told Patty and Taylor to wait while she went to the Bounder to get them some clean clothes.

They were sitting on a bench outside the bathhouse when Taylor recognized the freight wagon that almost ran them off the road.

"Patty! Look! Isn't that the rig that almost ran us over?"

"*I'm* not sure," answered Patty, even though she knew that it was. She had cooled off and didn't want any more trouble, and knowing Taylor, she knew that he would confront the driver. She remembered her dad and Taylor sparring in the front yard. Jake had taught him how to fight at a very young age, and they were always horsing around and boxing. She had seen Taylor in action a couple of times in school, and she knew what he was capable of.

Suddenly the driver of the freight wagon came out of a bar next-door and started across the street toward the rig.

Taylor sprung to his feet and dashed into the street, and with his temper flaring, he yelled, "Hey, mister, wait a minute."

"No, Taylor, don't," Patty said trying to stop him.

The man looked toward Taylor and said, with an obvious Southern drawl, "I'm in a hurry, sonny, what the hell do you want?"

Taylor approached the driver with conviction and said, "You almost ran us off the road earlier, and you were acting like a wild man. You could have killed someone."

The driver, who was tall and lanky, poked his finger in Taylor's chest and warned, "Look, kid, y'all had just better back away and shut your damned mouth." He gave Taylor a shove, and that was all it took to send him into action.

There was a small crowd gathering around by now to watch the ruckus. Eldene walked up just in time to see Taylor square off and give the driver two short jabs in the nose with his left fist and a strong quick punch with his right.

The driver hit the ground, looked up at Taylor, and decided to stay there.

The crowd was cheering as Eldene rushed in to see if the man was okay. Taylor was standing in a ready position in case the guy decided to get up.

Things cooled down after the sheriff, who came to see what was happening, was satisfied when Taylor and other witnesses explained what happened. The crowd broke up, and Eldene and the sheriff helped the driver to his feet and made sure he didn't have a broken nose.

The driver looked at Taylor and, while rubbing his chin and wiping blood from his nose, said, "Damn, kid, where'd y'all learn to fight like that?"

Taylor looked at him and, with pride, answered, "My dad taught me. He was the best teacher in the whole wide world."

The driver shrugged and said, "Man, y'all sure do pack a wallop. I'm sure sorry about the trouble I caused y'all this morning, I—I—I r-reckon I had this coming."

Taylor looked at him and said, "Yes, sir." He turned and walked toward Patty who was still waiting on the other side of the street.

Eldene caught up with Taylor and said, "You could have probably handled that a little differently, you could have gotten into some trouble there."

"I'm sorry, Mom, I was only going to give him a piece of my mind until he poked and shoved me."

"Well, I guess he might think twice before he tries to run someone else off the road again," she added as she patted him on the back. "Let's go get our baths and have something to eat."

"Yeah," Patty quipped, "all of that excitement has sure made me hungry. That was pretty intense for a minute or two. That guy didn't even know what hit him, y'all shore do pack a wallop thar, sonny," she said while swinging her fists at Taylor.

He looked at her with a somber expression. "Come on, smarty-pants," he said as he put his arm around her shoulders and messed up her hair. Patty wiggled loose from his arm, poked him in the ribs, giggling as she ran into the ladies' side of the bathhouse. Eldene was pleased with the way they were teasing each other. *Things are going to be just fine*, she thought as she followed Patty.

After their baths and a good steak dinner, with a slice of apple pie for dessert, they headed back to the Bounder to continue their journey. They thanked Bill for watching the Bounder and started out again.

They traveled a few more miles and noticed the wagon traffic had picked up considerably. Eldene knew that the road that they were on was well traveled, but she didn't expect it to be this busy. There were freight wagons and stagecoaches going both directions. There were several types of covered wagons traveling west. They had come upon a wagon train of about a hundred wagons or so. She decided that the best thing to do would be to stay in line. They continued until dusk and then found a suitable place away from the road to stop for the night. There were other wagons camped nearby, and the smell of food cooking filled the air.

The next morning, they got an early start so they could be ahead of the other wagons. They were able to pass the long wagon train. They made good time each day with very few incidents.

The evening before, Taylor had cut some long poles, about two inches around, to attach to the canvas flaps on the sides of the Bounder. He cut and peeled some shorter ones, about one and a half inches around, for the braces. This would give them a lean-to type shelter to roll down each time they camped. Now all they needed to do was attach the canvas to complete it.

The Bounder seemed to be the best equipped wagon on the road. They got comments from other drivers as they traveled and met people along the way. People of all walks of life and nationalities were going west to start a new life. All of the other women and girls wore long dresses and bonnets. Some of them made remarks about the way Eldene and Patty were dressed, but they just ignored them or told them that they were quite comfortable and that they were not ashamed of the way they looked.

There were people of all religions, and some of them were pretty set in their ways. Some of the men would just look at them and shake their heads in disgust. Eldene would just look them in the eye and say things like, "So you've never seen a woman in pants before, huh? Well, you have now." And then just go on about her business.

Patty was having a harder time accepting their comments, but she stayed close to Eldene and Taylor. She was learning how to deal with people from her mom. Although she had learned a lot about different personalities in the dress shop, it seemed there was always someone that was hard to satisfy, no matter how hard you tried. She was finding out you just cannot please everyone all the time.

The Bounder rolled into Cumberland, a busy railroad hub. They arrived early enough and were able to find a livery stable to bed down the livestock and store the Bounder. After they got the animals and wagon settled and attended to, they asked directions to the telegraph office and headed there first. They sent messages to both the Sweenys and CJ. They asked the telegraph official where a good hotel could be found and made that their next destination, laughing and talking about their trip.

The hotel had a bath area and a café, so they rented rooms for the night. After supper, they roamed around town and realized that there was a lot of construction going on. After inquiring they learned that they were starting construction on the railroad. They planned on going through Cumberland Gap and building the railroad on west. There were a lot of Oriental people employed by the railroad, and it appeared that they had a good start on the construction. Eldene had heard train whistles in the distance as they were traveling toward Cumberland. Also there was a rumor around town that they had discovered gold in California, and a good many people were headed there to stake a claim.

Eldene now realized what most of the traffic was about. People were going to California to strike it rich. She looked at Taylor and Patty and said, "I'm glad that we aren't looking for gold. I believe that people have no idea about the problems that they're going to have. We are going to head for Oregon as soon as we are able to." Taylor and Patty were both happy to hear that.

Eldene was thinking about the money that she had hidden on the Bounder. She was hoping that the metal box she had it in was secure and hidden well enough to not be found. Big Jim had bolted it to the undercarriage, and the lock was a heavy-duty tempered steel lock. She knew that the box couldn't be easily broken into, but she also knew that if, it was discovered by the wrong person or persons, they would stop at nothing to get it. They decided that they would go check the Bounder before they went to the hotel rooms for the night. They walked over to the livery stable. It was getting dark by now and pretty cold. The moon was beginning to light up the night, and you could see your breath.

The horses and mules were calmly roaming around in their stalls, and the goats were huddled in a corner of their little stall. The chickens had bedded down for the night. Eldene heard a shuffle near the Bounder and realized that her concern was probably more like a woman's intuition.

She touched Taylor's and Patty's shoulders and put her finger to her lips and whispered, "Shh, I think someone is prowling around the Bounder. We need to be careful and surprise him." She motioned for Taylor to go around one way, while she went the other. She told Patty to stay where she was.

They snuck around the Bounder, being as quiet as possible, when suddenly, a large tomcat jumped off the fence as he let out a loud *meow*! Taylor and Eldene both almost jumped out of their skin.

"GOOD GRIEF," yelled Taylor, "that scared the bejesus out of me, I almost peed my pants."

"Me too." Laughed Eldene as she collected her senses.

Patty was laughing so hard she was doubled over. Eldene and Taylor looked at each other and burst into laughter.

"I guess that's one thief that got away," Eldene joked.

They checked over the Bounder, and everything was still in order. Taylor decided that after he bathed, he would sleep in the Bounder, and they could let his room go. Eldene agreed, and it made her feel much better than leaving the Bounder unattended.

Another good story for my journal, she thought as they walked back to the hotel. Eldene had decided, before they left Baltimore, to keep a daily account of their trip out West. The journal also helped her keep up on the date. Just before they turned in for the night, she wrote, "March tenth, three months after my sweet Jake's passing w—" She drifted into deep thought. The journal slipped from her hand and fell to the floor, startling her into reality. She picked up the journal, finished her daily entry, and blew out the light. She fell asleep reminiscing about Jake and how she missed his strong arms around her.

The next morning, they got an early start and headed toward their new destination. According to their map, the next town would be Brownsville, Pennsylvania.

They would have to cross the Appalachian Mountains. Eldene was hoping that they won't get caught in a rain/snowstorm like they did coming over the Catoctin Range, traveling between Frederick and Cumberland. March can bring some bad weather sometimes, and she's praying that they don't get any more of it.

They passed by railroad crews as they hammered away at the earth to dig a bed for the railroad tracks. Eldene wondered how long it would take them to reach the West Coast. The war with Mexico has been going on for a year and a half now, and it has taken a toll on construction projects of all kinds. She was glad that Taylor is still too young to join the army.

Eldene was thinking about how much she loves her two children. *I am so thankful for them and the way they love life and each other.*

Taylor and Patty were riding side by side, chatting and joking back and forth, as they followed the Bounder up the mountain road. The terrain was rugged, and the mountains seemed to stretch out and up forever. The road was well constructed, and Jack and Jenny didn't seem to have much trouble pulling the Bounder along. The eighty miles or so to Brownsville should take them about four or five days. She figured they should be there by the fifteenth or sixteenth. They were making good time, and the weather was nice for this time of year. There were several Conestogas and prairie schooners traveling west, and there were still several stagecoaches and freight wagons going both directions.

The mountains were beautiful and the air was so clean and crisp. Eldene began taking deep breaths, trying to inhale as much of the crisp fresh air as she could. Breathing in the cool fresh air made her feel refreshed and full of energy.

The sun shining on the trees brought out all sorts of different colors. The oaks and tamaracks were beginning to get their leaves and needles. The alders and willows were budding, and she loved the fresh smells and sounds of the forest. She was enjoying the scenery and thinking that only God could create something as beautiful as this. Everything fit together so perfectly.

The road followed the terrain along the Potomac River and weaved back and forth across the river on stone arc bridges. Whenever they met a freight wagon or a stagecoach at a bridge crossing, Eldene would pull over and stop and let them cross first. There was probably enough room to pass, but she felt safer by stopping.

Eldene and Taylor traded off driving the Bounder for the next five days. They pulled into Brownsville on the morning of the fifteenth of March. There were so many wagons that the main street was lined with them. The hotels seemed overcrowded, and the boardwalks were lined with people. Eldene discussed it with Taylor and Patty, and they decided that they were going to continue and find a suitable place to stop for the night. They didn't need any supplies, and they still had several hours of daylight left. According to their map, it was about thirty miles to the next town of any size. They could probably get another ten to fifteen miles down the road before they would have to stop for the night.

Once in a while, Patty would ride in the Bounder and study her schoolbooks and read. She wasn't able to bring very many books, but she loved to read. She figured that she would be able to get new books as they traveled from place to place. *There doesn't seem to be an overabundance of libraries in these small towns*, she thought. *As a matter of fact*, she thought, *I don't recall seeing any at all.*

She began wondering about her friends at school and how they were doing. Her mind drifted off into deep thought about how she missed school and the dress shop. She was missing Aunt CJ and her daddy. She used to have so much fun with her dad at family picnics and church gatherings. She remembered one time when they were having a three-legged race and she and her dad tripped and got all tangled up with each other. They were laughing so hard that they had trouble getting up. She was smiling and thinking, *I don't think we won that race.*

Eldene had ridden on ahead to find a good spot for the night. About a mile down the road, she noticed a wagon that was leaning badly to one side. There was a man, a woman, and two younger people standing by the wagon. Eldene rode up to them and noticed that they had lost a rear wheel off the wagon.

"It looks like you might have a bit of a problem."

"Yep," answered the man, "I think we lost a wheel bearing."

"Well, my son and daughter are coming right behind me. Maybe we can help you out."

"That would be mighty neighborly of y'all if you could do that, we have an extra bearing and all. It's going to get dark pretty soon, and we sort of got the road halfway blocked."

"Why don't you unhook the team and let's find a long pole for leverage and get this thing jacked up and see if the wheel is okay," suggested Eldene.

By the time Taylor and Patty pulled up, they had everything ready to try to raise the wagon. Taylor jumped down off the Bounder and tied off the mules, and Patty rode up and tied Socks to the Bounder.

After everyone was introduced, Eldene suggested, "How about if my son and yours apply the leverage, and you and I put blocks under the axle?"

"Sounds okay to me," answered the man, "'cept I ain't used to a woman doing a man's work, ain't you afraid you will hurt yourself?"

"I'll be careful," answered Eldene. "I'm getting pretty used to doing a man's work by now."

Taylor grinned and said, "Yes, sir, she's pretty darned tough, she scared off a bandit, back there in Frederick, that was trying to get into our wagon. She sure sent him packing."

Eldene looked up at Taylor and just shook her head and rolled her eyes. Taylor started laughing and picked up the leverage pole. He placed the pole on the blocks, and he and the other boy pushed down on the pole. The wagon started rising up, and Eldene and the man pushed the blocks under the axle.

"That went slicker'n' a whistle," said the man as he scratched his head in amazement.

The woman took her daughter and Patty and began building a fire aways off the road. They finished changing the wheel bearing just as the sun was beginning to sink over the mountaintops. They were able to hook the disabled wagon up again and pull it off the road.

Taylor found a spot for the Bounder and took care of the animals for the night. They decided that fresh hot goat's milk and cocoa would be good to cap the evening with. They combined their supper and visited for the rest of the evening. They found that their new friends were heading out West to find some land to farm and raise their family on.

Patty and Sue, the daughter, exchanged notes and promised to try to stay in touch. Patty gave Sue her grandpa's address so the mail she sends could then be forwarded, by him, to their new home. Finding out they were going to be farmers made Eldene happy that they were not chasing gold.

The next morning, they had an early breakfast. They said goodbye to the other family and headed west toward the town of Washington. The sky was clouding up a little, and it looked and felt like it might rain. Eldene was praying that it wouldn't. They were lucky; the weather held and there wasn't anything more than just a few sprinkles. They passed a tippling house or two, but they decided not to stop. Eldene wondered why they called them tippling houses. They were mainly a bar and store and sometimes a café.

She shrugged and snapped the reins, yelling, "Giddyap there, Jack and Jenny, let's get on down the road."

As they pulled into Washington to replenish their supplies, Patty was excited to see a whole section of the mercantile dedicated to books and periodicals. Eldene said she could go and look for some books to buy while she and Taylor loaded the supplies. Patty skipped happily off down the aisle, looking at all the books. All too soon the Bounder was loaded, and it was time to go. Patty gathered up her purchases and climbed aboard the Bounder, excitedly showing Eldene the favorites of all the ones she had bought.

The 150 miles between Washington and Wheeling, Virginia, was very mountainous, and the road was a continuous uphill climb. They had a few delays because of rain showers and snow flurries, but they were able to make it to Wheeling according to their time-scheduled plan. They arrived on April 2, which just happened to be Eldene's birthday. Wheeling is a very busy river town situated on the Ohio River. There are boats and barges lined up on the river, waiting their turn to dock and load and unload their goods. Some of them carried people, and some of them carried freight or livestock. But most of the livestock had to be driven over land and cross the rivers at its low spots because of their great numbers.

Families going west were gathering to catch a paddle wheeler down the Ohio to the Mississippi River. Most of them were settling in the fertile valleys of Ohio, Indiana, Illinois, Tennessee, and Missouri. But some of them were going on west to the California gold mines or the Oregon territories.

They were able to find a livery stable to take care of the animals and a place to park the Bounder.

"We are so lucky to find a livery with all of these people traveling," said Eldene.

"I wonder where their wagons and animals are," said Taylor

"Look at all the people lined up at the riverboats," said Patty. "It looks like they are getting on them."

"You're right, honey, they seem to be traveling by riverboat."

They found a café near the river's edge and decided to have an early supper. They entered the café and found a table. Taylor excused himself and went over to the cook and whispered something to him, then returned to his seat, all smiles. They were eating and chatting and watching the steamboats and flatboats.

Eldene looked at Taylor and Patty and asked, "Do you know what I've been thinking? I am wondering how much time we could save by renting a flatboat and going onto the Mississippi by boat."

Taylor answered with a puzzled look on his face, "You've got to be joking, Mom, we could never handle one of those things."

"Yeah Mom," added Patty, "we would surely drown ourselves."

"Wait just a minute, you two. Let me explain what I am talking about. I'm thinking that we could rent the boat with the crew to guide it down the river."

"Well, I don't know, Mom, that could cost us a lot of money."

"Let's just check into and see if we could do it," said Eldene as she finished her steak. "If we could afford it, it would be a good experience and a welcomed rest away from that wagon seat for a while."

Patty perked up and announced, "I'm all for that, my butt could use a rest for a while." They all laughed and agreed to give it a try.

After they had finished their meal, Taylor signaled the cook, and he brought over a small cake with one flaming candle on it.

He sat the cake down, and Taylor raised his glass of water and said, "To the best mom in the whole wide world."

Patty agreed and gave Eldene a huge hug and a big happy birthday kiss.

"I love you, Mom."

Taylor withdrew a small package from his pocket and handed it to his mom. "This is just a little something from Patty and me." There was a small silver bracelet with two heart-shaped charms in the package.

"Thank you, I love you both very much." She hugged and kissed them.

Everyone in the café applauded.

They found a hotel so they could have a bath and get a good night's rest. They have a busy day planned for tomorrow, and Eldene wanted to be refreshed and ready to bargain.

Taylor bathed and said, "I'm going to the Bounder, I'll see you in the morning."

He has slept in Bounder since the incident with the cat. He knew that it made Eldene rest easier, and it made him feel better too.

The next day, they roamed the docks, talking to boat owners and pilots, trying to find a suitable barge. They learned that most of them were hauling cargo or already booked. There were lot of people traveling by riverboat. Most everyone was settling somewhere on the east side of the Mississippi River. However, there were several barges equipped to carry one or two families, including their covered wagons and their livestock, but it seems they were all taken.

They were just about ready to give up and go on by wagon when a stranger approached them.

"I hear that you folks are looking for a flatboat to rent."

Eldene held out her hand and introduced herself to the stranger, "Yes, sir, if the price is right and the crew is adequate, we sure are."

"I have what you might be looking for," he answered, "except you will need to share it with another family."

Eldene looked him in the eye and asked, "Do you think it would it be possible to meet the other family and take a look at the boat?"

"Of course, Mrs. McGrady, follow me. By the way, my name is Henry, Henry Collins."

They walked downriver a ways to a long flatboat that had been converted from a side-wheeler. There were steering quarters next to the big paddle wheel and livestock housing at the rear.

There was enough room for two covered wagons. Eldene noticed a privy next to the livestock huts and another small shedlike structure not too far from the privy.

Mr. Collins noticed the puzzled look on her face and said, "That shed, a ways down from the privy, is for bathing. I figured that people would appreciate a place to freshen up on the long trip to the Mississippi River."

"What about sleeping quarters?" asked Eldene.

"That, I'm afraid, will have to be in your wagons."

Patty looked at Eldene and said, "Well, at least we won't be bouncing around on a horse or a wagon seat for a few days, and my poor butt can sure use the rest!"

"I agree wholeheartedly!" Laughed Taylor.

"We need to join a wagon train in Springfield, Illinois, so where would be the best place for us to get back on the trail?" asked Eldene.

"Well, the best place would probably be Cincinnati," answered Henry. "And coincidently, the Thompson family are supposed to catch a wagon train there too. This could work out pretty good for the both of you."

"Well, I guess it could," stated Eldene. Let's go meet the Thompson family and see if we can make a deal."

"All righty, they're camped not too far from here," said Mr. Collins as he led the way.

Chapter 4

The River

The Thompson family was relaxing around their covered wagon as they waited for Mr. Collins to return. Eldene noticed that the woman and her daughter were dressed in long dresses and bonnets. The dresses had fluffy shoulders and sashes tied in a bow in the back, and the bonnets were tied in a bow under their chins. She thought that they looked more like they were going to church than traveling across the country in a covered wagon. The man and his son were clothed in more appropriate attire for traveling. She was wondering if they would accept the way she and Patty were dressed.

Mr. Collins introduced everyone and said politely, "I will leave y'all to get better acquainted and talk about what you want to do. I'll check back with you in the morning."

"Just a minute, Mr. Collins," said Eldene, "before you go, I need to have an idea of a price for your services."

"Well, as I told Mr. and Mrs. Thompson, I have a three-man crew, and there will be feed to buy for the animals and coal for the steam engine. I figured that it will take us about five to seven days, depending on the weather, to reach Cincinnati. The river is big and fairly slow-moving, and my engine is pretty small. It will cost ten dollars each for the horses, mules, and cows and five for the goats and two for the chickens. The wagons will be twenty-five dollars each, and for each person, it will cost ten dollars. It's your responsibility to make sure that your water barrels are full each day. Each evening we will pull into the bank and tie down for the night, and you will be able to build a fire, heat water, and cook your evening meal. If that suits ya, I will need half of the payment up front and half when the trip is finished."

"You seem to have things pretty well figured out, Mr. Collins. We'll have an answer for you in the morning."

While Eldene was talking to Mr. Collins, Taylor and Patty were getting to know the Thompsons. Eldene noticed that Taylor seemed to be enamored by the young girl who seemed to be about his age. Patty was talking with the young boy, who seemed to be about her age. She watched them for a moment and realized that new friends their own age might be just what they need. It could be the turning point for Patty, she thought.

After a couple of hours, Eldene decided that the Thompsons were a nice Christian family and would make good traveling companions.

"Well, Mr. and Mrs. Thompson, what do you think about traveling together?"

Mr. Thompson looked at Mrs. Thompson, and she nodded her approval. "Well, by golly, Mrs. McGrady, we think it's a danged good idea. It's going to be a downright real pleasure traveling with you and your children!"

"Okay, we'll see you bright and early tomorrow morning then."

"You can call me Harold, and my wife is Mary. Our children's names are Carrie and Randy."

"Okay then," Eldene responded, "I'm Eldene and this big brute"—as she put her arm around her son—"is Taylor, and this youngster"—putting her other arm around Patty—"is Patty."

"They sure seem like a very nice family," said Eldene as they walked toward the hotel.

"Yeah," answered Patty as she poked Taylor in the ribs and teased, "My, my, big brother, you seemed kind of smitten by that Ms. Carrie,"

"You looked pretty engrossed with Randy too, little sister!"

"We were just talking about how we miss our school friends and all," answered Patty.

"How come you're blushing then?" asked Taylor.

"Me! Your face is redder than mine!"

"Okay, you two," Eldene interrupted, "let's have some supper and get some much needed rest." Patty poked Taylor in the ribs again and ran into the hotel café.

Eldene was up early the next morning, eager to get the day moving. She woke Patty up and explained, "I am going to the Bounder to wake Taylor." As she reached the bottom of the stairs, she saw Taylor sitting in the lobby, waiting for her and Patty to come down for breakfast. He had already gotten the Bounder ready and had it waiting in front of the hotel.

"My goodness!" exclaimed Eldene. "You are quite the early bird, young man."

"Yes'm, I woke up before sunup and decided to get things ready."

After breakfast, they gathered their suitcases, loaded them onto the Bounder, and headed down toward the docks. Mr. Collins was on the side-wheeler, waiting for them. Harold and Mary, with their rig, showed up at the same time.

"Good morning, Mr. Collins!" said Eldene. "We've decided to take you up on your offer."

"Wonderful news," he exclaimed. "I'm sure I couldn't find a nicer bunch of folks to make the trip with!"

After they had settled the finances, Mr. Collins, introduced his three crew members as Lefty, Pete, and Vern.

"Y'all bring your covered wagons and animals to be loaded on the boat. It will take us the rest of the morning to load everything and get the wagon's wheels chalked and tied down."

After everything was loaded, Mr. Collins checked and double-checked to make sure all was secure and ready to go. "Good work, everyone. It looks like we are ready to go! Let's meet back here after we have some lunch, and we'll get underway."

"It's sure going to be good to be on the move again," said Eldene

"It sure enough will," answered Harold.

"Shall we all have lunch together?" asked Eldene.

"Sounds good to us," answered Harold. "There's a café a short distance from here."

Taylor and Carrie sat opposite each other. After the waitress had filled their water glasses, Carrie removed her bonnet and straightened her dark-auburn hair. Taylor noticed that her long hair framed her beautiful round face and made her brown eyes sparkle like a diamond reflecting off the sun. The dimples on her cheeks made her even more beautiful, and her perfectly lined teeth made her smile mesmerizing.

Taylor felt like he had been hit by a bolt of lightning. *She is so gorgeous*, he thought as he fumbled his fork, and it fell to the floor. He bent over to pick up the fork and accidently knocked over his glass of water.

The cool water ran onto his lap, and he jumped up, exclaiming, "Dang, now I'm all wet!" He simultaneously reached for the glass and knocked Carrie's glass over. The water ran onto her lap, and she jumped up, startled and wet. They just stood there, looking at each other with their mouths agape.

Everyone started laughing.

Taylor and Carrie burst into laughter, and the situation became an experience to remember. They finished their lunch and returned to the boat laughing and talking.

Mary nudged Eldene and whispered, "My, my, it looks like we have a couple of smitten children there."

"Yes'm, I was noticing that myself," Eldene whispered back. "They are so young, I'm sure it's just puppy love."

"We'll see," added Mary. "We'll see."

Eldene shrugged, and they walked on toward the boat. They all boarded the boat, and Mr. Collins told the crewmen to start untying the lines so that he could maneuver the barge into the proper position to head downstream. The crew had stoked the boiler, while everyone was having lunch, so there would be enough steam.

Blaaaaat, the air horn blasted.

"That was really loud," Patty yelled, looking around to see everyone with their hands over their ears.

"Yep, it takes some getting used to," said Vern.

The animals were frightened by the loud blast and started rearing and tugging at their ties.

"We had better go calm those critters down," said Harold

Taylor and Randy followed him. It only took them a few minutes to get the animals settled down again.

"Boy, that was exciting," said Randy as he whipped off his hat and wiped his brow.

"Yeah," said Taylor, "for a minute there I thought we were in big trouble."

"Good job, boys, we did it," said Harold as he patted them on the back.

"Sorry, folks!" exclaimed Mr. Collins. "I guess I'll think twice before I do that again."

"No harm." Laughed Harold. "Just give us a little warning next time!"

After the animals settled down, everyone relaxed and started talking and enjoying the scenery as they floated down the big river. There were several paddle wheelers and barges going both directions, but even with all the traffic, the afternoon was so peaceful. The faster craft kept toward the center of the river which allowed them plenty of room to pass. Toward the evening, the traffic began thinning out, and the flatboat ride was smooth and steady. The sun began its decent behind the trees and displayed a beautiful golden-reddish-orange display across the horizon. The trees along the riverbank become dark silhouettes against the darkening sky. A large flock of blackbirds were dancing in perfect unison, making different formations as they perform their extraordinary ballet in the sky against the beautiful sunset. Back and forth, up and down, around and around, as if they were dancing to a musical symphony.

"What a gorgeous sunset," said Eldene. "Look at those blackbirds. Isn't it amazing the way they all move together at the same time?"

"Yes," replied Mary, "I wonder how in heaven's name they keep from colliding."

"It's almost unbelievable, isn't it?" replied Eldene. "It's like someone is giving them directions."

Eldene saw that Taylor and Carrie were standing next to the railing on the edge of the flatboat, watching the birds and talking and laughing. She was glad to see Taylor so happy. His father's passing had been very hard on him. He had always been a happy-go-lucky kid, taking the bumpy roads of life in his stride, she thought, but this was something different.

Sighing, she said to herself, "I think perhaps Mary is onto something and that my little boy might be falling in love."

She looked over at Patty and saw that she and Randy were also talking and laughing. *He is a handsome boy*, she thought, tall, lean, and muscular, with dark wavy hair and deep blue eyes. It seemed as if they too were becoming good friends rather than falling in love. *After all*, she thought, *they are barely teenagers.*

She began reminiscing about Jake and her at fourteen. *I suppose that we were falling in love then*, she thought. *We used to have so much fun together. I'll never forget the good times we had. Jake was so wonderful and handsome.* She wiped away a tear and returned to reality. Eldene realized that Patty had met her match in this boy, who is as full of vim and vigor as she is. She smiled as she watched them looking over the railing, laughing and joking with each other. *Patty is beginning to show signs of a change for the better*, she thought.

Eldene's thoughts were interrupted by Mr. Collins' yelling.

"May I have all y'all's attention, please? We are going to pull into the bank and tie off for the night. Could everyone please sit on the benches along the railing? I have to put the bow in first, and after we tie it off, we have to let the boat swing around so that the side opposite the paddle wheel will be against the bank. It's an easy maneuver and should go smoothly, but I sure don't want a jolt to send anyone into the river," he added.

The turnabout went smoothly. After the flatboat was tied down, Mr. Collins asked Mr. Thompson if he and Taylor would take care of the animals while the crew lowers and secures the off-ramp.

"Sure thing," answered Harold.

"Right behind you, Mr. Thompson," said Taylor

After the ramp was in place, Eldene and Mary gathered the food and cooking utensils ashore to the camp space. Randy and the girls went ahead to gather firewood and build a couple of cooking fires. After everyone had eaten and cleaned up their dishes, they sat around drinking coffee and goat's milk and talking about what a great first day they had.

Eldene looked at Mr. Collins and said, "I must say, you really know how to handle this river, Mr. Collins."

"Well, thank you, Mrs. McGrady. Please call me Henry, or Captain Henry if you prefer."

"Captain Henry it is then," she answered.

Everyone raised their cup and said, all together, "To Captain Henry and his great crew."

"Thank you very much," they said, bowing and tipping their hats. Everyone broke out in peals of laughter.

The next morning dawned a little differently. Clouds had drifted in during the night, and the air was quite nippy. The wind was blowing slightly, and the river was a little choppy. After breakfast, just about sunup, everyone secured their belongings back on the boat, and Captain Henry and the crew swung the boat around into the proper position. Taylor, Harold, and Randy took care of the animals, and they were underway once again.

After a couple of hours, Eldene noticed that the clouds were getting darker; they were swirling restlessly and changing positions with one another.

"Those clouds seem to be mad at one another," said Patty.

"Yeah, like they're fighting over their place in the sky," said Eldene. "It's beginning to look like we could get some lightning and thunder. The wind is getting stronger, and it's beginning to sprinkle, and those big dark clouds do look pretty angry."

"I think you're right," said Mary, we should probably recheck and make sure everything is where it should be and tied down!"

"Good idea," said Harold.

Suddenly a flash of lightning lit up the sky, and thunder began rumbling. The lightning began a display of spectacular light shows across the darkening sky. The thunder roared as the lightning bolts split the sky. In a matter of minutes, the rain was coming down so hard that it was difficult to see.

Eldene and Mary took shelter under the wagons. The animals were getting excited and becoming restless. Taylor, Harold, and Randy made sure that they were tethered tightly to the hitching rail provided. A storm like this could cause the horses and mules to get too unruly and could cause them to do a tremendous amount of damage. Taylor made sure that they were separated as much as possible. Suddenly a big flash of lightning split the sky. A loud clap of thunder roared overhead.

"My gosh," yelled Taylor, "that was too close, right above us!"

"Yep, it was right over our heads," yelled Harold.

Jack, Jenny, and the other mules began kicking and thrashing. They kicked the boards loose on the side of the shed behind them. Taylor and Randy were trying desperately to calm them down, while Harold took care of the horses. After several intense minutes, they managed to get them settled down.

"Wow, that was exciting, wasn't it?" exclaimed Taylor.

"You can say that again," answered Randy. I wasn't sure we were going to be able to settle them crazy mules down."

Taylor put his arm around Randy's shoulders and stated, "We did it, buddy, we did it." Harold had also managed to keep the horses from doing any damage.

Just when they thought the storm had passed, another series of blinding lightning and roaring thunder dominated the sky. This time, it was a little farther away, and the animals didn't go into fits of fear. The wind had become increasingly stronger, and the flatboat was violently bobbing up and down. Suddenly the paddle wheel stopped turning, and Captain Henry was losing control. The flatboat started to turn sideways in the river. Captain Henry reefed on the large steering wheel, trying to steer it straight.

He yelled to the crew, "Run to the bow and get ready to jump ashore and wrap a line around the closest tree trunk." He knew he had to get the flatboat tied down before the raging river could do any damage or ram the boat into the bank. As they approached the riverbank, the flatboat had turned enough that the port bow was going to hit the embankment first.

"Jump," yelled Vern as they approached the riverbank.

They all jumped off the flatboat and quickly made several wraps around a good-sized tree.

"Hang on to the line, y'all," yelled Vern. "The dadburned boat is a gonna start swingin' around." The line held and the flatboat began turning.

Taylor motioned to Randy. "Come on, let's grab the other rope and wrap it around that tree yonder."

They waited for the right moment and jumped ashore and wrapped the line around the tree. *Cur thud,* the flatboat hit the embankment and stopped moving downstream. The water was still rough, causing the flatboat to bob up and down, but thanks to Captain Henry's quick thinking and everyone's fast action, the dangerous situation was over. After they made sure that everything was shipshape, Captain Henry looked at everyone and remarked with a sigh of relief, "Good grief! That was a mighty close call." He wiped his brow and thanked everyone for their cooperation and quick action.

"We're soaked and uncomfortable, but we seem to be okay," said Eldene.

Eldene looked at Taylor and Randy. "That was a mighty brave thing you two heroes did out there."

"Thanks, Mom, we were only doing what we thought was right.

"Mom, where are Patty and Carrie?"

"Oh my god!" exclaimed Eldene. "I don't know. I thought they were with Mary. It was storming so violently I couldn't see much."

"Here we are," yelled Patty, as she and Carrie came out of the bath hut. We were hiding from the lightning and trying to stay dry."

"Thank God," said Eldene. "I was beginning to panic a little. Hopefully there won't be a next time, but if there is, please stay with me."

"You too, Carrie," said Mary, "I thought you were with Eldene!"

"Okay, Mom," said Patty. "We were just frightened and found the closest place and ran for it. I'm sorry that I worried you."

"Me too, Mom," said Carrie, "that was scary beyond words. We just grabbed each other's hand and made a bee-line for the bath hut."

"I guess all's well that ends well. You're alive and safe, that's the main thing." said Eldene. She hugged Patty and kissed her forehead.

Captain Henry shook the boys' hands, and patting their shoulders, he said, "Thank you for your much needed help, you two would make a great riverboat crew! I am extremely grateful to you and your families for the all the help."

The wind began dying down, and the dark sky began to show some welcomed blue patches. The storm seemed to be moving on. After a while, the sun began shining, and the clouds had moved on to the north, and the river was calming. It once again became a slow-moving body of water.

"We might just as well spend the rest of the day here since we are already tied down," suggested Captain Henry.

Eldene looked at Harold for approval and said, "Sure, we are ahead of schedule anyway, and it would be nice to build a fire and get out of these wet clothes."

"Sounds good to me." said Harold.

As Patty and Carrie were the only dry ones, they gathered firewood and started the cooking fire. Soon everyone had dry clothes on and had hung the wet ones on bushes to dry. Then they gathered around the fire to warm up. Mary made a large pot of coffee. Everyone was having coffee and talking about the storm.

"That was a hell of a storm, said Harold. "I thought there for a minute we were going to lose a couple of those dad-burned animals."

"Yeah, me too, those mules were a little hard to handle," said Randy.

"We did, though," added Taylor. "They didn't damage anything that we can't fix."

Mary whispered to Eldene, "May I speak to you in private."

"Sure," answered Eldene. "Mary and I are going to take a short walk. We'll be back shortly."

"What is it, Mary?" asked Eldene as they walked.

"Well, I-I was wondering if you would help me alter some men's clothing. That confounded dress weighed a ton when it got wet, not to mention how miserable I felt. I know that Harold won't like it, but I'm just tired of dragging a dress around, and you and Patty seem to be so comfortable in your men's attire. I've decided to stand up to Harold, and when we get to Cincinnati, I am going to trade my cumbersome long dresses for something more practical for both Carrie and me."

"I think that would be a smart thing to do," answered Eldene, "I'll do my best to help you."

That night Eldene updated her journal. She entered the events of the day and fell asleep thinking of how proud Jake would be if he were here. He would be proud of the way she and the children were taking charge of their lives.

Eldene awoke the next morning to the noise of the flatboat crew repairing the steam engine. Apparently a drive belt had slipped off during the storm and caused it to stop operating. Captain Henry was directing the crew as they repaired whatever damage was done. They were able to build up enough steam to get underway by about midmorning.

Mary came over to the railing beside Eldene and said, "I explained to Harold what I intend to do when we reach Cincinnati. At first it was not acceptable to him. He didn't want anyone ridiculing me or Carrie. 'A woman should look and act like a woman,' is what he said, but when I asked him if he thought that you and Patty acted like men, he rubbed his unshaven chin and said, 'Well, I can't rightly say that they do.' Then I told him that the nights might be a bit colder if he had to sleep alone under the wagon. I think that little ultimatum may have been the clincher, and he finally said, 'Well, come to think about it, it seems like a fair idea.'"

Eldene answered with a chuckle. "You won't be sorry for the change." Then they both began laughing. They laughed and joked and talked about yesterday's events as the flatboat floated down the huge river.

Cincinnati was a busy river port with numerous paddle wheelers and barges docked along its piers. Longboats, flatboats, and paddle wheelers were manufactured all along the river's shores, so employment was not a problem if you liked to build boats or crew them. It seemed as if it was a very prosperous place, and people were busy going in all directions.

Captain Henry pulled into an open spot at the pier, and the crew secured the flatboat. It took a while for them to get the animals and wagons ready to off-load. They spent the rest of the afternoon off-loading everything. After they finished, Taylor remarked, "It feels like I am still floating down the river. My legs are trying to float out from under me," he joked.

"I feel a little wobbly too," said Patty, as she slowly went around and around with her arms stretched out.

"Me too," said Carrie, as she twirled behind Patty.

Captain Henry began laughing and said, "It appears that everyone has sea legs, you'll all feel fine in a couple of hours."

"I hope so," joked Taylor as he put his arm around Randy, using him for a crutch, as he wobbled on bended knees. They both stumbled and nearly fell. Everyone began laughing.

Patty and Carrie laughed and joked with Taylor and Randy as Eldene and Harold settled up with Captain Henry. They all said their goodbyes to Captain Henry and the crew.

Captain Henry remarked, "I enjoyed the trip with y'all, and I just wanna wish ya good fortune on your journey out West."

They decided to find a suitable place to set up camp for the night and then go into town the next morning to do some shopping. Each family had to replenish their supplies, and Eldene and Mary wanted to shop for some suitable men's clothing. Mary was filled with excitement the next morning and anxious to go into town. Carrie still wasn't too convinced, but she had been talking to Patty and decided to give the boys' pants a try.

Patty admitted, "I was reluctant at first, but now I'm kind of glad that Mom insisted that I do it." She assured Carrie that she would be much more comfortable than in their cumbersome dresses.

She didn't admit it to Patty, but Carrie was more worried about what Taylor would think of her than anything else. She was wondering if he would think she looked too much like a boy with the boy clothes on. She looked at Patty and Eldene and realized that they looked very much like women the way they had tailored their clothing to fit. That realization made her feel a little better, and she decided that she would look just fine and be a lot more comfortable. They spent the day in town, the women shopping for clothes and the men shopping for supplies. Eldene had given a list to Taylor and knew he would be responsible and get everything they needed. Eldene and Mary were able to sell the dresses that they had to the mercantile and raise enough money to buy most of the men's clothing they needed for Mary and Carrie. Everyone met back at the wagons when they were done.

"Would you please clean up the dishes and store the things that you bought today?" Eldene asked, looking at Taylor. "Patty and I are going to help Mary and Carrie with something."

"Sure, Mom, what is it?"

"You'll see soon enough. We'll be back later."

"Okay," said Taylor, a little bewildered.

When Eldene and Patty arrived, Harold was cleaning dishes and storing supplies, while Mary and Carrie were getting the clothes ready to alter.

"Doing a woman's work is not what a man is supposed to be doing," griped Harold. "I still have to feed the animals and milk the cow."

"The cow and the mules will still be there when you're finished, my sweet," said Mary.

"Yep, and my wife will be dressed like a dad-burned man!"

Taylor, on the other hand, was used to doing whatever needed doin' and didn't mind. Randy just followed Taylor's example. Taylor had sort of become his hero. He loved and respected his dad, but there was something about Taylor that made him want to be like him. They were close enough in age to have a good friendship. Randy thought that there probably wasn't anything that Taylor couldn't do. Taylor suggested Randy help his dad by feeding the animals, and Randy took off on the run. The women worked on the clothes until it was too dark to see.

"We'll finish tomorrow while the men are busy getting things ready for the trip to Springfield," said Eldene.

Eldene was pleased with the clothes they were able to buy. They were good-enough-fitting pants to only have to take in the waist areas and shorten the legs. They had to shorten sleeves on the shirts and sew in some pleats in the front and waist areas. When they had finished, Mary and Carrie were happy with their new look.

They packed away the dresses that they had on, and Mary said, "I feel good, I hope that Harold likes the way I look."

"You're comfortable, that's the important thing," said Eldene as she spun her around to make sure the clothes fit.

"Harold will get used to them soon enough," Mary said.

Patty looked at Carrie and said, "I'll have to admit, you are very cute in men's pants." They both giggled.

Carrie looked herself over the best she could, with a small makeup mirror, and exclaimed as she ran her hands over the sides of her body, "Well…here goes nothing."

She turned and walked out of the makeshift dressing room that they had made by hanging blankets around the lean-to that Taylor had put on the Bounder.

Mary jumped up and said, "Wait for me, honey, I don't want to go out there alone." Eldene and Patty followed out behind them, giggling. They were all excited and talking and laughing as they walked toward where the men were sitting around the campfire, having coffee.

Harold looked Mary and Carrie over and remarked, "Somehow men's clothes look a might different on you two than they do on us men. I can't say I don't like the way y'all look, but it will take some getting used to."

Taylor saw Carrie and thought she was even more gorgeous in the tailored pants and shirt. He stood and took a backward step and tripped over a rock. He stumbled and spilled his coffee as he struggled to keep his balance. He recovered, hoping that the reason for his clumsiness wasn't too obvious.

"Ex-cuse m-me," he stammered, "I have to go finish getting the Bounder ready for the trip." He backed toward the Bounder with the coffee cup still dangling from his finger.

Patty saw that he was embarrassed and said, "Wait for me, Taylor, I'll help you."

The next morning, they headed for the wagon trail that led to a place called Terre Haute. It was on the main road near where it ended. Taylor and Patty decided to walk with Carrie and Randy behind the wagons. Eldene let Harold and Mary take the lead.

Taylor was a little quiet. Carrie took his hand and asked, "Do you like my new clothes?"

"Yep, you look downright nice," said Taylor, slightly blushing.

"Thank you, I feel a lot more comfortable." She fluttered her big brown eyes, and poor Taylor melted.

Soon all four were laughing and joking as they walked, enjoying one another's company. They were all holding hands and swinging their arms back and forth. Taylor gave Patty's hand a slight squeeze and winked at her. She knew that he meant thanks for her support last night in his embarrassing moment of need. She loved her big brother, and she knew when to tease and when not to.

It's about a 180 miles from Cincinnati to Terra Haute, mostly on a wagon trail that hadn't been traveled very much. Eldene figured that they would get to Terra Haute in about fifteen days. *That will put us there about the twenty-seventh or twenty-eighth of April,* she thought. After four or five miles of bouncing around in the wagon, Eldene asked Taylor if he would take the reins for a while. With her folks' permission, Carrie climbed up to ride in the Bounder next to Taylor. Patty and Randy decided to ride the horses, but Eldene wanted to walk for a ways to stretch her legs and get some exercise. Taylor couldn't have been any happier. He felt like he could conquer the world singlehandedly.

Carrie locked her arm in his and turned her head to look at him and said, with a sparkle in her eyes, "Okay, handsome let's get on down the road."

Taylor, blushing slightly, snapped the reins. "Giddyap, Jack, giddyap, Jenny!" he yelled.

"May I join you, Eldene?" Mary shouted.

"Sure thing!" Eldene hollered back.

Eldene enjoyed looking at all the different kinds of colorful scenery. She was able to recognize several different kinds of trees and flowers, and the ones that were unknown to her, she would point out and ask Mary if she knew what they were.

"I love the smell of spring," Eldene said.

"Me too, it's so refreshing. By the way," Mary added, "thank you for helping me with the clothes. I couldn't have done it without you. As a matter of fact, I wouldn't have even tried it if I hadn't met you."

"Well, you are quite welcome, and you look fine and comfortable."

As they walked, they were calling out names of trees and plants. "Those are sycamores," said Eldene, pointing at a grove of tall trees. "I can see oaks, honey locusts, wild plums, and horse chestnuts."

"The ones with the white flowers are dogwood," said Mary. "That grove over there is alders."

"What beautiful country," said Eldene.

There were squirrels chattering and cottontails running into the bushes. She saw a couple of wild turkeys run into the bushes too.

"Looks like we may have rabbit stew or wild turkey for supper," she said. "Taylor could pick one of them off with his sling." She recalled how expert he was with a sling, another of the many things Jake had taught him.

"Sling?" asked Mary

"Yes, he always carries one in his back pocket. Why, I have seen him pick off many a wild turkey with it."

"My, my, that boy is quite a wonder," said Mary.

"Yep, he sure is," agreed Eldene, laughing. "A turkey dinner would be real tasty."

They walked a while longer, and then Eldene traded off with Taylor again. Mary climbed back onto her wagon with Harold. Taylor and Carrie walked for a while and then traded off with Randy and Patty, who had still been riding the horses. That's how the rest the of the day went, everyone taking turns riding and walking. After they had traveled about ten miles, Eldene suggested that they find a good spot to set up camp for the night. Everyone agreed that it was a good idea to get set up before dark. They found a nice open area protected by a canopy of trees and began to set up camp. Just as they were finishing, they heard a gobbling sound in the distance.

Eldene said, "Taylor, grab your sling, and you 'n' Randy go out there and see if you can bring back a big fat turkey for supper!"

Taylor took his sling from his back pocket. Randy looked at him in astonishment and exclaimed, "Really! You mean you actually can hit something with that thing?" He had never seen anyone use a sling. "Is that like the one that David killed Goliath with?" he asked.

"Yep," answered Taylor, "just like it."

Everyone watched as Taylor and Randy snuck through the trees. After about five minutes, Taylor put his finger up to his lips and whispered, "Shh, there's one right over there in that tree."

He had a nice round rock in the sling pocket. He motioned for Randy to stay back while he took aim. One strap of the sling was attached around his middle finger. He grasped the other strap in the palm of his hand while the rock hung below in the sling pouch. He twirled the sling once around his head and let go of the strap in his palm. His index finger was pointing at the turkey. The stone went whistling toward the turkey with lightning speed. They heard a thud as the rock hit its mark, and the turkey fell to the ground.

"Wow, that was incredible!" yelled Randy. "You have to teach me how to do that."

"Okey dokey," answered Taylor. "I think we will have plenty of time for that." They ran over to the turkey, picked it up, and headed back to the camp. Everyone was applauding and praising Taylor for his marksmanship.

He smiled and said, "Patty is pretty good with one of these things too."

"Yep," answered Patty, "Taylor taught me how back in Baltimore, where we used to hunt rabbits and wild turkeys."

They boiled some water and plucked the turkey. After it was all cleaned Eldene put the bird on a spit over the campfire.

"Patty, honey would you turn the turkey once in a while so the rest of us can do the chores."

"I'll keep Patty company," said Carrie.

Eldene had picked up some wild asparagus that was growing along the trail.

"Roast Turkey, asparagus, mashed potatoes with gravy and biscuits topped with homemade butter!" said Mary as she set down a pot of potatoes that she had cooked while the turkey was roasting.

"Boy, it just doesn't get much better than this, does it?" remarked Eldene.

Patty and Carrie set out plates and utensils, while Harold and the boys washed up for supper.

"This is good, good food," said Taylor as he took a big bite.

"It sure enough is," said Harold, "thanks to you and that dad-burned contraption of yours."

"I ain't ever seen anything like that before," said Randy.

"I reckon none of us has" said Harold.

"Taylor said he would teach me how to use it," Randy said excitedly.

"Well, good," said Harold, "maybe I can sit in on some of those lessons too!"

After supper, everyone turned in for the night. Later on, after everyone was bedded down for the night, Eldene heard a strange noise near the Bounder. Then she heard the livestock starting to thrash around. The horses were snorting, and the mules were becoming unruly.

She tiptoed to the back of the Bounder, woke Taylor, and whispered, "Do you hear that? Something is scaring the horses." Taylor got out of the Bounder. The mules and the horses were beginning to raise a ruckus. They were rearing and stomping, whinnying, snorting, and braying and trying to break loose from their ties. The goats were running around their stake downs, and the chickens were cackling and trying to get out of their cages. Thompson's cow was bawling and tugging at her rope. Taylor came around the rear of the Bounder and saw Harold and Randy coming with their muskets. "What's going on, what's all the ruckus about?"

Taylor heard a grunting sound near where the campfire was and looked up to see a large black bear.

"Look, it's a bear," he called out.

The bear grabbed the remains of the turkey that was left on the spit above the cooking grate.

Boom! Harold fired his musket in the air, and the bear took off running with the turkey—spit and all—in his mouth. They chased after him and watched as the bear disappeared into the moonlit woods. Eldene, Mary, and the girls were calming the livestock as the boys walked back into the camp.

"What was it?" they asked in unison!

"It was a dad-burned bear!" answered Harold.

"Yeah," added Taylor, "and he stole the rest of the turkey."

Eldene and the other girls looked at the boys and started laughing.

"What's so funny?" asked Harold.

They looked at one another and realized that they were standing there with their rifles and nothing else on except their long underwear and boots.

Eldene, still laughing, said, "It looks like I have another great page for my journal, and next time, I will remember to pack away the remains of supper.

"This was worth it, even if we did lose the rest of the turkey," said Mary, chuckling.

Patty and Carrie were laughing so hard they couldn't speak.

The next morning, they checked to see if the bear had done any other damage and found that everything was okay. They packed up camp and started northwest toward Terre Haute and the Wabash River.

Eldene breathed in deeply. *Spring is in the air. Chipmunks are chattering, and the robins are hopping around, looking for bugs and worms. Sparrows are flittering from tree to tree, and squirrels are leaping from branch to branch.* *Oh, if only Jake could be here to enjoy this peaceful feeling,* thought Eldene. *He would love it so much.* Her thoughts drifted into daydreams and memories as the Bounder bounced over the rough trail.

Chapter 5

On to Springfield

They pulled into Terre Haute on the twenty fifth of April, three days ahead of Eldene's estimated schedule. It seemed that the whole city was teeming with people going in all directions. Stagecoaches, freight wagons, covered wagons, surreys, buckboards, and men riding horseback filled the streets. Pedestrians were crossing the street whenever they could dodge their way through the traffic without getting trampled. Eldene was glad that Taylor and Patty were riding in the Bounder with her.

"Look at how busy this place is!" said Taylor. "It's almost like Baltimore."

"I think that even Baltimore was a little more settled than this," said Eldene.

"Yeah," said Patty, "all these people look like they are in a mighty big hurry to get somewhere."

"The Thompsons must want to go on through," said Eldene. "They don't seem to be looking for a place to stop. Maybe we should just follow them and try to get past all this craziness!"

After about an hour, they had made their way through town, and the Thompsons pulled over and stopped. Eldene pulled up behind them.

Harold approached the Bounder. "Wow, that's a dad-burned busy place back there!"

"Yep," said Eldene. "I'm wondering just what's going on there."

"Well, I didn't want to stop in the middle of all that ruckus, so I figured we'd just keep on a movin'."

"What do you say we find a spot to camp for the night?" asked Eldene. "If you will keep an eye on the Bounder, Taylor, Patty, and I will walk into town and see what's going on."

"The kids and I will go with you, if you don't mind," said Mary.

"Sounds fine to me," said Harold, "I don't care to get in the middle of that mess, I'll take care of things here."

"Okay then," said Eldene.

"Yeah," said Taylor, "it'll be fun."

It was midafternoon, and the streets of Terre Haute were still bustling with people, going to and fro.

"We need to find a telegraph office or a postal office," said Eldene. I need to wire my parents and sister, CJ."

"I need to send off a letter myself," said Mary.

Eldene stopped a gentleman and said, "Excuse me, sir, could you tell me where the telegraph office is?'

"Sorry, ma'am, I...don't think we have anything like that here in Terre Haute."

"I was hoping to send a wire to my relatives in Baltimore."

"I'm afraid I don't know what you mean, ma'am."

"What about a postal service where I can send a letter?"

"Oh, that would be about ten buildings down the street on the left. It's inside the Terre Haute Mercantile."

"Thank you for your help, sir. By the way, what are all these people doing in town?"

"Well…a lot us are getting ourselves ready to leave town because of the new Wabash-Erie Canal construction. A lot of people don't want the canal to come through here and are pretty mad about it. We like things the way they are, and the canal will bring in more and more people. They are planning on coming through Terre Haute and going on to the Ohio River. The dad-burned canal workers have taken up all the hotel rooms and now are camping everywhere. There are a lot of folks moving on west, away from Terre Haute. They were planning on building the road on to Vandalia, Illinois, but the newsprint said they ran out of money. I don't see why, they seem to have plenty of money to build that damnable canal."

"Thanks again for your help, sir," said Eldene, sensing it was time to move on.

"Glad I could be of help," he said, tipping his hat and walking away.

"Looks like there is going to be a change for these people," said Mary. "I'm glad we are just passing through."

"So am I," said Eldene, "so am I."

The kids were looking in the store windows and laughing and having fun. Eldene noticed that Taylor and Carrie were holding hands, and in fact, so were Patty and Randy.

"Looks like our children are having a good time," she said.

"They seem to be enjoying one another's company," said Mary.

Yeah, maybe a little too much, too soon, thought Eldene. They seem to be getting pretty close to one another. As they approached the mercantile, a commotion of some sort broke out further down the street.

"Wait here on the walkway while I take care of business," said Eldene.

"Okay, Mom, we'll be right here watching the ruckus," said Taylor.

Bang, bang, rang out just as Eldene and Mary came out of the mercantile. They looked down the street just as a man fell to the ground.

"Look, that man running away has a gun in his hand," said Taylor. "He must have shot that other man."

"There goes a couple of deputy sheriffs after him," said Randy.

"Okay, come on everyone, I think we have had enough of this town of Terre Haute! Let's head on back to the wagons and get ready to move on," said Eldene.

"Let's wait and see if they catch that fellow," said Taylor.

Carrie tugged on Taylor's hand. "Let's do what your mom said, shall we?"

"Yeah, Taylor," said Patty, "I think we've seen enough."

Even though Taylor was curious, he knew that they were right. "Well…okay, let's go then," he said reluctantly as he let Carrie pull him down the street, with Patty behind, pushing on his back.

"Dang, I was hoping we were going to stay," said Randy.

Patty ran from behind Taylor and tagged Randy on the shoulder. "Come on, I'll race ya!" She took off running, and Randy chased after her. Taylor and Carrie followed suit.

"Where in the world do they get all of that energy?" said Mary

"I don't know, but they seem to never run out of it," answered Eldene.

Harold had all of the animals taken care of and a campfire going. They relaxed and visited the rest of the day and turned in early, so they would be well rested for the long days of traveling ahead, as they had decided to leave the National Road and take a less-traveled route northwest toward Springfield, Illinois.

They all got up early and discussed their trip while having breakfast.

"According to the map, it looks like Springfield is about two hundred miles or so," said Eldene.

"Yep, we should be able to make it there in about two and a half or three weeks," said Harold. I reckon we should get to Springfield around the fifteenth of May."

"That'll give us about two weeks to get our wagons taken care of for the trip into the wilderness," said Eldene. "I want to have the bearings greased and have some new brake blocks put on the Bounder."

"Me too," replied Harold. "I want to be ready for that trip. I heard that it can get pretty danged rough between Kansas City and Oregon. We need to be ready for just about anything and everything, I reckon."

"We're a pretty tough bunch, we'll make it okay," said Eldene emphatically!

"Yep," added Taylor, "we're not going to let anything stop us."

"All righty then," said Harold, picking up Eldene's slang, "I reckon we're ready to hit the road."

"Make sure the fires are out," Eldene said to Taylor, "and let's get going."

By the time the camp was all cleaned up, Patty was mounted on Socks, and Barney was saddled and ready for Taylor. Randy was in the Thompsons' wagon with Harold and Mary, but Carrie was riding in the Bounder with Eldene.

"HEEYA. Giddyap there, Jack, giddyap, Jenny," yelled Eldene as she snapped the reins. HEEYA." Jack and Jenny followed her command and headed the Bounder toward the trail.

Thweet, whistled Harold. "Move out, mules," he hollered as he pulled in behind the Bounder.

They traveled north along the Wabash River until they found a suitable place to take the wagons across. Eldene guided Jack and Jenny to the river's edge and stopped.

"Taylor, ride Barney out a ways to see how deep the water is," said Eldene.

"All right, Mom," Taylor yelled back. "Come on, Barney, let's go, boy," he said as he made a clicking sound with his tongue. "Easy now, Barney, easy, boy," he said as Barney waded forward into the water." It looks like a pretty good place to cross, Mom. It only comes up to Barney's knees," Taylor yelled as Barney climbed up the opposite bank.

"Okay then, come on back and take the goats across, and then you can come back and get the Thompsons' cow."

"All right, I'll be right there," shouted Taylor.

"Follow behind him Patty, and then have Taylor bring Socks back to get Carrie and Randy. Is that okay with you and Mary?" asked Eldene, looking at Harold.

"That sounds like a dad-burned good-enough plan to me," said Harold.

"I think I would rather ride Socks across too, if that is okay with you," said Mary. "We haven't crossed a river this big yet, and I'm a little nervous about riding across in the wagon."

Eldene took the money bag out of the steel box mounted under the wagon so it wouldn't get wet while they crossed.

After Taylor had shuttled everyone across, he said, "Do you want me to bring the Bounder across, Mom?"

"No, I think I'd like to try it myself," Eldene hollered back.

"Okey dokey, just take it nice…and…easy, Mom," Taylor shouted.

"Yeehaw there, Jack! Yeehaw, Jenny!" she yelled as she snapped the reins, and the mules pulled the Bounder into the river. She was midway when she saw something coming downriver toward the Bounder. "What is that coming at me?" she yelled at Taylor.

"It looks like a big log!" Taylor hollered back

He grabbed the lasso tied to his saddle and yelled, "Let's go, Barney," and galloped up the river's edge and entered the water just above the large log. There was a large limb sticking up from the log.

"Come on, Barney," he yelled as he twirled the lasso. He tossed the lasso, and the loop went around the limb.

"Let's go, Barney, show us what you're made of, boy. Come on, boy," As he wrapped the rope around his saddle horn, he headed Barney toward the opposite shore, pulling the log. "Keep going, Barney. Come on, boy, keep on pulling."

Barney was able to pull enough of the log onto the shore to stop it from ramming the Bounder. Everyone was applauding, whistling, and praising Taylor and Barney from both sides of the river.

"You never cease to amaze me, son," said Eldene proudly. "That was nothing short of a miracle. I was sure that log was going to ram right into the Bounder!"

"Twer'nt nothin', my lady," quipped Taylor as he laughingly retrieved his lasso to hide his embarrassment at all the attention and then crossed the river once again. Moments after they got the Bounder and the Thompsons' wagon across and up on the far bank, the log broke loose and floated on down the river.

"That could have been bad," said Harold. "That boy's a quick thinker."

"The chickens sure got a little scared." Laughed Patty. "They broke two eggs." She held up the only unbroken one. "Looks like I'll have to clean the coop."

They traveled downriver again until they came across the wagon trail that headed toward Springfield. The trail seemed to be little more than a crude rutted path made by wagon wheels and animal tracks, as it headed across the prairie.

Eldene stopped and yelled back at Harold and Mary, "This seems to be the right trail, but it hasn't been traveled much lately."

"It might be a little rough going!" Harold yelled, "But I reckon it'll get us there sooner or later."

"Yep, I suppose it will! Yeehaw, Jack and Jenny, let's get going."

Later that day, when they were setting up camp, Harold commented, "I reckon that wasn't too dad-burned bad, we got about nine or ten miles in today."

"Yeah, but my behind sure feels more like twenty," said Patty, rubbing her behind. Everyone laughed.

"Mine too," said Carrie, I think I sat in that wagon seat for way too many hours. I think we need to get a couple of horses when we get to Springfield. Do you think we could, Pa?"

"Well... I don't know if that would be possible," said Harold, scratching the back of his neck, "I think maybe they might cost more than I can afford."

"Can we at least look and see?" asked Carrie.

"Yeah, Pa, let's at least see what it would cost," said Randy.

"Well... I guess it won't do no harm to look."

"Yippee ki-yo ki-yay!" Carrie yelped.

"I said we'd look... I didn't say we'd buy!"

"I know, Pa, I know." She gave him a big hug.

The next morning, Taylor let Carrie ride Barney. He decided to walk alongside and then maybe spell Eldene on the Bounder. Patty was riding Socks, and Randy was walking beside her. Taylor noticed a patch of wildflowers next to a pond, off the trail a ways, and decided to pick some for Carrie.

"I'll be right back," he said as he ran toward the flowers.

As he was picking the flowers, he noticed several yellow jackets flying around. The yellow jackets began zipping past his head, and he began to panic a little. He decided that the flowers weren't worth getting stung for. He stood up and started to head back to the trail when he stepped into a hole near the edge of the flower patch. He looked down, and his leg was completely covered with yellow jackets.

"I've stepped in a yellow jackets nest," he yelled.

"Hey, everybody, Taylor's in trouble," screamed Carrie.

The yellow jackets were attacking Taylor with a vengeance.

"Eee yikes!" Taylor screamed as he flailed his arms and began to run. He was blinded by fear, and the yellow jackets were relentless in their assault. Carrie jumped off Barney and ran to help Taylor. Taylor was flailing away in a panic.

"I'm coming, Taylor," she screamed.

The yellow jackets began to attack Carrie. "Yeeow." She ran toward Taylor and tackled him. They went flying into the pond. There were hundreds of angry yellow jackets fluttering around in the water, and hundreds more swarming around the nest.

"Oh my god, come on, Carrie, let's get out of here," he said as he swam toward the opposite side of the pond.

"I'm right behind you." She gasped.

Taylor helped Carrie out of the water and threw his arms around her. "Thank you, thank you, thank you, that was mighty daring and brave."

"I didn't know what else to do. Those crazy bees were trying to kill you."

"You saved my life," he said as he held her closer. "Did you get stung?"

"Yeah, they got me a couple of times," she said as she squeezed him. "Did you get stung?"

"Yep, they got me good."

"Are you all right, Taylor?" Eldene yelled.

"I think so, Mom. We'll be there in a minute."

Carrie looked up at Taylor and saw that his face was beginning to swell. His left eye was almost swollen shut. "Oh, dear god, you're starting to swell something awful. Let's go get some dry clothes and get you taken care of." She grabbed his hand and headed around the pond toward the Bounder, making sure that they were far enough away from the yellow jacket nest.

Eldene looked at Taylor and realized that he had been stung several times. "Your face is swelling beyond recognition, son. You'll have to ride in the Bounder and stay quiet until some of that swelling goes down." Eldene looked at Carrie and saw tears running down her face. "I saw what you did over there, and I think it was one of the bravest things I've ever seen," she told Carrie as she hugged her.

"Is Taylor going to be okay?" Sobbed Carrie.

"He's a tough boy, he'll be just fine." She soothed Carrie.

"He looks terrible, Mrs. McGrady, I'm afraid for him. Sometimes those yellow jacket stings can make you really sick."

"He'll be fine. I think he looks worse than he feels. Why don't you go get some dry clothes on and check back a little later?"

"Okay, ma'am. I'll be back in a little while." She tethered Barney to the Bounder and followed Mary back to their wagon.

Patty looked at Taylor and said, "My goodness! You look like you've been beat up, Taylor. Don't you know better than to take on an army of yellow jackets?"

"I geth nop," he said, trying to talk through his swollen lips. "I'b lerben I hobe."

"You look kind of miserable."

"I ab kyd ob mibberble."

Patty couldn't keep from laughing.

"Whab's tho fubby thiter deaw. I don thig ib's fubby."

"I'm sorry, it's just that you sound and look so different with your face so swollen. I really don't think it's funny." She kissed him on his swollen cheek.

Randy was waiting at a distance, trying not to laugh.

"Come on, Randy," said Patty. "You can ride Barney.

Eldene made sure that Taylor was comfortable and said, "Okay, folks, we are ready to go once more."

"Okay!" yelled Harold. "If Taylor is okay, let's do it!"

Carrie ran back to the Bounder. "May I ride with you, ma'am?"

"Of course, dear, hop on."

"Heeya, Jack! Heeya, Jenny!" she yelled and snapped the reins. Carrie looked in on Taylor to see if he was all right.

"Mrs. McGrady!" she yelled. "Taylor is burning up with fever. I think we had better stop and take care of him."

Taylor was moaning and acting delirious.

"Whoa there, Jack Whoa, Jenny!" yelled Eldene.

"What's wrong?" Patty asked.

"It's Taylor, honey, we have to stop and take care of him. Ride up and tell the Thompsons."

"I'll do it," yelled Randy, "go ahead and help your mom."

"Okay," said Patty as she dismounted.

"You're right, Carrie," Eldene said, feeling Taylor's forehead. "He's burning up with fever. Patty, get some cold water."

Eldene began unbuttoning Taylor's shirt and realized that the yellow jackets had stung him on his neck and head.

"Look," said Carrie, "there are yellow jackets inside his clothes."

"Oh, good Lord in heaven, help us, this boy has been stung too many times. The little monsters inside his clothing are still stinging him.

Patty brought the water. When she saw Taylor's condition, she began to cry. "Mommy! We've got to do something, he could die." She gasped.

"What's going on?" Harold inquired.

"Taylor is really sick, Mr. Thompson," said Patty. "We've got to do something."

"There's a creek up ahead," said Harold. "I'll fetch some mud from the bank, and we'll pack him in cool mud."

"Would you step out of the wagon, sweetie? I have to undress Taylor, and he would never forgive me if you saw him naked."

"Yes, ma'am, I understand," said Carrie as she wiped tears away.

Harold returned with the mud and handed it to Eldene. "We will have to change the mudpack every once in a while in order to keep him cool. The mud should help draw out the poison from them dad-burned wasps and get his fever down."

Not knowing whether it would work or not, Eldene agreed to try it. Eldene worked the rest of the day and through the night, trying to break Taylor's fever and get the swelling down. Patty, Carrie, and Randy kept bringing cool water and fresh cool mud. Harold and Mary took care of the animals and everything else.

"How's he doing, Mrs. McGrady? Is he getting any better?" asked Carrie.

"He's not doing any worse, but he's still burning up with fever. I won't stop until he's broken this high fever."

Eldene kept swabbing Taylor's face with cold wet cloths. Taylor was still deliriously moaning and writhing in pain.

The early morning hours were pretty cold, and everyone was wrapped in blankets to keep warm.

Just before daylight, Taylor began shivering. "What's happening, Mom? Where am I? What's this stuff all over me? Is this stuff mud? Yikes, am I naked?"

"Oh, dear god, thank you," said Eldene as she felt Taylor's forehead. You were delirious and burning up with fever. We kept you packed in cool mud to get your fever down and draw out some of the yellow jacket poison in you. It seems to have worked. Your face isn't as swollen, and your lips seem to be working pretty good."

Taylor tried to rise up. "My head is splitting, I think I'm going to puke."

Eldene grabbed a nearby pot and put it under his chin.

"What's all the ruckus?" asked Harold. "Is everything okay?"

"Well, his fever has finally broken, but he isn't feeling very good right now. We probably should camp here for a day or two so he can get his strength back. You folks could go on ahead if you want to, we could join up again at Springfield," said Eldene.

"No, Daddy, please," said Carrie, "we can't go without them. They need our help."

"She's right," said Randy, "we can't leave them behind."

"We're making good time, so I reckon a couple of days won't hurt none," said Harold. "Dad-burn it, we ain't goin' nowhere without you folks. We're gonna make camp right here until that boy can travel."

"All right then," said Eldene. "First thing I have to do is make a comfortable place for Taylor under the weather flap on the Bounder. I'll need more water, kids, so that I can clean the mud off and get him into some clean clothes."

After they got Taylor set up under the weather flap, Eldene and Patty began cleaning up the mud mess in the Bounder.

"Good heavens, what an awful mess," said Patty, "we may never get this place back in order."

"We'll make it, dear, just keep cleaning."

"Maybe in a week or two," Patty said jokingly.

Everyone was tired after a long night without sleep.

"We should all get some rest while Taylor is quiet," said Eldene. "Patty and I will watch him and make sure he is taken care of."

"I would like to help, if you don't mind," said Carrie.

"Okay, but you should probably get some rest first. I'll take the first shift while you and Patty rest."

Carrie slept for a few hours and then returned to the Bounder to take her turn.

She didn't get more than ten feet away from him for the rest of the day and most of the night.

"I'm really worried about Taylor, Mrs. McGrady. He's too quiet. Don't you think he should be moving around by now?"

"I think he's finally sleeping," said Eldene as she felt his forehead. "The swelling is going down, and he doesn't seem to have a fever. I think he has won his battle."

She had no more than finished when Taylor started rubbing his eyes and stretching his legs and arms.

"What's going on, Mom? I'm hungry."

Carrie heard his voice. "Thank God he's all right. I'll fix him something to eat," she said with tears of joy running down her cheeks as she walked away.

Taylor started to get up when he realized that he was in his underwear. "I think I'm ready to get dressed," he exclaimed.

"Are you sure you feel up to it?" asked Eldene "You've been a pretty sick boy."

"I'm feeling pretty good. I think I could eat a horse," quipped Taylor.

"I guess I should go hide Socks then," joked Patty.

"Maybe we should start with some oatmeal and goat's milk," said Carrie.

"That's a good idea," said Patty. "I'm not ready to give Socks up yet."

"Ha ha smarty-pants, maybe I'll just eat one of the mules!"

"Well, obviously you're feeling much better, young man," said Eldene. "I guess maybe we can get back on the road tomorrow morning."

"We're all mighty glad to see that you're okay," said Harold. "We were getting pretty worried there for a while. Them dad-burned wasps did their damndest to do you in, young feller."

Carrie began spoon-feeding Taylor when suddenly, he realized what she was doing. "I can feed myself," he said as he grabbed for the spoon.

"Just be still and open your mouth," said Carrie, pushing his hand down. "You can feed yourself tomorrow."

"Yeah, that will give me time to hide Socks and Barney," joked Patty.

The next morning, Taylor was the first one up. He put the harnesses on the mules and saddled the horses. Everyone was amazed when they got up and smelled fresh coffee brewing.

"Come on, sleepyheads, let's get on to Springfield. It's going to be dark pretty soon," joked Taylor.

"You, big dummy." Yawned Patty. "The sun isn't even up yet."

"You're feeling your oats today," said Eldene. "I'll fix some eggs and biscuits while you milk the goats, and we'll get back on the road."

*****

The next few days were good for traveling. There were several creeks and rivers to cross, but it was mostly sunny and warm, and the relatively flat terrain wasn't difficult. All of the poplar trees had sprouted new leaves, and the evergreens were beautiful with their light-green needles growing on the tips of their branches. The flowering trees were in bloom, and the meadows were bursting with different colors as the wild flowers popped open to soak up some of the daily sunshine.

Oh, how I wish that Jake was here with us, thought Eldene as she looked out over the beautiful surroundings.

"Hey, Mom, look what I got us for supper today!" yelled Taylor as he rode up alongside the Bounder, startling Eldene. "I got some meat to fry up," he said, holding up four cottontails. "I was teaching Randy how to use the sling, and he got one of them by himself. You should have heard him hoot and holler. He was doing cartwheels and jumping around like a chicken with its head chopped off. He got so excited that he forgot that he was riding Socks, and he ran off and left her. I had to go round her up. I was laughing so hard that I almost fell off Barney!"

"I'm glad you boys are having a good time. It looks like you have enough there to invite the Thompsons for dinner tonight."

"I was hoping you would say that," said Taylor.

Patty poked her head out of the flap and said, "I know what you're up to, big brother. You just want to spend some time with Carrie."

"Yeah, well, guess who else will be there, little sister. Someone that you seem to like being around a lot."

"Okay, kids, let's talk about the weather or something else," said Eldene, smiling.

Later that day at supper, Randy began bragging about his experience. "When I saw that rabbit, I jumped off Socks and whirled that sling around my head, just like Taylor taught me." He whirled his hand around his head, pretending that he had a sling, as he continued, "I let go and the danged rabbit just sat there chewing on a wild flower, looking at me. I realized that I had forgotten to load the danged sling. I found a nice round rock, and this time when I let go, the rabbit toppled over. I was so excited that I forgot I was riding Socks, and Taylor had to go round her up." Everyone was laughing as he went through his dramatic antics and gestures while telling his story. "I thought that when we started out on this trip that things were going to be boring and depressing, but they have been fun-filled and exciting since we started traveling together. I'm happy that we met up and became friends."

"I agree," said Mary, "I am mighty proud to be part of this adventure!"

"We appreciate your kind words," said Eldene, "but I think we are the fortunate ones to have friends like you all. We have a good many miles left to go, and we couldn't ask for better companions."

The next several days went fairly smooth, and they were able to make up some of the time that they had lost.

Chapter 6

Springfield At Last

It was the fifteenth of May, and they were camped on the bank of a fairly deep river.

"We must be getting close to Springfield," commented Eldene. "I think this is the Sangamon River. It runs southeast of Springfield just a few miles."

"I reckon all we have to do is find a dad-burned place to cross the confounded thing. I walked downriver, and it's to dad-burned deep. We'll have to go upriver and find a spot to cross," said Harold.

"Mommy, may we stay here for an hour or two longer so that we can find a private place to bathe?" asked Patty.

"That's a good idea, sweetheart," said Eldene. "How about if we girls go upriver a ways, and you boys can go downriver."

"Good, grab some soap and clean clothes, Carrie, and let's go play in the water," said Mary.

They found a secluded spot that was easy to wade into. Patty shed her clothing down to her long johns that Eldene had altered, and took a running jump into the water. "Yippee!" she yelled.

Carrie followed Patty, stripped to her petty pants. "Oh my god!" she screamed. "This water is so cold."

Eldene stuck her toes in the water and quickly jerked them back. "Are you guys crazy? This water is freezing." She slowly lowered herself into the cold water, yelling, "Oh my god, oh my god, oh my god!"

"Come on, Mom," yelled Carrie.

"I'm c-c-c-c-c-com-m-ming," said Mary as she lowered herself into the cold water.

"It's not too bad once you get used to it," said Patty as she soaped herself. "It feels refreshing"

Everyone was having fun, chatting and bathing when suddenly, Patty let out a bloodcurdling scream. "Eek, a snake."

Everyone was screaming and rushing to the bank. The snake slithered its way to the opposite side of the river and disappeared in the tall grass.

"Wow, that was scary," said Patty. "I wonder what kind of snake it was."

"I don't know," said Carrie, "but I don't want to be in the same river that it's in. Those things give me the shivers."

"Me too," said Mary.

Everyone was stammering and talking at once. Eldene and Patty in their short-sleeved and short-legged long johns, and Carrie and Mary in their petty pants and camisoles.

"Likewise!" exclaimed Eldene. "I think maybe bath time is over."

"Yep, I'm done!" exclaimed Mary as she grabbed her towel and stepped behind a bush. "I'm not bathing with any snakes."

Everyone stepped behind bushes, dried off, and redressed.

"That was refreshing, though, we'll have to do that every time we cross a river," quipped Patty.

"Yeah, but without the snake!" exclaimed Carrie.

The boys had the wagons hitched up and ready to go when they returned to camp.

They followed the trail upstream until they came to a suitable place to cross the river.

"Watch out for snakes," Patty joked. The girls all started laughing.

They crossed without incident and headed northwest to Springfield.

Springfield, a city of about four thousand residents, is the capitol city of the state. As you enter the city, the capitol building is the first thing that you see. The white dome stands majestically above the surrounding buildings.

"Wow, Mommy," said Patty, sitting next to Eldene in the Bounder. "Look at the beautiful buildings and wide streets. It's almost like a dream. Everything looks so clean. Look at those two guys with the handcart going around, cleaning up horse poop." She laughed.

"Yeah, I wonder what they do with it. There are a lot of horses and other animals to clean up after. It's a little different than the hustle and bustle of Terre Haute, though," commented Eldene. "It looks like we may enjoy the next couple of weeks here while we wait to join the wagon train West. Taylor!" she called. "Would you ride back and tell Mr. Thompson that we are going to go on through town and find a place to camp?"

"Sure, Mom."

They found a place about a half-mile west of town and set up camp.

"Looks like we are plenty early for the train West. I don't see a lot of dad-burned wagons lining up anywhere," said Harold.

"I think we should see if we can find Mr. Gerard and find out where they are going to form the wagon train," said Eldene. "We may have to move our camp."

"I reckon you're right about that, be right smart to do that before we go to all the trouble of setting up just to have to tear down and move."

"Let's just get enough gear out for tonight, and we'll go into town tomorrow and check things out and mail some letters," remarked Eldene.

"Well, sounds like a dad-burned plan. I think we could use a night of rest. We'll see y'all in the morning."

The next day was bright and sunny. The early morning sun made the dome on the capitol building stand out like a glorious watchman overlooking the large red brick building. The building was in the center of a large plot of land that separated it from other structures. They were walking down a street named Adams.

"I'll bet this street is named after the second president of the United States," said Patty.

"I think you are probably right," said Carrie. "There are probably Washington and Jefferson streets here somewhere."

They turned the corner at Sixth Street in front of a large four-story building. Taylor was holding Carrie's hand and looking around at the sights

"Look ou—" said Carrie.

"Oomph." Came a deep voice from above Taylor.

Taylor looked up at the tall thin man that he had crashed into. "Oh, excuse me, sir, I guess I bettered watch where I am going."

"No harm done, young man," the tall thin man said as he bent over and picked his hat up and brushed it off. "You folks have yourselves a nice day." He turned and walked through the big double door.

Taylor noticed the sign above the doors that read "LINCOLN-HERNDON–Law Office."

"I guess that man must be a lawyer," he said as they walked away.

"He sure is tall, and there is something about him that makes me think that he is an important person in this city," said Carrie.

"All I know is that he is about the tallest man I've ever seen. I'm over six feet tall, and he looked down at me."

"Okay, everyone, I'm going to find out where the wagon train is forming and see if I can find Mr. Gerard. I'll see you all back at camp later," said Eldene.

"Mary and I will tag along with you," said Harold.

"Okay, then you young'uns can have a day of fun while we get things sorted out."

"Okay, Mom, we'll be okay," said Taylor.

Remembering that Carrie and Randy had asked their dad about a couple of horses, he said, "Come on, let's go look at some horses."

A passerby told them that the livery stable and black-smith shop was on the north side of town. The blacksmith was busy shoeing horses.

"Excuse me, sir, do you know where we can find a good deal on a couple of horses?" asked Taylor.

"As a matter of fact, I do, young feller," answered the blacksmith, a large man with a friendly smile and one bushy dark eyebrow across both eyes. His dark hair curled out from under the brim of his funny little short-billed cap. "I just happen to have a couple of fine young horses for sale myself." He pointed toward the corral. "That nice buckskin gelding with the white-striped face and the Appaloosa filly with the white mane and tail are just over three years old and broken to ride."

The four of them went over to the corral to get a better look at the two horses.

"I like that Appaloosa," said Carrie.

"What are you looking to get out of them?" asked Randy. "I like the looks of the buckskin."

"I want seventy-five each with saddles and bridles."

"I don't think my dad has that much money to spare. I guess we'll have to talk it over with him."

"What are all of those horses in the other corral?" asked Patty. "Are there any of them that are less money?"

"None of those have been broken to ride yet. Are any of you young'uns able to ride a bronco? I'm kind of short-handed right now, and maybe I can offer y'all a deal on the appaloosa and the buckskin. There are eight horses there that need to be trained to ride. If y'all think you can handle that, I'll give you the two horses with saddles and bridles."

"How soon can we start?" asked Taylor.

"Y'all can start anytime you want to. You young ladies can keep the animals fed and watered, help cool them down after the boys git through with them."

"Taylor!" Patty whispered excitedly. "You don't know how to ride a bronco."

"It can't be that hard," quipped Taylor. "I can do it. How about it, Randy, can you ride a bucking horse?"

"I-I don't know, but I don't think Pa will go for it."

"Let's not tell Pa and Ma," said Carrie. "Let's make it a surprise. We'll tell them that we got a job at the livery cleaning out the stalls and feeding the animals a few days, to earn money for the horses."

"What if they get their nutty necks broken?" asked Patty, twisting her lips. "Then what will we do?"

"We'll be careful," said Taylor. "We'll have it done before you know it."

"Okay then, Mr. Rodeo Pants, let's give it a try. I can see that your mind is made up," said Patty. "You know that Mommy will not approve."

"She'll be busy getting things ready for the wagon train, and she won't need our help all day, every day. We can work things out. We've got two weeks to get it done."

"Okay, sir, we'll tame the horses for you. We'll start tomorrow morning."

"All righty then, young man, I'll see you then. My name is Pete."

"Okay, Pete, I'm Taylor. This is Patty and Randy and Carrie."

As they headed back to the camp, Randy asked, "Boy, just what have we gotten ourselves into?"

"I don't know," said Patty, "but Mr. Rodeo Pants here thinks he does."

"Well, they don't have the $150, and they want the horses, so I guess we'll just have to learn fast," said Taylor.

Carrie squeezed Taylor's hand, looked up at him, batted her big beautiful brown eyes, and whispered, "I think you're wonderful."

He squeezed her hand and winked.

When they got back to camp, Eldene, Harold, and Mary were talking to a couple of men. Eldene introduced them as they approached. "These two gentlemen are the wagon train bosses, Mr. Gerard and Mr. Childs."

"Pleased to meet you," said Taylor. "I'm Taylor." He extended his hand.

"I'm John, y'all can call me Tripper," said Mr. Gerard, "and this young man is Jerome, but we call him Romy."

Everyone introduced themselves and shook hands all around.

"Mr. Gerard said that the train will be forming in this very meadow and that we are the first ones here. We'll be the lead wagons."

"That sounds great, I guess it pays to be early," said Taylor.

"The folks will start coming on a regular basis anytime now, and we'll probably be ready to head West in about two weeks," said Tripper. "Romy and I will be having several meetings to get everyone informed of the rules and regulations and places in line."

"All righty," said Harold, "we'll be sure and be ready for y'all."

Eldene seemed to be in a daze of sorts. "You okay, Mommy?" asked Patty.

"Yes, honey, I'm okay. I was just thinking about your dad," she lied, knowing that she must be blushing. *Oh my god*, thought Eldene. *What's wrong with me? My heart's pounding, and I'm feeling something that I shouldn't be. Jake's only been gone since March. I can't be thinking what I'm thinking. It's much too soon.*

Romy tipped his hat, looked Eldene in the eyes, and said in his kindly Southern manner, "It's been a downright pleasure to meet you nice folks, and I'll be keeping in close touch with y'all for the next few months. I think we are going to get along very well," he added as he turned and walked away.

Eldene stepped up into the Bounder, trying not to be obvious. She wanted some privacy to clear her thoughts.

"Well, Patty, we need to milk the goats and feed the mules and horses," said Taylor. "I think Mom needs to be alone for a while."

"We need to take care of things too, kids," said Harold. "We'll see y'all in the morning. Carrie, you help your ma, and Randy can help me with the cow and mules."

Later that night, Taylor and Patty told Eldene about their jobs at the livery stable.

"It's getting dark later, so I'll be able to work on the wagon each day after we finish at the livery," said Taylor.

"All right but we can't let things get in the way of our work here," said Eldene. "We have to be ready to go when Romy—er—I-I mean Tripper says so."

"Okay, Mom"—noticing her stammer but smart enough to ignore it—"I promise we won't let you down."

They could hear Harold talking loudly to Carrie and Randy. "Okay then, dad-burn it, you can work at the con-founded stable, but you better not let your chores here fall behind. I'm going to be busy with the wagon, and I'll need some help when I get ready to pack the dad-burned wheel bearings. Your ma's going to need your help too, young lady."

"Yes, Pa, I'll be here every day after we finish, I promise," she said as she hugged him and gave him a big kiss on the cheek. "Gosh, Pa, you need to shave!"—rubbing her face—"Your whiskers are sharp."

"Them dad-burned animals better be worth it."

"Things will be all right, dear, let them earn their way. How else would we be able to get a couple of horses? They've been working pretty darn hard, and it would be good to have a couple of horses for the trip," said Mary as she cupped Harold's cheeks in her hands and kissed him on the lips.

"All right, dad-burn it anyway. I said they could do it. There's no call to get all mushy in front of the kids," said Harold, being a little flustered.

Taylor was up early the next morning, feeling anxious and nervous. He had the animals taken care of and the coffee brewing on the campfire when Eldene and Patty got up.

"You're up early this morning," said Eldene, yawning and stretching.

"Yep, I want to get an early start at the livery stable."

Patty wandered over to Taylor and whispered, "Have you got your rodeo pants on this morning?"

"Yep, and I see you have your smarty-pants on."

"Yep, I sure do," she said quietly as she poured two cups of coffee. "Here's your coffee, Mommy." She sashayed over to the Bounder and handed Eldene one of the cups, sticking her tongue out at Taylor.

"Are you two at it already this morning?" asked Eldene, noticing Patty's gesture.

"No, we're just happy," said Patty.

"We're ready to go to work," said Carrie as she and Randy approached their camp.

"Okey dokey, we'll be back early, Mom."

Pete was ready for them when they arrived at the stables. "I got four mustangs ready for y'all to work with today. There's a saddle and bridle with a bit and a twitch iff'n y'all need it. I put a couple of shovels and pitchforks out for the gals to start with. I'll be a' leaven y'all to your jobs whilst I go shoe some horses over at the Double D ranch. Y'all have a good time, and I'll see y'all later."

After Pete was out of sight, Taylor looked up toward the sky and said, "Well, dear lord, we're gonna need your help today."

"Okay, Mr. Rodeo Pants, ride 'um, cowboy!" exclaimed Patty, slapping her thigh as she jumped up and down like a bucking horse.

"All right, sister dear, don't stab yourself with that pitchfork while y'all are cleaning up horse poop." He held his nose and was being snide.

Everyone started joking and laughing.

Taylor managed to rope the first mustang. He quickly wrapped the rope around a post in the center of the corral and kept pulling it in until the bucking, stomping mustang's head was close to the post.

"Randy! Come and hold onto the rope while I try to put a saddle on him!" yelled Taylor.

"Okay, I got him!" yelled Randy.

The mustang was snorting and tossing its head and trying to pull away.

"Whoa, boy, whoa," said Taylor, trying to calm the frightened animal. "Whoa there, now whoa," he said as he rubbed the horse's neck and patted him.

The horse began settling down, and Taylor gently laid the saddle blanket on his back. The horse tried to pull away.

"No, you don't, big fella," said Randy, tightening the tether. "Stand still, boy."

Taylor gently sat the saddle on and waited to see what the horse was going to do.

"Easy, boy, easy…" said Taylor as he reached under the mustang's belly to get the saddle strap. "Whoa, boy, whoa, I just have to cinch up the saddle, and we can get you back to your stall."

He cinched up the strap, and the wild horse began stomping and pawing the ground and rearing his hind legs. "Whoa, boy, whoa," said Taylor. The horse began calming. "Easy, boy, just let me put this bit into your mouth." The mustang wasn't having any part of the bit in his mouth; he shook his head, snorted, and stomped around. "I guess we'll have to use the twitch on him. He's just too danged strong. I've helped my dad use one, so I think I can do it."

"Okay," said Randy, handing him the twitch.

Taylor put the twitch around the mustang's upper lip and began twisting it. "Whoa, boy, whoa." The wild horse stopped jumping around and began trying to get rid of the thing around his lip. "Whoa, boy," Taylor pleaded as he cinched up on the twitch. The horse settled down.

Working together, they managed to get the bridle on the unruly horse. "That was not easy," said Randy, panting and puffing.

Taylor released the twitch and slipped the rope from around the horse's neck. He quickly tied the reins to the post. "Whew"—wiping the sweat from his forehead—"I don't like using that danged twitch. I'm not going to do that again. I don't want to hurt them, I just want to ride them," he said, shaking his head. "I don't know if I'm going to like what comes next, but here goes anyway." Taylor stepped into the stirrup and pulled himself onto the saddle, grabbing the reins, at the same time releasing the mustang from the post.

The horse didn't move. "He must be tired or some—th—ing," said Taylor, just as the bronc lowered his head, turned, snorted, and began to buck. He reared up his hind legs and came down with a thud and jumped into the air with all four hooves. His head was between his front legs, his back was bowed, and he was twisting, turning, and bucking. He was kicking up dust and neighing and snorting, trying to get rid of whatever was on his back.

"YAHOO!" Taylor yelled as he hung on with every ounce of strength that he could muster.

Patty and Carrie couldn't stay away. They were standing on the corral rails, cheering him on and screaming, "Yippee ki-yo, ride 'um, cowboy."

Randy was jumping up and down, doing somersaults and half-cartwheels and yelling, "Stay with him, Taylor, hang on, EEYAHOO!"

"Oh my gosh, he's doing it, he's riding him," yelled Patty. "That's my big brother, YAHOO!"

"This is so exciting," exclaimed Carrie! Look at him go, EEYIPPEE!"

Taylor hung on until the mustang stopped bucking. He rode him around the corral several times. "Well, I reckon that's one down," said Taylor as he dismounted and fell to his knees, realizing that he had no feeling in his legs. "Whoa, I can't stand up."

"Are you all right?" asked Carrie as she ran to his aid.

"Yep, I'm just fine. I just can't seem to walk, m-my legs don't want to work right, I can't seem to keep them under me."

"Maybe you should lie down and let me rub your legs, I think you have lost the circulation in them," pleaded Carrie, being concerned.

"Oh my god!" he exclaimed. "My legs are starting to tingle and hurt real bad." He stood up and began rubbing his legs. "I think they went to sleep like when you sit on a fence rail too long. The circulation is coming back, and it hurts like hell. Ow, ow, ow!" he yelped as he crippled around in a circle, rubbing his legs.

"Well, maybe those aren't your rodeo pants after all," commented Patty with a smirk.

"Those are sure enough your smarty-pants, though," said Taylor, still wobbling in circles, trying to get all the feeling back into his legs and feet. Everyone laughed and joked while Taylor recovered. Randy took care of the mustang while Carrie and Patty helped Taylor.

"Okay, let's get back to work," said Randy, leading another mustang. "We've only got a few hours left."

"OH GOD, this is harder than I thought it was going to be." Moaned Taylor as he tried to move.

"It's my turn," said Randy.

"Are you sure?" asked Taylor. "It's kind of painful."

"I'm sure, just help me get the saddle on him."

They struggled with this horse, just like the other one, but they managed to get it done. Randy got onto the saddle, and the mustang reared up on his hind legs and came down on his front legs and kicked his rear end into the air with a strange twist.

"YEOW!" Randy screamed as he went flying through the air, landing face-first in a large pile of horse dung. "Eeyuck!" he yelled as he wiped dung from his face.

Everyone was laughing so hard they could barely stand up.

"What's so dad-burned funny," Randy commented as he spat and sputtered.

Patty led him to the water trough to wash up. "Oh my goodness, you have poop in your hair and in your ear and all over your face." She was trying not to laugh but couldn't help it.

Randy dunked his head in the water and cleaned up. "That was just dad-burned nasty," he quipped. "That dad-burned critter ain't getting away with that," said Randy as he grabbed the reins, jumped back into the saddle without even touching the stirrups. "EEYAHOO!" he yelled as he spurred the mustang into action.

The rest of the day was pretty rough, as they worked with the other three mustangs.

"We managed to get two of them rideable today, that leaves six more," said Taylor as they walked back toward camp. "I feel like I've been dragged through a knothole or something, but I guess I'll live through another day."

"Me too, but my knothole was full of horse manure," quipped Randy.

Everyone started laughing.

"You sure were covered in poop." Laughed Patty.

"Yep, I reckon I was, and it tasted terrible, EEYUCK," retorted Randy, wrinkling his face and spiting.

Patty put her arm through his and whispered, "I think you are bold and brave."

Randy felt proud. "Thanks, Patty." He put his arm around her and kissed her on the temple. "That means a lot to me."

Patty blushed and smiled. "I'm just glad you didn't get hurt."

Back at camp, they did their chores, and even though they were sore, Taylor and Randy were able to keep their secret.

The next day, Eldene and Harold were working on their wagons. Romy rode up and, tipping his hat, said, "Howdy, folks."

Eldene looked up, and her heart started pumping faster. She knew she had to show some indifference. "Hello, Mr. Childs. How are you today?"

"I'm fine, ma'am," he said as he dismounted, "but it's just plain Romy."

"Howdy, Romy," said Harold. "What can we do for you today?"

Eldene thought, *Oh my god, he's getting off his horse and coming over here, I have to collect myself and straighten up.*

"I stopped by to tell y'all that a few wagons are going to be lining up behind you folks. We want them to camp in the order that they will be traveling in when we start out for the Mississippi. You folks will be first in line. The next few days will be kind of busy around here, so Tripper and I will be moving our camp to a spot near you."

"All righty, we'll help out any way we can," said Harold.

Meanwhile Eldene was trying to mount a wheel on the Bounder.

"Let me help you with that wheel, ma'am." He took the wheel and lifted it onto the axle. "There you go, ma'am, all done."

"Thank you, mister—er—I mean Romy. I appreciate your help."

"It's my pleasure, ma'am."

"You can call me Deeny."

After Romy left, Harold looked at Eldene and said, "He's a downright handsome young feller, ain't he?"

"I suppose so. I hadn't really noticed," she lied, busying herself, finishing with the wheel. Seeing she had the job under control, Harold turned and, with a smile, headed back to his camp.

The next few days were a little hectic as the wagons began lining up. Romy and Tripper camped ahead of the Bounder, not more than fifty feet away.

Eldene kept herself busy with the Bounder and the tack for the animals. She decided that Romy was a perfect gentleman, and he knew how to use finesse. She caught him looking at her now and then, but he was always polite and unassuming. *I like this man*, she thought. *I think we are going to be very good friends. I like his deep Southern drawl, the way he carries himself with pride and confidence without arrogance.* She stood there a moment with her hands on her hips. "Yep, I like him," she said under her breath.

Eldene was awakened the next morning by the noise of more wagons pulling into the meadow, and people setting up their campsites. The kids had already left for the stables. She was pouring herself a cup of coffee when she noticed Romy approaching.

"Good morning, Deeny. How about a cup of that good-smelling coffee?"

"Sure," she said, pouring him a cup. "Looks like we are getting quite a few wagons for the trip West."

"Yes, ma'am, we were supposed to have fifty-six, but we've picked up fifteen more. It looks like we have seventy-one so far. By the way, I stopped by to tell you that your son and Howard's and Mary's son are doing a fine job breaking those wild mustangs that we are buying from the livery stable."

"They're doing what? I don't know anything about any wild mustangs," said Eldene with a surprised look on her face.

"Uh-oh, I guess I let the cat out of the bag. I reckon Pete made them a deal on a couple of young riding stock if they break the mustangs for him. I went by there yesterday, and they were working on the last one. I guess all they have to do now is ride them around so the horses will get used to someone riding them."

"I am going down there right now, and I may wring someone's neck," said Eldene.

"I'll walk with you, just let me tie my horse to a tree. May I ask why you and the kids are going out West?"

"Well, sometimes I have a hard time talking about it, so I will give you the short version. My husband was killed by a runaway freight wagon, and I decided that I didn't want to live in Baltimore any longer, so here we are."

"I have noticed that you and your daughter and Mrs. Thompson and her daughter are dressed a little more practical than any of the other women in the train."

"Yep, we want to be comfortable, and so we altered some men's clothing, and I'm glad we did. Things are a lot easier to do when you're not fighting a dress."

"Well, for what it's worth, I think you look beautiful, and I like the way y'all are dressed."

They approached the livery corral as Taylor was just about to mount a mustang.

"Oh, hi, Mom, what's going on?"

"How about you tell me what's going on, young man?"

"*Well*, I was just about to get up on this horse."

Just then Patty and the others came around the corner of the building. "Uh-oh," exclaimed Patty, "looks like we've been caught."

They told Eldene what they had been doing. "Do you realize that you could have been maimed or killed? What in the world were you thinking?"

"We're just fine, Mommy," said Patty. "And Carrie and Randy now own two beautiful horses for the trip West. Please don't be mad at us."

"Well, I'm thankful you're all okay, but I'm not happy about you doing something like this behind my back."

"I'm sorry, Mom. I guess we weren't thinking so much about the danger," confessed Taylor. "We should have been more thoughtful of your feelings. I'll be more careful in the future. I take full responsibility. Patty tried to tell me it was a bad idea, but the excitement of the adventure got the best of me."

"Well, we got eight good mustangs out of the deal," Romy interjected. "You've got a bunch of remarkable youngsters here, Deeny."

"Yep, I reckon we have," she agreed. "You kids finish up here, and starting tomorrow, we have to finish getting things ready to head into the wilderness."

Everyone worked hard for the next few days. Harold didn't say too much, but you could tell that he was proud of his children and their accomplishment. Carrie and Randy were excited about their horses. Mary was glad that everyone came out with no major injuries.

Mary approached Taylor and said, "I want to thank you for helping Carrie and Randy and for taking Randy under your wing and keeping him safe."

"Randy is pretty danged capable, he saved my hide a few times. I was mighty glad he was there," said Taylor. "I'm proud to call him my friend."

"I'm glad that we are crossing the wilderness with you folks," said Mary as she gave Taylor a quick hug.

Later that evening, Romy came over to the camp and said, "Tripper wants everyone to gather at his camp after breakfast. He wants to talk about the rules of conduct."

"We'll all be there," said Eldene.

"All righty then, I'll see you all in the morning."

Eldene watched as he walked away. "You kind of like that feller, don't you?" whispered Mary.

"It's that obvious, huh? I guess I'll have to be more careful."

"Well, he is quite a handsome young man, and he's got some education from somewhere. You would probably have to go a long way to do better. If I were you, I would stay close to that one."

"Good night, Mary dear, I'll see you in the morning," said Deeny with a smile.

"Good night, Deeny, sweet dreams," said Mary, smiling as she walked away.

Chapter 7

Wilderness Bound

"Good morning, everyone," greeted Romy. "Please gather in as close as y'all can so that y'all will be able to hear Cap'n Tripper. We'll be leaving the United States of America in a few days, and it's important that everyone knows the rules and regulations of travel'n' in a wagon train. I've met most of y'all, but for those that I haven't met, I'm Jerome Childs, better known as Romy. I'm the one that y'all will come to if you have a problem. I try to be fair with everyone, but I will *not* tolerate any conflict. It is very important that we all get along.

"There are 71 wagons, 183 men, women, and children, 86 mules, 26 oxen, 125 chickens, 37 milk cows, 28 goats, 98 horses, and 12 dogs. We also have 2 cowboys driving a small herd of 40 beef cattle, *Everyone* will be expected to take care of their own animals. They are your best friends out here and are *extremely* important for your survival. Cap'n Tripper is well known for his ability to get wagon trains to their destination safely and with very few casualties. He will not tolerate any sort of abuse, animal or human. Y'all listen close to what he has to say. Captain?"

Romy walked over to Eldene and winked. "Do you mind if I stand here next to you, ma'am?"

Eldene looked at him and commented with a small smile, "Why no, Mr. Childs, sir. Make yourself comfortable."

He grinned and tipped his hat and whispered, "Thank you, Deeny."

"Good morning, all, I'm John Gerard, better known as Tripper or Captain. I'm the wagon master of this here wagon train. My job is to get everybody to their chosen destination in one piece! As Romy told y'all, we will be entering into the wilderness country in a couple of days or so. There are things out there that most of you have never seen before and probably haven't even heard of. When we cross over the Mississippi River, there are no laws to abide by, so we have our own laws. They will be strictly enforced by me and my people. We will not tolerate theft or fighting. Under our laws, thieves are tried and punished if convicted. If anyone kills another person that is a member of this train, he or she will be tried by a jury of six chosen people and turned over to the authorities in the next town. But I have to say, in all of my years as a wagon master, we have never had this happen."

"What about Indians?" someone yelled.

"Yeah," yelled another person, "are we gonna run into Injuns?"

"There is that possibility," answered Tripper. "If that happens we'll fight them off. From now on, everybody needs to keep their guns within reach. If you own a sidearm, you need to have it strapped on at all times. There are critters out there like bears, wolves, rattlesnakes, badgers, scorpions, vinegarroons, deer, elk, coyotes, antelope, wild sheep, and other critters that can cause a world of hurt and harm. If you are on horseback, be sure to have your rifle and sidearm handy at all times. We don't shoot animals for anything other than food, unless we absolutely have to. My camp is always open if you have a problem or a question. Romy will fill y'all in on the wagon lineup."

Romy stepped up beside Captain Tripper again. "Everybody will be traveling in the order that they arrived," said Romy. "The only time we don't travel in a straight line is when the wind is blowing dust made by the wagons in front of ya. It's okay to spread out in that case, but you can't pass anyone, and this usually only happens in the flatlands of the prairies and deserts. In case of a severe dust storm, we will circle the wagons, tie the animals down, and cover everything that ya can with tarps and wait out the storm."

"When do you suppose we will be head'n' out?" asked Harold.

"We're going to be leaving Springfield in two days," answered Romy. Make sure that y'all are well stocked with food that don't easily spoil and keep your water barrels and bags filled. It won't take long for everybody to learn the dos and don'ts of the trail. We'll be travel'n' twelve to fifteen miles a day. That should get us over the Rocky Mountains by September. If all goes well, we'll be in Western Oregon by December. If any of y'all want to reconsider, we'll surely understand, and you'll get a full refund, but I'll need to know by three o'clock today. I'll be available for the next couple hours, if you have any questions. Now y'all have a good day."

Everyone left, discussing what Romy had told them. Eldene started to walk away when she heard Romy say,

"Hold up a minute, Deeny, I'd like to walk with you if you don't mind."

"It's okay, Mom, we'll see you later," said Taylor.

"Okay then, Romy," she said as she swayed from side to side with her hands in her back pockets. "What's on your mind?"

"Nothing to fret about, pretty lady. I just thought y'all might like to have some company," Romy said with a smile. He reached out and took Eldene's hand which quickly disappeared in his large one and said, "Let's walk over there by the creek and talk a spell."

They were standing on the creek bank overlooking the sparkling brook. It was running so clear you could see the fish as they swam by.

"It sure is peaceful here, isn't it, Deeny?"

"Yep, I think so," said Eldene, looking a little puzzled.

"Deeny, I have never met anyone like you before, and I-I-I am growing quite fond of you," said Romy nervously.

"I like you a lot too, Romy," she said, trying to put him at ease.

He put his hands on her shoulders and looked into her beautiful hazel eyes. He quickly leaned toward her and kissed her on the lips.

Eldene thought, *Oh my god, what am I doing?* At first, she was shocked, but she couldn't stop herself from putting her arms around his neck and melting into a long passionate kiss. It had been so long. *Oh, dear god, can this really be happening?* she thought as they stood there, embracing. Backing away and recapturing her composure, she looked at Romy and said, "That was nice, and I won't deny that I liked it, but I have been widowed for only a few short months, and I think we need to take things a little slower. I need time to get over Jake's death, and even though I like the feelings I have for you, I want to be sure that they are genuine."

"I think I understand, Deeny," said Romy, holding her hands in his. "I will respect your wishes and try to be the gentleman that I am. We have plenty of time to get to know each other, and I think that you are worth the wait, no matter how long it takes."

"Thank you for understanding."

"Does this mean that I won't be able to come calling?"

"Well, I guess I don't see any harm in an occasional walk in the moonlight," said Eldene with a smile as she took his arm and headed toward the Bounder

*****

The wagon train arrived at the Mississippi River in just over two days after they left Springfield. The McGradys and the Thompsons were the first ones to cross over to Hannibal Missouri.

"This is a huge beautiful river," commented Eldene.

"It sure as hell is," replied Harold. You can see river for miles, both north and south. I wonder where all that dad-burned water comes from."

"We learned in school that almost every river and stream on the east side of the Rocky Mountains and almost every river and stream on the west side of the Appalachians run into the Mississippi River," stated Patty. "It's the longest river in North America."

"Yep, Pa, it goes from Canada to the Gulf of Mexico, down in Louisiana," added Randy.

"Looks like we've got ourselves a couple of real scholars here, don't it, Mom?" Taylor said.

"Yep, and we'd be doing well to let some of it rub off on us, don't you think, young man?" commented Eldene.

"I reckon you're right about that. I could probably learn a lot from Ms. Smarty-pants here," said Taylor as he put his arm around Patty and kissed her on the cheek.

Patty just looked at him, rolled her eyes, and shook her head.

It took three days to get all of the wagons and livestock across the big river. But luckily there were no mishaps. The wagon camp was just north of Hannibal and well able to handle the large wagon train.

"This is a beautiful country," said Mary, "but I wouldn't like living so close to this big river."

"I don't think I would like it much either," said Eldene. "I think that the land here would be too expensive. I'm looking forward to picking up some good land with a nice timber stand and a good place to open a sawmill."

"A sawmill? My goodness, I would've never guessed that you would want to start a sawmill," Mary said, bewildered. "I kind of figured you for a mercantile or a supply store of some sort."

"Nope, not me. I was raised by a logger-turned-mill-owner, and my dream is to bring fine lumber products to the West. Someday my father and mother will be joining us, and I want to be ready for them."

"How exciting that sounds," commented Mary. "We ain't sure where we'll end up yet, but Harold has his heart set on some good farmland. Maybe we will be able to find something close to where you and Taylor and Patty will be."

"That would be wonderful, and it doesn't look like we'll be separating those children anytime soon," said Eldene.

"Yes, I reckon they are getting pretty well attached to one another. I've noticed that Taylor and Carrie are spending a lot more time with each other, and Randy is pretty fond of Patty."

"They all get along so well together and seem to be very good friends. Patty was not very happy before we joined up with you folks, and she is more like the happy young girl that she was in Baltimore. I think we would be foolish to lose sight of one another. I'm sure that there is plenty of good farmland in Western Oregon, and besides maybe Harold would like the milling business," said Eldene. "We've got about two thousand miles to talk to him about it."

Mary smiled a big smile and said, "That just sounds so exciting to me."

Meanwhile the kids were sitting on the bank of a nearby creek.

"That water looks mighty inviting," quipped Taylor as he stood up and acted like he was going to jump into the water.

Carrie stood up, and Taylor quickly lifted her in his arms and jumped into the water. "EEYAHOO!"

"EEYAA!" Carrie screamed as they hit the cold water. They began splashing around and laughing and giggling.

Randy looked at Patty with a mischievous look.

"Oh no, you don't, buster," yelled Patty as she took off running with Randy chasing her.

"Gotcha," said Randy as he grabbed her arm and quickly jumped into the water, pulling her in after him.

"Eeyikes!" screamed Patty. "This is war." She began splashing water in Randy's face. They played and swam for a while and then headed back to camp, happy but soaking wet.

Later that evening, Romy stopped by and said, "I reckon we'll be moving out early tomorrow morning. We just got the last wagon across, and Tripper wants to get an early start."

"We'll be ready to go," said Eldene as she handed him a cup of coffee. "You look like you need a little break. Would you like to get off your horse and rest a bit?"

"Sorry, Deeny, but I reckon I have to keep on moving." He took a couple of sips of the hot coffee and handed the cup back. "Thanks for the invite, though. I'll see y'all later when I have more time. Besides, pretty lady, it looks like a good night for a walk in the moonlight."

Eldene watched as he rode away. *There is something about that man that makes me feel good*, she thought.

Eldene noticed two men riding toward Romy. She had not seen them before. She watched as the three men chatted, and Romy rode off. The two men rode toward the Bounder. She could see that one of them was an Indian. She had seen Indians before, but none that looked like this one. He had long black braids that ran behind his ears and over his shoulders and a leather band laced with colorful beads, supporting three feathers, around his head. He appeared to be about six feet tall and sat straight in the saddle with his deep-brown eyes looking directly at Eldene. He wore buckskin clothes and carried a bow and a quiver of arrows. A knife was strapped to his side and a rifle across his saddle.

"Good morning, gentlemen," she said as they started to ride past the Bounder.

"Good morning, ma'am. Whoa, boy."

The Indian kept riding. "Wait up a minute, Moons, the lady wants to talk to us."

"Well…okay, Bill," the Indian said in perfect English, "but only for a minute. It's going to get dark soon, and we have a long way to go."

The man dismounted and said, "My name is Bill Winters, and my friend is Joseph Many Moons. I call him Moons."

Eldene looked from one to the other. Bill Winters was six feet tall, muscular, with blondish-brown hair down to his shoulders. His eyes were light blue, and his teeth were slightly bucked, which didn't change the fact that he was handsome in a rugged sort of way. His leathery complexion caused vertical lines to form on his face when he smiled. He had a Colt revolver on his right hip and a knife on the left. There was also a rifle in a sheath on the side of his horse. He was wearing buckskins and a leather round-brimmed hat and a friendly smile.

"Pleased to meet you, Mr. Winters"—extending her hand—"you also, Mr. Many Moons."

"Just call me Bill, ma'am"—tipping his hat—"I'm not used to being called mister."

"All right then, Bill it is," said Eldene.

"You can call me Joe or Moons," said Many Moons. "I answer either way."

"I'm Eldene, and these are my youngsters," she introduced Taylor and Patty.

"We're the scouts for the wagon train. We're usually out in front about ten miles or so, and we come back in every so often to report to the captain or Romy."

"Good to meet you, Ms. Eldene," said Many Moons. "We have to go now, Bill."

"I'm a com'n. It was nice meeting you, folks. We'll get to know you better as time goes on."

That was interesting, thought Eldene as they rode off.

The train pulled out early the next morning, heading west from Hannibal on a trail toward St. Joseph. The sun was peeking over the treetops through a deep-blue sky. Everyone was excited to be on the road once again. The kids were riding their horses.

"You young'uns stay close to the train. We're not sure about whut's up ahead, and I want y'all to keep within eyesight," said Harold.

"Okey dokey, Pa, we will," answered Randy.

The trail seemed to be well traveled by previous travelers. The ruts were deep, and the brush was cleared out to about forty or fifty feet wide on each side of the trail.

Romy rode up to the Bounder. "Good morning, Deeny. You look mighty pretty today, as usual."

"Why thank you, sir, but flattery will get you absolutely nowhere," said Eldene as she tightened her grip on the reins. "I must say, however, that you are looking quite handsome yourself this morning."

"Well, thank you, miss," Romy replied. "And thanks again for the pleasure of your company last evening."

"It was a very pleasant evening, indeed, and I enjoyed it very much," said Eldene.

"Well, I have to get on with my duties. I'll catch up with you later."

"All righty, I'll be right here, in the same seat behind these smelly old mules for the next few hours," said Eldene, chuckling.

Eldene watched as Romy rode off toward the front of the Bounder.

Tripper was riding a little way ahead of the train. "How are things shaping up back there?" asked Tripper as Romy rode up beside him.

"They're looking pretty good. I still have to check on the rear, but I figured you might want to talk to me before I go."

"Nope, you're doing a good job, and I appreciate the way you step up to the challenge. I'm going to ride up ahead for a couple of miles and check out the trail."

"Okay, Captain. I'll get on back there and make sure the train keeps on movin'."

"By the way, Romy. I've been noticing that you have an interest in Mrs. McGrady."

"Y-yes, sir," said Romy cautiously. "I'm becoming quite fond of her and her family."

"Well, she seems like a right nice lady. I would move slow, though, if I were you. She's a young widow, and I don't want to see you bite off more than you can chew. Don't let romance cloud your judgment. I need for you to be alert at all times."

"I understand your concern, Captain, but you won't have to worry about that. Deeny, er, that is, Mrs. McGrady and I have a pretty good understanding, and we know where we stand with each other. Thank you for your advice, and I promise you, I'll always do my job to the best of my ability."

"Okay then," said Tripper, "I'll see you later in the day." And he spurred his horse.

Romy sat there for a minute, shrugged his shoulders, and then spurred his horse into a gallop toward the rear of the train.

Time passed by slowly as the Bounder bounced along the trail. Eldene began daydreaming about Jake. She was in deep thought when Taylor rode up to the Bounder.

"Hey, Mom!" he yelled, startling her.

"My goodness," she answered as she returned to reality. "What are you so excited about?"

"Well, actually I was just checking to see if you were all right. I thought maybe you might want to trade off for a spell."

"I'm all right, I was just thinking and enjoying the chitter-chatter of the squirrels and birds."

"All right then, how about some squirrel meat for supper tonight? There are hundreds of big red fox squirrels out there, and I could pick off four or five for a nice squirrel stew."

"Sounds good to me."

"Okey dokey!" yelled Taylor as he snapped the reins and spurred Barney into action. "I'll see you in a couple of hours."

Taylor approached Patty and the others in a full gallop. "Whoa, Barney," he said, pulling back on the reins. "Whoa, boy."

"What's the hurry?" asked Patty. "You were coming pretty fast. Is something wrong?"

"Nope, I just missed you, little sister, that's all," said Taylor with a snide smile.

"Okay, smarty-pants," asked Patty, "what's the real reason?"

"Well, okay since we only have a couple of hours before we stop for the night, I thought we could ride ahead and do a little squirrel hunting."

"That sounds like fun," said Randy. "I've been practicing with my sling."

The four of them galloped ahead of the train toward a likely looking grove of trees.

"All righty then," said Taylor, "let's tie up the horses and hunt in those trees over yonder." He pointed toward a large oak grove. "You and Patty go first, Carrie and I will hunt about fifty feet behind you."

"Okey dokey," said Randy excitedly.

Patty knew what Taylor was up to, but she decided to not say anything for a while.

As Randy and Patty walked past a tree, the squirrels would circle the tree away from them, and Taylor would down him when he circled to his side of the tree.

After Taylor bagged about four squirrels, Randy began getting a little frustrated. "How come you're getting all of those squirrels, and I'm not even seeing any?" said Randy. "What's your secret?"

Taylor started laughing. "What's so funny?" asked Randy, shrugging his shoulders.

"Are you going to tell him or am I?" asked Patty as she put her hands on her hips.

"Okay, you got me," quipped Taylor. "Let's trade places for a while."

"Whenever we pass a tree with a squirrel in it, the squirrel scampers around the other side of the tree, keeping out of sight, and when he appears on Taylor's and Carrie's side, Taylor picks him off before the squirrel sees them," explained Patty.

"Oh." Sighed Randy. "That's downright clever."

"All right, brother dear, let's see you get a couple big fat squirrels," said Carrie.

"You were in on this, weren't you?" asked Randy.

"Well…not really, but it didn't take long to figure out what Taylor was up to," said Carrie. "It was fun so I just kept quiet."

They traded places, and Randy was able to get four squirrels for their stewpot.

They walked back to their horses just as the wagon train was approaching.

Tripper rode up to the tack wagon and told the driver to circle the wagons at the next clearing. "We will be stopping there for the night!" yelled Tripper. "There's plenty of fresh water and lots of dead trees for firewood."

"Yes, sir, Cap'n Tripper," answered the driver.

Later that evening, after all the animals were bedded down, and everyone was finished with their chores, Romy came over to the Bounder and announced that there was going to be a shindig at Captain Tripper's campsite. "Everyone is invited," he said, "and be sure to put on your dancing shoes."

"That sounds like a lot of fun!" shouted Mary. "I haven't danced since I was a young'un."

"Me neither," announced Harold, "and I don't figure on start'n' now."

"C'mon, you old stick in the mud," said Eldene. "It's time we all loosened up a little."

"C'mon, Pa, let's go see what going on," said Carrie as she grabbed his hand.

Mary grabbed Harold's other arm and said, "Let's go have some fun, dear."

"Confound it anyhow, I reckon I'm out numbered, dad-burn it," griped Harold as he reluctantly surrendered.

Taylor took Carrie's hand and led her toward Tripper's campsite. Randy did the same with Patty.

Eldene and Romy followed close behind. "This is going to be lots of fun," stated Romy.

"I haven't danced for a long time," said Eldene. "I hope I can remember how."

They arrived at Tripper's camp to find almost everyone in the train whooping, hollering, and dancing to a four-man band consisting of a fiddler, banjo, mandolin, and guitar player.

"They sound good," commented Eldene.

Romy took Eldene's hand and said, "Yep, c'mon, pretty lady, let's go kick up our heels."

Mary pulled Harold toward the dancers. "If they can do it, we can do it. Let's go pretend that we're young'uns again!"

"Aw, dad-burn it, Mary." Balked Harold as he followed her toward the music.

Everyone was having a good time when Eldene thought she heard someone screaming. "Romy, did you hear that?"

"Yes, I reckon I did. I think maybe we should check it out."

"I think you're right. It sounded like someone in trouble. It sounded like it came from one of the wagons over there."

"Come on then, let's hurry," said Romy as he grabbed Eldene's hand.

As they approached the wagon where the screams were coming from, a young man yelled, "Thank God! Please help, my wife is having the baby!"

Eldene climbed into the wagon and saw a young girl lying on the wagon bed, perspiration running down her face. "Get me some clean towels and hot water and hurry! What's your name, honey?" asked Eldene.

"Penny," she groaned.

"Okay, Penny, I want you to do as I say"—as she positioned her—"can you do that for me?"

"Yes…ma'am, I, I think *so*." She panted.

"Okay then, here we go. I want you to take deep breaths and blow out in short breaths, starting now."

"*Okay*." Gasped Penny as she sucked in her breath and blew it out in puffs.

"Good girl, keep doing that and begin pushing real hard when I tell you to."

"*Oh*, it hurts!" screamed Penny. *Oh* God…it…hurts!"

"Start pushing, honey, it's almost over. One more good hard push."

"I—I *can't*."

"Yes, you can, *push hard!*"

"Yee!" screamed Penny.

"That's it, honey!" Eldene said, as the baby slipped into her waiting hands. "It looks like you have a very pretty little girl."

Eldene laid the baby on Penny's tummy and finished up the birthing. She cleaned everything up and then wiped Penny's face with a clean warm cloth. I'll check back with you before I turn in for the night, okay?"

"Oh...she's beautiful, thank you, thank you, thank you."

"That's okay, honey, you did all the hard work, and I'm glad I could help."

"Axel!" yelled Penny. "Come and see our new baby girl."

Axel and Penny Ward were a young couple who lost their parents in an Indian uprising and only have each other. Axel is twenty years old, well built, about five feet, ten inches tall. His big blue eyes sparkle with enthusiasm, and his long brown hair runs down to his shoulders. Penny is a brown-eyed blond-haired girl, nineteen years old. She is five feet, two inches tall and is full of vim and vigor.

Eldene changed places in the wagon with the awe-struck new father.

"Wow!" said Romy. "You never cease to amaze me!"

"Well, I've been in that particular predicament myself a couple of times." Laughed Eldene. "Let's get back to the party and let the new parents enjoy their baby girl! Do you think it would be possible to move their wagon closer to the front of the train?" asked Eldene. "They're about twenty wagons back, and that new baby is going to be breathing in a lot of dust."

"I reckon we can move them up a ways. I'll talk to the cap'n," answered Romy.

They arrived back at the shindig, and everyone had a hundred questions about what was going on.

"Well, it looks like Axel and Penny Ward have a brand-new baby girl!" yelled Romy. "And this pretty lady right here was the one that delivered her."

"Yahoo, yippee," everyone cheered and clapped.

The next morning at sunup, everyone was awakened by a ruckus. Romy was positioning the Ward's wagon so that they could move in line behind the Thompson's rig.

"That was quick." Laughed Eldene. "You sure enough don't let any grass grow under your feet."

"Nope, I reckon I don't." Romy chuckled. "Gotta keep this train movin'."

"Looks like no one had a problem moving back a space," said Eldene.

"Nope, everybody was okay with it, so here we are."

"I'm glad that they are going to be closer. Penny is going to need some help with that sweet little baby girl. Thanks again, Romy."

"My pleasure, pretty lady. I'll see y'all later. I gotta go see the cap'n and get this wagon train a movin'. Yee-haw there, Rebel, giddyap!" yelled Romy as he spurred his horse and sped away.

Chapter 8

The Open Plains

Eldene was behind the reins on the Bounder, guiding the mules over the trail along the banks of the meandering Platte River, when Taylor rode up beside her.

"This country goes on forever! It's so dry, the ground is like a powdery dust. The grass and trees are starving for water. I wonder if it ever rains in this part of the country. It's downright eerie."

"Yes, it sure is! Here we are next to a river, and the plants are thirsty. It's ironic," quipped Eldene. "Ride back and see how the Wards are doing with that new baby."

"Okey dokey, be right back. C'mon, Barney, let's go, boy, hyah!"

The sun was bright, and even the air was warm. You could see for miles. The heat was unbearable. The vast plains seemed endless, and the bushes and grass were yellowing for lack of moisture. The trees looked forlorn with the dust clinging to their leaves. They were just standing there on the flat terrain, as if they were waiting for something to happen. The only thing moving was the wagon train and a few sparrows, flitting from tree to tree, looking for insects.

"Good morning, Mr. Ward! I'm Taylor, Eldene's son! She asked me to see how you folks are doing with the new baby in this dusty country?"

"Howdy, Taylor, you can call me Axel, and my wife's name is Penny. We're doing pretty good so far. Penny is keeping the baby covered, and she's staying inside with the canopy flap tied down so that the dust can't get in. Tell your mom thanks for everything. We owe her a lot!"

"I'll tell her, but I'm sure she believes that you don't owe her anything! She is just such a great caring person, and I know she was glad to help," said Taylor. "I'm proud to be her son!"

"I can see why you feel that way," said Axel. "She's pretty darn amazing. My gosh, this sure is a big country we're going through. It looks like miles and miles of nothing but more miles and miles! I hope that it's not dusty like this all the way across!"

"Me too!" answered Taylor. "Hey, I'll talk to you later, Mr. Ward! Oops! I mean Axel! I'll tell Mom that you're doing okay. If you need anything, just holler! Hyah! Barney, let's go!"

"They're doing fine, Mom, Mr. Ward, er, I mean Axel says thanks for everything."

"Okay, I'll see them tonight when we circle up. Thanks for checking on them for me, son!"

"No problem, I'll see you after a while," said Taylor as he rode off to be with Patty, Carrie, and Randy."

Taylor noticed some big dark clouds forming in the distance. "Those clouds up ahead look like they might have some thunder 'n' lightning in them," he said as he rode up to the others.

"We were just talking about them," said Carrie.

"Yeah," Patty interrupted, "they seem to be getting darker and darker!"

"And closer and closer too," said Randy.

"Wow, look at the two dust trails up ahead. It looks like a couple of riders, riding at a full gallop toward us," said Taylor, pointing toward the obvious storm. I wonder if they are the train scouts?"

"I don't know," said Patty, "but by the way they are riding, we will know in about ten minutes or so!"

The two figures came into shape as they got closer.

"Yep, it's the scouts! There must be something wrong for them to be riding so hard, and they are hollering!" said Taylor.

"I think they are saying circle the wagons!" said Patty.

"Yep! That's what they are saying," said Carrie. "They're yelling, 'Circle the wagons, a bad storm's a comin'!'"

"C'mon, y'all!" yelled Bill as they sped by. "Thar's big trouble in them clouds up ahead. We have to circle up and tie down!"

They rode to Captain Tripper, yelling, "Cap'n, Cap'n, thar's twisters in them thar clouds, we gotta tie down!"

"Circle the wagons!" yelled the captain as he bolted toward the chuck and tack wagons.

Romy started riding from wagon to wagon, yelling the order!

"Put them in a double circle!" yelled Tripper.

"Yes, sir, Cap'n!"

Soon the wagons were circled in two tight circles. Romy rode up to Eldene and said, "It looks like there may be a tornado or two in that storm, that's there in the distance. Tie everything down tight and make sure the animals are tied tight too! Put everything in or under the wagon and leave room for you and the young'uns under the wagon!" He rode off to tell all the others.

Everyone was working hard, getting things taken care of, when Harold yelled, "I just saw a dad-burned bolt of lightning out there! I didn't hear any thunder, though, so it's still pretty dang far away! I guess maybe we had better hurry up and get this done and brace ourselves for this confounded storm!"

"Yep! It looks like it could be a bad one, the clouds are getting darker and darker." Mary joined in.

Suddenly Taylor yelled, "Look, that must be a tornado"—pointing toward the storm—"it looks like a big funnel coming down!"

"Good Lord in heaven!" yelled Eldene. "Everyone get under their wagons and lie as flat as possible!"

People were scrambling to get themselves braced for whatever was going to happen. Women were screaming, children were crying, and men were trying to calm down their nervous animals. Taylor, Harold, and Randy were trying to settle their animals down when they heard the deafening noise of the twister as it came closer and closer, tearing up everything in its path! Eldene ran to the Ward's wagon. Axel was busy with the animals. "C'mon, honey, you and the baby come to our wagon!" She took the baby, and they hurried to the Bounder!

"I'm so scared." Cried Penny as she took the baby from Eldene!

"Oh god, me too!" yelled Patty as she put her hands over her head. "Yeek, me too!"

"Let's not panic!" yelled Eldene, trying to be calm. "Everything is going to be okay!"

Mary and Carrie were under their wagon, lying on their stomachs. "I'm scared, Mom!" screamed Carrie!

"Me too, honey, me too!" She put her arm around her.

The twister's roaring was so loud you can't hear one another screaming! The rain was coming down so hard that the ground was becoming saturated and beginning to form huge mud puddles! The river started swelling, and the strong winds were blowing the rain sideways, and everyone was getting drenched! Eldene made sure that Penny and the baby were well protected from the water rushing around the Bounder.

"Hang on, everyone, here it comes!" she yelled.

The twister passed within an eighth of a mile of the wagon train. The wind was blowing so hard that the canopy on the Bounder was whipping, and Eldene thought it was going to get ripped off its ties. After what seemed like an hour, but really was only a few minutes, the deafening sound began to fade away, and the twister passed by and went on its destructive way.

"Is everybody okay?" asked Eldene as she stood up and began helping Penny and the baby.

"That was too scary for words, I'm soaked to the skin," said Patty as she held out her hands and looked at herself in disgust!

"I guess we all are, honey, but thank God we're alive and kicking!"

"Is everyone okay?" asked Taylor. "That was pretty darned intense! I thought we were going to get blown off the earth! Is everyone okay over there?"

"Yep, I reckon we're all in one piece! That was just downright scary!" yelled Harold!

"Man alive, it sure as hell was!" exclaimed Axel as he ran over to the Bounder. Are you and the baby okay? I was worried sick, but them dad-blamed animals wouldn't settle down! I saw Eldene come and get you, so I reckoned you were better off than under our wagon by yourself!"

"We're just fine," answered Penny, "thanks again to Mrs. McGrady!"

Romy rode up just then. "Everyone okay?"

"Yes, we're all just fine," said Eldene. "How about the rest of the folks, did everybody make it okay?"

"One little boy got a broken arm, and we had to round up some of the animals, but I guess we're okay. If Cap'n Tripper hadn't doubled the circle, we would have lost some wagons on the south end. A twister came within a couple hundred feet of the train, and if they had been spread out in the normal circle they would have been hit by it. We sure are a lucky bunch of people!"

"Yeah, lucky, thanks to the experience of a very good wagon train master and God in heaven!" commented Eldene.

"Amen to that," said Harold!

"I'll see y'all later, glad all y'all are okay," said Romy as he turned and rode off. "Gotta get back to work."

Taylor and the others began stringing lines to hang clothing and bedding on to dry. "I hope we don't see any more of those things. That was like being in a raging river!"

"Me too!" said Carrie. "I have never been so scared!"

"Yeah, and the noise was so deafening, I couldn't even hear my own screaming!"

"It took all my strength to keep them two mules from running away, and they are so dumb they would probably have run right into the twister! I didn't think I was going to make it," said Randy.

"Yep, me too," said Taylor, "they were pretty dang panicked."

"I think you both are the bravest men in the world," said Carrie as she winked and gave Taylor a kiss on the cheek.

"Me too," said Patty, kissing Randy on the cheek.

Randy looked at Taylor and said, blushing, "I reckon I'd go through another one of them storms for another one of those."

"Yep, me too," said Taylor as he winked at Carrie. "Me too!"

They could still see the storm as it moved to the northeast. It was as intense as ever and leaving a path of destruction.

"Well, that's our first tornado, and I hope it's our last!" said Eldene.

"I can do without another experience like that," said Mary, with tears running down her cheeks. "I've never been so terrified! We were in a wildfire one time, and it was terrifying, but at least, we could fight back. There's no stopping something like a tornado. They just run right over you and kill if they can!"

"Well, it's gone now," said Eldene, putting her arm around Mary. "We'll be out of this country pretty soon, and this will all be behind us."

"I guess things aren't so dry now," said Taylor as he wrung out his kerchief. "Next time we'll be careful what we wish for, huh?"

The next morning, the sun was peeking over the horizon, as if it was apologizing for hiding during yesterday's storm. The river was receding, and the ground surface was beginning to dry out. The air smelled fresh and clean. There weren't any dust devils skipping across the plains and the trees, and shrubs were washed of all the dust that was covering them. You could hear men talking about the storm as they scurried around, harnessing the animals and hitching up their wagons. Women were busy gathering the dried laundry and repacking, getting their wagons ready to head out once again.

"Howdy, ma'am, how are y'all getting along?"

Eldene looked up and recognized Bill Winters. "Well, howdy, Mr. Winters. We are doing just fine, thank you for asking. Are you and Mr. Many Moons on your way out again?"

"Yes, ma'am, we're off to the wild blue yonder," he said as he waved his hat.

"Thank you and Mr. Many Moons for saving our lives. If it weren't for you two brave men, we may have been swallowed up by one of those terrifying monsters! We owe you a great debt of gratitude!"

"No, ma'am, we were just doing our jobs!"

"Yep," said Many Moons, "just adoing our jobs. C'mon, Bill, we have to git goin'."

"Okay, Moon, I'm a comin', I'm a comin'. See you next time, ma'am, y'all have a good day!"

The two men rode off toward the West, waving their hands in the air. "You like that redheaded squaw, don't cha?" inquired Moon.

"She's a downright handsome woman, and she seems to come from good stock, and yep, I do like her. So what, nosey?" answered Bill with a bit of attitude.

"Well…just so you know, Romy and her are seeing a lot of each other, so I think she is probably off-limits. You may be barking up the wrong tree," said Moon.

"Damn it, Moon, why'd ya have to go and tell me that! Ya done messed up my whole damned day!"

"I figured that it would be better to tell you now so you won't be getting your hopes up for nothin'," quipped Moon.

Bill's disappointment was obvious. "Can't say that's the best news I've ever heard, but I reckon it's what I needed to hear." Bill was feeling sad and hurt as they rode in silence for several miles. Many Moons knew it was time to hold his tongue and let things soak in for a while. Bill finally spoke up. "Okay, Moon, I guess we had better get on some higher ground and start doin' our jobs. I reckon I'm gonna be okay now."

"I'm right behind you," said Moon with a happy tone. "Let's get goin'."

The wagon train was having its own problems with muddy ground that the rains had left behind. Wagon after wagon was getting mired down in the mud. They were having to use horses and mules from other wagons that wasn't stuck yet to help the ones that were. It was a viscous circle.

"I sure will be glad to get out of this muddy flat country," said Eldene!

"Yup, me too," said Taylor. "I'm getting pretty durned tired of pulling people out of the mire and the muck."

"Just look at my boots, I'll never get the mud off them, they're a mess," complained Patty as she lifted her boot up to show Taylor and Eldene.

"Haha, you are a pitiful sight there, little sister, with your pant legs all rolled up. You're kind of a muddy mess!" Laughed Taylor as he took his finger and swiped mud on Patty's cheek!

"Eeyuck!" screamed Patty! "I'll get you for that." And she picked up a handful of mud and slung it toward Taylor!

"Whoa," Taylor said as he dodged. The mud went flying past him and hit Eldene smack in the face.

"What in the world!" yelled Eldene.

"Oh my gosh, Mommy, I… I'm so, so sorry." Patty gulped. "Tha…t w…was meant for Taylor!"

Eldene wiped the mud from her face. "I'll deal with you later, young lady. Right now we have to get these wagons moving! You two would do well to stop horsing around and get back to work!"

"Yes'm," answered Patty as she stuck out her tongue at Taylor. "I'll get you, smarty-pants," she said.

Taylor laughed and said, "I'll be waiting, Ms. Muddy Boots!"

The next two days were slow and tedious. Mud kept building up in the wagon wheels. "I'm shore enough getting tired of having to stop every hundred feet or so to clean this confounded mud out of the dad-burned wagon wheels!" Grumped Harold.

"Yeah, me too," said Axel and Eldene simultaneously!

"It's beginning to get on my nerves," griped Axel as he dug mud out of his wheels. "Penny is having a hard time with the baby inside the wagon, with it bouncing around in this mud and muck!"

Ever optimistic, Eldene remarked, "We'll be out of this soon, the ground is beginning to dry out, and we are going to be on higher ground. It looks like we're headed for a bit of an incline!"

"I hope so!" yelled Taylor, "my back's getting sore. The poor little goats are solid mud. I don't think I'll be able to find their teats to milk them!"

"Take them down to the river and lead them into the water," said Patty. "That'll clean you and the goats at the same time!"

"You take them to the river, Ms. Muddy Boots," joked Taylor. "You need a bath more than they do!"

"Oh yeah, well, Mr. Smarty-pants"—laughed Patty—"you're beginning to smell like them smelly goats!"

Taylor looked at Patty with an I'm-going-to get-you look and ran toward her. "Gotcha!" Taylor yelled as he tackled her!

"Yikes!" squealed Patty. "You're getting mud in my hair!"

Eldene heard the ruckus and stopped the mules. She saw Taylor and Patty rolling around the muck. "What in heaven's name are you two doing? Just look at you, you're mud from head to toe!"

Both of them were laughing so hard they couldn't answer. They just sat there in the mud, looking up at their mom.

"Well… I guess you both can go give the goats a bath and wash yourselves while you're at it!" said Eldene with a smirk.

"Yes'm," they both answered at the same time.

"I'll get you for this, Mr. Smarty-pants," said Patty as she untied the goats from the Bounder.

The Thompsons were all laughing at the comedy going on.

"Them two young'uns have too much dad-burned energy." Laughed Harold.

"Yep, you're right, Harold, I don't know where in the world they get it all!" said Eldene.

"I don't remember havin' that much gumption," quipped Mary.

Romy rode up to the Bounder. "Whoa, boy, looks like they're having a lot of fun!"

"Yeah, they sure do get carried away!" remarked Eldene.

"Well, they'll be able to use some of that energy soon. We're going to be climbing out of this bottomland in a couple of hours. We're going up California Hill, and that's a long trip. We'll be in Wyoming country pretty soon, and things are a little different there. They've got critters there that'll make your skin crawl."

"Oh good, that's just what I need is to make my skin crawl! What kind of critter are we talking about that could do that?" asked Eldene.

"Oh, pretty lady! There is some of the ugliest critter on the face of the earth. I can't even explain how ugly some of them are!"

"You're not making me feel very good about going through Wyoming. Is there any other way?" Eldene shuddered.

"Afraid not, but you don't need to fret none. I'll be around to protect you. I'll see y'all later. Hiyah, boy, let's go!" He spurred his horse, and as he rode away, he looked back and winked at Eldene. She promptly stuck out her tongue at him!

They circled the wagons a short distance from two large rock formations that resembled buildings. About ten or twelve miles further west, you could see a tall peak that looked like a chimney protruding from a haystack. The McGradys, Thompsons, and Wards were all sitting around the campfire discussing the odd-shaped peaks.

"That one over yonder"—pointing toward a pointed peak—"is kind of like a big stack of hay. I wonder if that's the needle in the haystack that people talk about when they can't find something?" joked Taylor. Everyone laughed!

Romy rode up and dismounted. "I see y'all are settled in for the night."

"We are, we were just wondering about those odd-shaped peaks," said Eldene. "We were noticing how they resembled buildings!"

"Well…by golly, they do have names like buildings. The one over there on the right is called Courthouse Rock, and the one on the left is called Jailhouse Rock!"

"Dad-burned if that don't beat all," quipped Harold. "Why in tarnation did they ever get names like that?"

"I'm pretty certain that two of them were named after the courthouse and jailhouse back in St. Louis. I reckon the other one just looks like a chimney," answered Romy.

"I reckon that it makes sense when you think about it," said Harold.

"I stopped by to tell you that Cap'n Tripper said we are going to have to start earlier in the morning and stop later in the evenings. We are behind schedule due to the storms, and we have to make up for the lost time. We don't want to have to spend the winter on this side of the Rockies," said Romy. "It would be a mighty long wait until spring."

"We're doing ten-hour days now," said Axel. "Any more would be mighty hard on Penny and the baby."

"Well, the only option is for you to lag behind, and that would be disastrous," said Romy. "We are going to be going from daylight till dark and stocking up again at Fort Laramie. We'll stop there for one day and move on toward a place called Independence Rock."

"We'll help out with the baby," said Patty as she put her arm around Penny. "Everything will be just fine."

"You all are so good to us," said Penny with teary eyes. "I'm so thankful that we are on this train with you, wonderful people!"

"We'll make sure that we all make it together," said Mary

"Yes, that's a fact!" said Eldene. "We're not going to let anything happen to you and that precious little girl!"

"I am so proud to be acquainted with all y'all, and I reckon we'll be able to keep up with y'all's help," said Axel. "By the way," he continued, "we want y'all to know that we have decided to name the baby Eldene Patricia Ward. We're gonna call her little Deeny!"

"Oh dear god in heaven," said Eldene as tears welled up in her eyes. "I feel so honored, I... I don't quite know what to say." Tears ran down her face as she hugged both Axel and Penny and kissed little Deeny on her soft cheeks. "Th-thank you!"

"Oh wow, me? A baby named after me! I can't believe it!" yelled Patty. "I feel like dancing or something!" She started jumping around, singing!

"Sounds like a good idea!" yelled Randy as he took Patty's hand and began jumping around with her. "Yahoo!"

Taylor grabbed Carrie's hand, and they joined Patty and Randy, whooping and hollering. "Yahoo, yippy, yahoo!"

Romy took Eldene's hand and said, "Let's take a moonlight walk. It may be awhile before we get another chance to walk and talk. He turned to the kids. "Y'all don't mind, do you?" He tipped his hat as he led her away from all the hullabaloo at the campsite.

Chapter 9

Into the Wild Country

It's four o'clock in the morning, and everyone was stirring around, trying to wake up so they could get on the road. The moonlight was shimmering off the rippling waters of the river, and the frogs were croaking back and forth in rhythm. An owl was hooting in the distance, and you could see the bats fluttering across the water, diving for insects in what seemed like perfect time with the frog's rhythm and orchestration.

"Gosh, Mom," said Taylor, "it's still kind of dark out. Don't you think we're a little too early?"

"Yeah, Mom," moaned Patty, stirring as she peeked out of the Bounder. "I'm not ready to get up yet."

"Well, you heard what Romy said. We need to be on the road by first light. It'll be light before you can say Jack Robinson's cow's dead," joked Eldene.

"*What!*" said Patty with a puzzled look. "What in the world does that mean?"

"It's just an expression, dear. It means it's almost sunup, and we need to be ready to roll. So you need to get up and grab yourself some biscuits and gravy and help your brother with the harnesses."

"Yeah, sleepyhead," said Taylor, "I've already fed the horses and mules and milked the goats. It's time to get your britches on and move your butt."

"I've got my britches on, smarty," said Patty as she turned her bottom toward Taylor and wiggled her butt at him.

Randy and Carrie walked up to the Bounder just in time to see Patty's bottom sticking out of the canvas flap and wiggling back and forth.

"Dad-burned, that's something you don't see every day!" exclaimed Randy as he and Carrie broke out laughing.

"Yeek!" screamed Patty as she turned beet red. I—I—I didn't know you were here."

"We came over to see if everyone was all set to hit the trail. We weren't expecting to see a sideshow." Giggled Carrie

"I—I—I was joking around with my smarty-pants brother," said Patty, wrinkling her nose and lips.

"We'll be ready in a few minutes, we just have to harness the mules and hook them to the Bounder," said Taylor.

"I'll help you," said Carrie as she picked up the collars.

"Come on, Patty. I'll help you saddle the horses," said Randy, taking Patty's hand.

"Okey dokey," said Patty as she grabbed a biscuit.

Eldene finished packing everything away while they hooked up the team.

Romy rode up and tipped his hat. "Good morning! Are y'all ready to get on the road to bigger and better things?"

"Yep, I reckon we are," quipped Eldene, trying to mimic Romy's Texas drawl. "Would y'all like to step down for a hot cup of java?" She looked up at Romy, smiled, and winked.

"Well… I reckon I can't turn down an invite like that, pretty lady, now can I?" And he dismounted.

"Wyoming doesn't look much different than the country behind us!" exclaimed Taylor.

"It looks like there's a lot more sagebrush," said Carrie.

"Yup." Randy piped up. "I rode out early this morning, away from the river, and I ran into sagebrush that seemed to go on for what looks like miles and miles."

"Yep," said Romy, "there's a few miles of sagebrush in these parts. I reckon we'll be going through it for a couple of weeks. We'll probably see herds of antelope and buffalo and a few other critters. You'll be able to have sage hen for supper whenever you want it."

"Yippy!" yelled Randy as he swung his sling around. "I'll be able to sharpen my aim."

"Have you ever tasted rattlesnake before?" asked Romy.

"Eeyuck!" exclaimed Eldene. "I can't imagine ever doing anything like that."

"It's pretty durned good," claimed Romy. "You just skin it and cut it into steaks, roll it in an egg batter, and fry it up in some hog grease, and you have a mighty fine meal."

"I'm thinking probably not," said Eldene, shaking her head and wrinkling her lips.

"I might try it," said Harold as he and Mary walked up to the Bounder. "It don't sound half-bad."

"Hi, you two," greeted Eldene. "Are you kidding me? You would actually eat a rattlesnake."

"Dad-burned if I rightly know, I ain't never tried it, but I might if I get a chance."

"Well... I ain't cookin' no rattlesnake, so don't plan on eatin' one anytime soon," said Mary.

"There's diamondbacks out there big enough to feed three families," said Romy. "Maybe we'll try one before we get out of these parts."

"Yikes," said Patty, "a snake that big might have us for supper."

Everyone laughed and began making comments all at once. "Rattlesnake! Eeyuck, blech, not me," "Me neither."

Romy and Harold both scratched their heads and chuckled.

"Well...folks, this is fun, but it's daybreak, so we gotta get going. I'll see y'all later on down the trail."

Just as Romy started to mount his horse, Patty let out a bloodcurdling scream. "*Eeks*, oh m-gosh! Oh m-gosh! *Eeks!*"

Romy dropped the reins and went running toward Patty, as did Eldene and everyone else.

Patty was screaming and jumping up and down and rapidly shaking her hands. "Oh my gosh! Oh, eeks!"

"What's wrong, Patty?" asked Eldene, trying to calm her down.

L-look at that! What is it? It was on my saddle blanket!" yelled Patty as she pointed to a huge bug-like creature trying to bury its wobbling head in the dirt.

Everyone looked at the giant bug. "I don't know what it is, honey, but it sure is a scary-looking thing," said Eldene. "What is it, Romy?"

"Well, folks, that's one of them critters I was telling y'all about," said Romy. "It's called a vinegarroon."

"A vinegar what?" asked Taylor.

"They are part of the scorpion family. It's a good idea to check your clothing and bedding every day from now until we get out of these parts. Check y'all's shoes before you put them on too. Scorpions like to hide in places like that."

"I want to go back to Baltimore," said Patty. "That thing is awful. We never had any bugs big enough to eat you. I feel creepy all over."

"Me too," said Carrie. "I'm not going to put my feet on the ground until we reach the mountains."

"We'll just have to be careful," said Harold. "There's been people through here before, and I reckon they must've made it okay, and I reckon we'll make it okay too. It's time to get on the road, folks, so let's mount up and git a goin'."

"Yep, Harold's right, folks. I'll see y'all later," said Romy as he mounted up and rode off.

"We've got snakes big enough to feed three families and bugs big enough to carry you off. What will we find next?" Piped Eldene as she climbed into the Bounder's seat. "I'm not liking some of these critters around here."

"Me neither," said Mary. "I can't wait to get out of this country."

"We'll be just fine, dad-burn it," claimed Harold. "It can't be much worse than what we done been through."

"We'll see you at the next stop. Hyah, hyah, let's go, Jack, giddyap, Jenny!" yelled Eldene as she snapped the reins. "I would like for you and Patty to stay close for a while, okay?"

"Okey dokey, Mom," said Taylor. "Let's go, Barney."

The kids were riding a couple hundred feet ahead of the tack wagon.

"There's a couple of riders coming toward us over yonder," said Randy, pointing toward the north.

"Yeah," said Taylor, "I was just wondering if they were Bill and Many Moons checking in." "They're not because they are leading two pack horses."

"It looks like they are wearing some kind of animal skins," said Carrie.

"Yeah, and I can smell them from here," Patty whispered loudly, covering her nose. "They smell like a barnyard or something."

The two riders rode on toward Captain Tripper. The one in the front had a coonskin cap and leather pants and coat. He had long scraggly brown hair and a beard to match. He looked angry and mean, and his piercing dark eyes seemed to look right through you. The second rider was a smaller man with leather clothing and long scraggly hair that appeared to be blondish. His beard was shorter than the first rider.

"Those fellows look like they've had better days," said Taylor. "That first one looked like he was mad at the world."

"I wonder what that pack horse was carrying?" said Randy. "It sorta looked like cow hides."

"I'll bet they're buffalo hides," said Patty. "Romy said there was buffalo in this part of the country."

"Yep," said Carrie, "and they smelled like they'd been living with the whole herd. Blech, I can still smell them."

"Me too," added Patty as she put her hand over her nose.

"Yeah, they left a stench all right," said Taylor. "C'mon, let's get on back to the wagons. I don't like the looks of those two characters."

Captain Tripper was to the side of the trail, talking to the two strangers. He was speaking loud and stern. "I don't care what you want, you can't join the wagon train. You'll have to move on."

"We done lost two of our pack mules back yonder to a bunch of renegade savages. All's we want is to tag along as fer as Fort Laramie," said the large man.

"Sorry but I can't take any chance of those Indians comin' down on my wagon train over a bunch of buffalo hides," emphasized Tripper. "You're gonna have to move on."

"You can't stop us from ridin' with y'all!" the large man yelled angrily. "We ain't a goin' back out thar to get killed by a bunch of damn savages."

Romy rode up beside Tripper. "You havin' a problem with these two, Cap'n?"

"Nope," said Tripper, "they were just getting ready to leave, ain't that right?" He moved his hand toward his pistol.

Romy noticed the smaller man reaching for his rifle. "You heard the Cap'n, it's time to move on, keep your hands away from your rifles and move on." He tapped his pistol grip with his index finger.

The two men turned slowly toward the rear of the wagon train and began to go with reluctance.

"Fort Laramie is the other direction. I don't want you two behind us," said Tripper. "I want y'all to head out in front of us so that I can watch y'all disappear."

The two men stopped and looked at Tripper and Romy, and the large man said, "You can't send us out th—"

"You heard me, get going," interrupted Tripper, pointing in the direction ahead of the wagon train.

The two men turned around. The large man said angrily, "Our blood is on your hands, sir."

"I ain't likely to forget this, mister," said the smaller man. "I'll be a-seein' y'all agin'. C'mon, mule, get to movin'." He spurred his horse and pulled on the mule's lead.

Romy and Tripper watched as the two men rode off. "Those two are nothing but trouble, they could bring down an attack on the wagon train," commented Tripper.

"What were they up to?" asked Romy.

"My guess is they were slaughtering buffalo, taking their hides, and leaving the carcasses for the wolves, coyotes, and buzzards. The Indians scared them off and took two of their pack mules that were loaded down with hides."

"I understand," said Romy. "If they're with the train, we'd be fighting off an attack for sure."

"Pass the word along for everyone to keep their eyes open for those two rank smellin' hombres," commanded Tripper. "Tell them to watch for Indians too. I'm a little concerned now that I know they're out there somewhere lookin' for those skinners."

"Yes, sir, Cap'n," said Romy.

"Bill and Many Moons are due in any time now, so they will know where the Indians are," said Tripper.

"Hyah, boy, let's go," said Romy as he headed toward the Bounder.

Taylor and Eldene had their rifles loaded and ready. "That sounded like it could have gone bad," said Taylor as Romy rode up.

"Yep, it sure enough could've," said Romy. "Y'all need to keep a sharp eye out for those two buffalo skinners. If you see them or any Indians around, let me know."

"Indians?" asked Eldene. "You mean we might get attacked by Indians?"

"It's not likely that a small band of Indians will attack us," answered Romy, "but if they think we have anything to do with those two smelly skinners, they might."

"Smelly is putting it mildly," said Patty, wrinkling her nose. "I can't seem to get their stench out of my nose."

"Me neither," added Carrie, "I'm still gagging."

"Haha!" Laughed Romy. "I reckon I'd better go on down the line and warn the rest of the people. Stay alert."

"Why are the Indians after those yahoos anyhow?" asked Harold. "They must've done somethin' to make them purty dad-burned mad."

"The problem is they slaughter the buffalo for the hides and leave the carcasses to the wolves and buzzards. The Indians use every single bit of the buffalo for food, shelter, tools, and clothing. The skinners come out here by the dozens and take away their livelihood. The government is trying to stop them, but they are hard to catch. There's no law against what they're doing yet, and the army can't really do anything about it," said Romy.

"It's a dad-burned shame, that's what it is," quipped Harold, "a dad-burned shame."

"Yep," added Romy, "it sure enough is. That small band of Indians that they call renegade savages are just a small hunting party. They are part of a much larger tribe that have a village north of here a few miles. If Cap'n Tripper let them travel with the wagon train, the whole tribe would come down on us."

The rest of the day was uneventful. Later everyone was sitting around the campfire, discussing the earlier happenings.

"Those buffalo skinners must never take a bath," said Patty. "I wonder how they can stand each other?"

"That's probably why the smaller one rides in front of the big one," commented Taylor.

"Yeah, I get it," Randy agreed, "that way he's not downwind."

Everyone laughed.

"How'd y'all's day go after all of the excitement?" asked Romy as he walked up to the campfire.

"It was a dad-burned long day," answered Harold. "We must've got in a good thirty miles today."

"Yep, we got in a good day," commented Romy. "If we keep this up, we'll get over the Rockies before the end of October."

"I've heard that it snows in August and September in those mountains," said Axel.

"Yep, it sure can. If we can't get over them by then, we won't be able to go until next spring."

"I reckon we danged well better get over them then," stated Harold. "I ain't a hankerin' to spend the winter in this dad-burned country."

"We'll make it," said Eldene. "All we have to do is keep on keeping on, that's what my daddy always says."

"I'm going up the river and find a place to freshen my sweaty self," said Patty.

"I'll go with you," said Carrie, "I want to freshen up too."

"Okay, honey, but don't go very far, it's starting to get dark," said Eldene.

"Okey dokey, we won't be too long," said Patty as she and Carrie walked toward the river.

"It's too open here," said Patty as they looked for a place. "Let's go further up the river so we'll have a little more privacy."

"Well…" stammered Carrie, "I… I guess it will be okay."

After they had gone up the river quite a distance, Carrie said, "Patty, I think we have gone far enough, we should stop here. There is plenty of cover here, and I don't want to get any farther away from the wagon train."

"Okay, this looks like a good spot to take a moonlight swim," said Patty. "The moon is so bright, it's almost like daylight."

Just as they started to take off their boots, Patty whispered, "Wait, I have a funny feeling that we are being watched."

"What do you mean?" said Carrie as she looked around. "You're scaring me. I *think* we should go back to camp."

"D-do you smell that awful smell?" asked Patty. "It smells like those buffalo hunters."

"Yep, I sure do. They must be pretty close," commented Carrie. "We gotta get back, c'mon."

Suddenly the two skinners jumped out of the bushes and grabbed the two girls.

"You two gals are a sight for sore eyes," said the smaller one as he wrestled Patty to the ground. "I ain't never seen nobody as purty as you."

Patty began screaming, "AAHEE, AAHEE! Let me go, you ugly smelly monster."

Carrie was fighting her captor for dear life and screaming, "AAHEE! Get your filthy hands off me." She stomped down on the man's foot as hard as she could. He yelled and relaxed his grip, just enough for Carrie to break his hold and drop down. She bolted toward the wagon camp as fast as she could.

Patty scratched the skinner's face and kneed him in the groin. "Yikes, you hellcat. I'll kill you for that." He backhanded Patty across the face.

Patty began sobbing and screaming as she kicked, scratched, and fought for her life. "Let…me…go, you dirty smelly puke!" she screamed.

The skinner that had Carrie yelled, "C'mon, Elroy, we gotta get the hell outta here. Thet other one got away, an' she'll git the whole damned bunch of them yahoos after us."

"Not till I teach this little hussy a lesson or two."

"If'n ya go and kill her, we'll be a runnin' forever. C'mon, let's get the hell outta here."

Taylor came running into view with his revolver in his hand. The big skinner grabbed his rifle and pointed at him, yelling, "Hold on there, young feller, stay where ya are, or I'll kill ya."

"Tell your ugly pardner to get his hands off my sister!" yelled Taylor as he started toward Patty.

"I said stay where you are," yelled the big man as he pulled back the hammer on his rifle.

Without hesitation and lightning-fast, Taylor raised his gun and pulled the trigger. The big skinner fell to the ground with a thud. Taylor looked at the other skinner and yelled, "Let go of my sister, or I'll blow your stinking ugly head off!"

"Ya done went and killed my partner, now I'm a gonna kill yer sister." He pulled Patty to her feet and grabbed her from behind as he pulled his skinning knife out of its scabbard. "I'm a fixin' to cut her damned throat."

Taylor calmly and coldly stated, "Get away from my sister, or you're a dead man," as he took careful aim.

The skinner raised the knife toward Patty's throat as Taylor pulled the trigger. The bullet hit the skinner in the forehead, just above his nose. He instantly went limp and fell to the ground, dead.

"Are you hurt, Patty?" asked Taylor.

Patty ran to Taylor, sobbing. "I... I... I thought...he was going...to kill...me. I... I'm so glad to see you." She threw her arms around Taylor's neck and buried her head in his chest and began sobbing.

Taylor just stood there, kind of in a state of disbelief. "Everything happened so fast," he said. "Geez, I just killed two men."

"How...did...you know where...to go?" asked Patty.

"Mom sent me to look for you two, and I met Carrie running for help. I sent her on to get Mom and the others, and I came to get you."

"I... I'm s-so glad that you're my brother. I love you so much."

Taylor looked at Patty and said, "Nobody is going to hurt my little sister. I wouldn't have anyone to kid around with. Hey, you're bleeding! It looks like you have a cut above you eye, and your eye looks swollen."

"Yeah, that smelly buffalo skinner hit me a few times, but I got in some good ones myself."

"You were fighting pretty darned good. He knew he had his hands full, that's for sure."

"I would have died before I would have given in. I wasn't about to let him have his way with me!"

Carrie and the others came, and Carrie put her arms around Patty and began crying. "Oh, Patty, I thought for sure they were going to kill us. I-I didn't want to leave you, but I had to get help. I… I'm so glad that you're alive, I was so afraid."

"What happened?" asked Eldene as she took Patty in her arms. "We heard the gunshots as we were running over here."

"Taylor saved my life," said Patty proudly. "You should have seen him, he was so brave."

"I was scared out of my wits," said Taylor. "All I could see was two men trying to hurt my little sister. I barely remember what happened, it happened so darned fast. I know that I just killed two men."

Romy and Captain Tripper and several other people came running.

"What the hell happened here?" asked Captain Tripper. "We heard the gunshots."

"Taylor had to shoot those two skinners," said Eldene. "They had Patty and Carrie and were trying to force themselves on them."

"I didn't have any other choice," stated Taylor, "they were going to kill Patty and me. That big one there still has his thumb on the hammer of his rifle, and that one over there still has the knife next to him that he was going to cut Patty's throat with. She's got the bruises to prove it. I did what I had to do," stated Taylor in his own defense.

Romy looked over the bodies of the two skinners and said, "It's like he said, Cap'n."

"Well, I reckon we need to take care of these two hombres and do something with the buffalo hides that they have on that pack mule there. I'll talk to you tomorrow about what happened. Y'all can go on back to the wagon train, and Romy and I will take care of things."

After everyone left, Tripper looked at Romy and stated, "Get a couple of the men and bury these two hombres."

"What about the animals and hides?" asked Romy.

"Well...go ahead and burn all of their gear, including their saddles and the hides," ordered Tripper. "Brush down the animals, and we'll mix them in with our stock. I don't want the Indians to suspect that we had anything to do with these two skinners. Bill and Many Moons are due back. They will know what the Indians are up to. If they were after these two hombres, they will know about it."

"After I finish up here, Cap'n, I'm going over to the McGrady's camp and have a talk with young Taylor. I know him pretty well, and I know he is feeling bad about what happened here."

"That's probably a good idea. You can tell him that he don't need to lose any sleep over these two troublemakers."

"I'll tell him, Cap'n."

Back at the Bounder, everyone was sitting around the fire. "Those two smelly buffalo skinners seemed to come out of nowhere," said Carrie. "They grabbed us and began pawing us and trying to have their way with us. The big one had such a tight hold on me that I thought he was going to break my arm, and Patty was fighting for her life. He had her on the ground, and she just fought all the harder. I was able to break free, and I just began running. I knew that I had to get help fast. That's when I saw Taylor, and he sent me after the rest of you."

Taylor was watching the sparks from the burning wood float up into the sky. They seemed to merge with the stars as they floated higher and higher.

Romy walked into the camp. "Howdy, folks, how are y'all holding up?"

"Not too bad under the circumstances!" exclaimed Eldene.

"How about you, Taylor? Are you okay?" asked Romy.

Taylor was quiet for a couple of minutes. He looked at Romy. "I *think* so," he stammered. I... I've never had...to kill...anyone before."

"I know how you feel. I've been in your boots once or twice myself, and it's not an easy thing to swallow," said Romy. I know you did what you had to do, and so does Cap'n Tripper. If you hadn't, Patty would be dead, and maybe you would be too. Those two were up to no good from the get-go. Cap'n Tripper said to tell you that there would be no trial or anything, and you shouldn't lose any sleep over those two."

"I think you are a very brave young feller," said Harold.

"Yep, me too," said Mary.

Eldene put her arm around Taylor's neck and kissed him on the cheek and whispered, "Your dad would be so proud of you. You are so brave, and I love you."

Everyone joined in and assured Taylor that he was going to be okay.

"Thanks, everybody. I... I feel much better now. I am going to be okay!" he stated with conviction. "I'm going to be just fine. I'll never let anyone hurt any of my family or friends."

"The cap'n will stop by tomorrow and talk to you about things," said Romy. "I'll see y'all tomorrow. We'll be hitting the trail at the same time. Bright and early."

"All righty then," said Axel. "C'mon, Penny, let's get some shut-eye."

"Yep, us too," said Harold. "It's been a dad-burned full day. G'night, we'll see y'all in the morning."

"Okey dokey," said Eldene, "we should all try to get some sleep. We'll be ready by daybreak." Eldene turned her attention to Patty. "I'll heat some water, and you can wash up inside the bounder. We need to get you out of those torn soiled clothes."

"Okay, Mommy, I want you to burn them. I'll never wear them again. They smell like that filthy buffalo hunter," said Patty as tears ran down her face.

Eldene put her arms around her. "Okay, honey, if that's what you want, we'll burn them and get you cleaned up. What about you, dear?" asked Eldene, looking at Taylor.

"No, ma'am, they didn't get close enough to touch me, thank God. I feel pretty good now, so I'm just going to turn off my mind and get some sleep."

"Okay, we'll be hitting the trail early," said Eldene. "Fort Laramie can't be too much farther."

Chapter 10

Running Wolf

Taylor was up early the next morning. He was still a little uneasy about what he had done to the two buffalo hunters. *I am sure that I did the right thing for Patty's sake*, he thought. He had finished taking care of the animals, and just as he was getting ready to milk the goats, a loud rattling sound startled the goats. The animals began to act a little crazy. "What the heck was that?" he said, talking to the goats. *Baa! Baa!* The goats began bleating and panicking.

"Whoa! What's going on?" yelled Taylor as he jumped out of the way. The rattling sound was more intense. He spotted the source just a few feet away. "Whoa, that's one heck of a big snake."

The large rattlesnake appeared to be around six or seven feet long and as big around as Taylor's forearms. It was coiled about eight to ten feet away and ready to strike.

Eldene came over to see what the ruckus was. "What's all the fuss about?" she asked.

"Stay back, Mom," said Taylor. "There's a huge rattlesnake over there. I'm afraid to move, he's so close. I'm afraid to reach for my gun, he may strike if I do."

"I've never seen a snake that big." Gulped Eldene. "He's huge and angry. What'll we do?"

"I'm not sure," said Taylor. "The goats are having a fit, and the snake doesn't look like he's going anywhere. I think I'm going to go for my gun and shoot him."

Harold heard the noise. "What's all the ruckus?"

"There's a huge rattlesnake a few feet from Taylor," whispered Eldene, pointing toward the snake.

Harold spotted the rattler and said, "Tarnation, I ain't never seen a snake that dad-burned big. Hold real still there, Taylor, while I get a good bead on him."

"Okay, but don't miss!"

Harold raised his rifle and took aim. *Kaboom!* The Snake started writhing and twisting around.

"Good shot," yelled Eldene, "you got him."

"Yup, it looks that way," said Harold. "Now what'll we do?"

The gunshot brought Romy running with his revolver in his hand. "What's going on over here!" he shouted.

"Harold just shot a huge rattler!" exclaimed Eldene as she pointed at the writhing dying snake.

People from all over the train came running toward the Bounder to check things out.

"Well...it looks like y'all are going to get to taste rattlesnake after all." Chuckled Romy. "Let's skin him out, Harold, and we'll cook him up for supper tonight."

"Okey dokey, let's git to it," said Harold as he reached for his knife. He held the snake up as high as he could and exclaimed, "Don't be alarmed, folks, it's just a big ole rattlesnake." The snake was still dragging the ground as he held it up for the crowd to see. "I reckon we're gonna have snake steaks for supper tonight."

"I think y'all are gonna be surprised at how good snake meat is," commented Romy.

Patty wrinkled her face and said, "I'm not eating any ugly old rattlesnake, yuck."

"Me neither!" said Carrie.

People in the crowd began commenting as they walked away.

"I'm not about to eat no snake."

"Not me!"

"Me neither."

"Blech."

Romy began laughing. "Y'all keep your eyes and ears open. Diamondbacks always run in pairs. This old boy has a mate around here somewhere."

"Oh, that's what we need," joked Eldene, "two big snakes to eat."

Later at suppertime, Romy made an egg and goat's milk batter to coat the snake meat and fried it in rendered hog fat.

"I'll have to admit that those steaks smell pretty darn good," said Eldene.

"I might have to try it," said Taylor.

"I'm ready," said Harold, licking his lips.

"I'm ready to try some," yelled Axel. "It smells mighty good to me."

Eldene made some mashed potatoes and gravy and cooked up some wild asparagus.

Everyone was anxious and apprehensive about tasting rattlesnake meat.

"Okay, everyone, let's give it a try. I'll go first to show that there's nothing to fear," said Romy. He cut off a bite and put it in his mouth. "Yum, this is excellent."

Harold took a bite. "Well, I'll be hornswoggled, that's downright good. It tastes a little like chicken."

Everyone took a bite, except Patty, Carrie, Mary, and Penny.

Eldene was reluctant to try it, but she gave in and tasted a tiny bite. "This is actually pretty darned good, girls, give it a try."

"Yeah, c'mon, it's good." Piped Taylor.

"It's good," said Randy as he held up a piece and popped it in his mouth. "Yum, yum."

"Yep, y'all are missing out on some mighty fine vittles," said Axel.

"That's okay, I'll pass," said Patty. "I'll just have some potatoes and asparagus."

"Yep, me too," said Mary.

"I'll stick with Patty and Mom," said Carrie.

"I'm nursing a baby, so I'll not be eating any snake," said Penny as she wrinkled her nose.

Bill Winters and Many Moons walked up. "Sorry we're late, folks," said Bill, "we got sidetracked by the cap'n."

"Howdy," said Romy. "I invited Bill and Moon over for some snake steaks, I hope you folks don't mind."

"Not at all," said Eldene. "I'll get you each a plate."

"Thank ya, ma'am."

"Yes, ma'am," said Many Moons.

"How is the trail ahead looking?" asked Eldene. "Are we going to have a rough ride ahead of us?"

"Well, by golly, ma'am, things aren't looking too bad," answered Bill. "The trail is in purty fair shape, aside from a few areas that have some deep ruts. I reckon it's from too many wagons havin' to go over the same dad-gummed spot."

"Are we going to have trouble getting through 'um?" asked Harold.

"We will if we get any heavy rains. I'm hopin' we can get through the narrow spots before that happens," said Romy. "We don't want to have any major breakdowns that'll hold us up."

In the distant horizon, Taylor saw a silhouette of an Indian on a horse. "What does that Indian fellow over there want? He seems to be looking us over pretty good."

"What? Where?" asked Romy as he jumped to his feet.

"He's right over there," said Taylor, pointing toward the silhouette. "He's just sitting there, looking at us."

"Tarnation," said Romy, "I reckon we had better go tell the cap'n. Y'all just act normal and do what you always do after supper. After y'all get packed up, move your animals to the inner circle and make sure they are tethered tight. Set your rifles where you can get it in a moment's notice with plenty of ammo."

"Are we going to be attacked by Indians?" asked Eldene.

"Probably not," said Many Moons. "They're looking for those two buffalo skinners that the cap'n told us about. They want them pretty bad."

"Yup," Bill interrupted, "Moon and me met them two fellers out on the trail, and the little one was a braggin' about how he had a fling with a purty little Indian squaw.

Well…me and Moon decided we didn't want to be close to them, so we moved on."

"Yes, ma'am," said Many Moons. "If they did something to an Indian woman, it was against her will, and those Indians over there are after their hides."

"If they think those two renegades are here with the train, they will attack us to get to them," said Romy. "The best thing for us to do is be ready for them. Me and the boys here will go tell the cap'n and warn the rest of the train. I'll be back in an hour or so, meanwhile be calm and keep your eyes peeled."

"Thanks for the vitals. That was mighty fine-tasting sage hen," joked Bill.

"Yes, ma'am. It tasted like rattlesnake." Laughed Many Moons.

Everyone laughed.

"There are four Indians over there now. And they are a little closer," said Taylor anxiously.

"Okay, let's go, boys," said Romy. "They may want to powwow. I don't think they are going to attack us. The tribes around these parts are at peace with the white man right now. They do most of their fighting with other tribes. We'll be keeping a close watch tonight, just in case."

"If they just want to talk to us, they'll wait till morning, won't they?" asked Harold.

"Yup," said Many Moons, "they won't do anything tonight. There's not enough of them to attack us right now. They're a small scouting party. If they are going to attack us, they will wait for the rest of their tribe to come. They won't attack us when we are circled. They will wait until we are strung out."

"That makes more sense," said Taylor, "that way we will be busy trying to circle the wagons and fighting them off at the same time."

"They're pretty darned clever, aren't they?" asked Eldene. "I'm sure that Captain Tripper has already thought of this, but it seems to me that as long as they are out there, we should stay circled and try to talk with them."

"I reckon that's probably what the cap'n will do," answered Romy. "It is the sensible thing to do."

After Romy and the others left, Taylor commented, "I don't know what everyone else thinks, but I think we should stand watch tonight."

"I'll trade off with you," said Randy.

"I'll take a turn," said Axel.

"Well…dad-burn, let's just figure on each one of us taking a turn every three hours, and that way nobody gets too danged tired," stated Harold.

"All right then," said Taylor, wanting to be on watch at dawn. "How about if Randy takes the first watch and then Axel, then you and me last?

"Okey dokey, that sounds okay to me," said Harold.

Early the next morning, the sun peeked over the horizon, causing a red-tinted sky with crimson clouds floating lazily by. Taylor was sitting on a log wrapped in a blanket, watching the birds flutter from bush to bush, chirping and pecking at insects.

"I brought you a nice hot cup of coffee," said Carrie.

"Whoa, you…scared me," said Taylor as he came out of his daydream, "but thanks."

"I didn't mean to startle you. I thought you could use some company."

"Yeah, thanks, it's a little chilly this morning," said Taylor as he made room for Carrie to sit down. "Mmm! This hits the spot."

"I guess we didn't get attacked last night." Chuckled Carrie. "We all seem to be in one piece."

"Haha! Yep, so far so good."

Taylor looked toward where they saw the Indians the day before, and there in the distance, four Indians were riding toward them, waving a white flag on the end of a spear.

"Look, Carrie, they want to talk to the captain. I'll go tell him."

Just then Captain Tripper, Romy, Bill, and Many Moons rode past the Bounder toward the four Indians. Romy was waving a white flag on the end of his musket. By now Eldene, Patty, and the rest of the bunch had positioned themselves around with weapons in hand.

"I think everyone on the train is ready if they decide to attack us," said Eldene.

"Yep, I think we will give them a fight they won't soon forget," said Mary.

"*Well*, let's hope it doesn't come to that!" exclaimed Harold. "I sure as hell ain't a hanker'n' to fight no dad-burned Indians!"

Three of the Indians stopped, and one kept riding toward the captain. One of the three was still holding the flag in the air. Romy, Bill, and Many Moons also stopped advancing, and Captain Tripper kept going toward the Indian. They met and began talking.

"I wonder what they are talking about," said Eldene.

"Yeah, me too." Chuckled Taylor. "I doubt that they're discussing the weather."

Eldene laughed. "I'm glad you still have your sense of humor, son."

After what seemed like an eternity, Captain Tripper turned and hollered to Romy, and he began galloping toward the Bounder.

"I reckon what that's all about, he sure is in a dad-burned hurry," commented Harold.

Romy approached and yelled to Eldene, "Cap'n Tripper sent me to fetch Taylor."

"Do you know why they want him?" asked Eldene.

"I reckon the chief wants to have a powwow with him about the two buffalo skinners. He'll be okay, I won't let anything happen to him."

"Do you feel up to it, son?" asked Eldene.

"I… I guess so. I'm not going to get scalped or skinned, am I?" joked Taylor.

"Not unless they scalp me first." Laughed Romy.

"Well… I reckon in that case, it'll be okay to have a powwow with the chief." Grinned Taylor.

"Mount up and let's get this over with then."

Taylor gave Eldene a hug and said, "Everything is going to be okay. I'll be back in a few minutes."

"Tie your wind strap tight so they can't get your hat off." Chuckled Patty. "That way it'll be harder to get to your curly locks."

"Thanks for the advice, little sister, I love you too."

Carrie, unable to contain herself, ran to Taylor and threw her arms around his neck and kissed him square on the mouth. "You better come back here in one piece." Suddenly noticing everyone looking a little astonished, she sheepishly backed away and put her hand to her lips, obviously a little embarrassed. "I… I just wanted to s-say g-goodbye."

Taylor grinned and winked at Eldene as he mounted his horse. "Let's go, Barney."

"You go on over to where the cap'n and the chief are," said Romy. "I'll stay here with Bill and Many Moons."

"Hello, Taylor," greeted Captain Tripper. "This is Chief Running Wolf, he's the high chief of all the tribes in these parts. They call him Hiamovi. He would like to ask you a few questions about those two buffalo skinners. I told him what happened, and he understands what you had to do. He speaks good English, so you won't have any trouble understanding him."

"Okay, Captain Tripper, I'm honored to meet you, Chief Running Wolf."

Taylor noticed that the chief was dressed in a vestlike leather top with turquoise beads up and down both sides and leather chap-like pants with leather strapping from the waist down. He had leather moccasins that covered his ankles, and he sat straight and proud on a beautiful pinto. He had long black braided hair with a leather band around his forehead with several feathers attached to it. Taylor thought he was quite magnificent-looking.

"You are brave *Kasovaahe*," said Running Wolf. "*Netonesoehe?*"

Taylor looked at Captain Tripper and said, "That don't sound like English to me!"

"He said you are a brave young man and asked your name."

"Oh, thank you, sir. My name is Taylor McGrady."

"It good thing you do for sister and friend. Cheyenne and other tribes owe great gratitude to young warrior. *Hatoa'e* hunters you kill bad *hetaneos, megedagik hatoa's.* Almost kill Wenona, Oota Dabun. Cheyenne are looking for them for many moons. Annazama be very proud of Taylor. You make search end, and Cheyenne want say many thanks and wish to give gift to *niaish.*"

Taylor looked at the captain and shrugged.

"He said the buffalo hunters you killed were bad men. They killed many buffalo and almost killed his firstborn child, Day Star. Your mama can be very proud of you, and he wants to give you a gift of thanks."

"Thank you, Chief Running Wolf, I… I only did what I had to do," said Taylor humbly.

Chief Running Wolf motioned to the three Indians in the near distance, and one of them began riding toward them. He rode up to the chief and handed him a rawhide necklace with a bone carving and a bow with a leather quiver full of arrows.

"*Me'tseha,*" said Chief Running Wolf, pointing toward Taylor.

The brave handed Taylor the gifts, smiled, and rode off.

"Cheyenne sleep much better. You and family welcome in Cheyenne camp anytime. You good *Hetane. Niaish. Nestaevahosenoomatse,*" said the chief.

Taylor looked at the captain. "He said you are a good man, and he thanks you again and said that he will see you again soon, he hopes."

"Thank you, sir. I am honored to accept your great gifts, and I hope very much to see you again soon too," said Taylor as he extended his hand to the chief.

Chief Running Wolf grabbed Taylor's arm just below the elbow. Taylor followed suit and grabbed the chief's arm in the same fashion. "We *dakota* now, *Kasovaahe*. Go with *Ma'heo'o*."

The chief spurred his pinto and rode off, waving to Taylor and Captain Tripper.

Captain Tripper looked at Taylor and said, "He told us to go with god and called you young man again. It seems you've made a friend for life. You wear that bone carving around your neck, and you will be welcome in all the tribes' camps from here to Oregon. Thanks to you, 'young man,' this wagon train will have no Indian troubles. Chief Running Wolf is famous among all the tribes and that carving is his signature. Yahoo!" yelled the captain. "Let's get this train on the road." And he spurred his horse into action.

"They're all coming back!" yelled Carrie excitedly. "Everything must be okay."

"Yep, it looks like it," said Eldene. "Let's get the teams hooked up. I'm betting that Captain Tripper is ready to hit the trail."

The captain rode straight to the Bounder and yelled, "You can be mighty proud of your son, Mrs. McGrady, he handled himself mighty good out there. He made a friend for life. I'll let him tell the story as y'all get your wagons ready to roll." He bowed slightly, touched the brim of his hat with two fingers, and spurred his horse.

"I'll catch up with y'all later," said Romy as he followed the captain.

Taylor explained to everyone what had happened and showed his gifts. "I was kind of nervous at first, but Chief Running Wolf is a really nice man, and I liked him a lot. He made me feel good."

"Here, big brother," said Patty as she handed him a plate of biscuits and gravy. "I have to keep my hero in good shape."

"Thanks, I am hungry." He took the plate and gave Patty a one-armed hug. "I'm plum glad that you are my little sister." He looked at Carrie and winked. "Say, Harold, do you think it would be all right for Carrie to ride on the wagon with me while I give Mom a break?"

"I reckon that would be okay, Taylor my boy, just keep both hands on the reins," joked Harold.

Taylor blushed a little and said with a big grin, "Yes, sir."

"C'mon, Mary," said Eldene, "you can ride along with me on Carrie's horse, and I'll ride Barney."

"Yahoo!" yelled Mary. "Let's hit the trail."

Randy and Patty rode on ahead a little way. "I'm sure glad to be on the road again," said Patty. "I was getting pretty nervous with those Indians looking us over."

"Yep, me too. I'm glad it's over. Now we can go back to having fun and just looking out for one another."

"I'm your huckleberry," joked Patty, "you watch me, and I'll watch you."

"I reckon that I'll never get tired of watching you," said Randy as he winked.

"Well, then watch this—hyah! Hyah!" She spurring Socks into a fast-paced trot.

"Oh, so you want to play. Yahoo, giddyap, boy. Haha, I'm still watching you," joked Randy as he caught up.

They reined in their horses to a walk.

"Well, I guess maybe I kind of like being watched by you." She leaned over from her saddle and gave Randy a big kiss on the cheek.

Randy was blushing. "Well, I… I… I reckon we had better not get too far ahead of the wagon train. W-we don't know what's ahead of us."

"Yep, I think you're probably right." And she batted her eyes. "You are probably right." She turned Socks and headed back toward the wagon train.

Chapter 11

South Pass

Fort John was a large impressive fort, constructed of thick adobe bricks, nestled in a strategic setting where the North Platte River joined the Laramie River. It was bordered by both rivers, which made it difficult to be approached on two sides. The two sides facing the prairie were protected by high adobe brick walls, the same as the trading post's tall buildings. There also are guard towers on the high walls facing the two rivers, manned with an armed guard in each one.

Captain Tripper had the wagon train circle about a hundred feet outside the main gate.

Romy rode up to the Bounder. "The cap'n wants us all to meet at his camp. He wants to talk to everyone before we go into the fort."

As soon as everyone was gathered around, the captain, who was standing in the tack wagon, called for their attention. "Fort John is mainly a trading post for Indians and wagon trains," he started. "Trappers and buffalo hunters also get their supplies here. The Indians don't like the buffalo hunters, and the buffalo hunters don't like the Indians, so they stay clear of one another. Once in a while, there is a buffalo hunter that comes in while the Indians are here, in which case there is always trouble. Today it looks like it's just going to be us. Let's hope it stays that way. We'll go in and get our supplies and get back to the wagons, as quick as possible, so we can get on the road to South Pass. It probably will take most of the day, so we'll plan on camping here tonight and start out early in the morning. There is a lot of us, so we'll have to go in twenty at a time, starting with the lead wagon. Romy will be in charge, so he'll let each of you know when it is your turn. Thank you, and y'all have a good day."

"I reckon we're first," said Harold. "I'm a hankerin' to git this over with. I don't want to be in there if any of those hunters or Indians show up!"

"Me too! First thing, I'm going to look for a place to take a nice hot bath!" said Eldene.

"Yeah!" yelled Patty. "I'll get my nice clean clothes!"

"Wait for us!" yelled Mary and Carrie.

"I reckon I'll be taking one too," hollered Taylor.

"I'll get my stuff!" yelled Randy.

"Tarnation," Harold moaned, "I reckon a bath ain't a bad idea. Wait for me, an' I'll be right with ya."

"I reckon we're going too!" yelled Axel as he and Penny walked toward the Bounder.

"I think me an' baby Deeny can use a nice warm bath," said Penny as she held the baby up.

"Well, then," said Eldene as she began the march toward the fort. "Let's be off to a glorious day!"

Inside the fort was set up like a small town. Buildings were lined along the riverside barriers, and the official's headquarters were on the other side. A tall lanky man was standing on the porch of the main office building. "You will find everything you need right here, folks. The main mercantile is the large building in the center, and the bathhouses are on the right. Enjoy your stay and have a good day."

"Seems like a nice fellow," said Mary. "I think I'm gonna like this place."

"Let's git to washing up and shopping and git our dad-burned stuff and git back to the wagons," said Harold.

"You seem to be in a big hurry, dear," quipped Mary incredulously. "We've been eating dust for days on end, and I want to enjoy this much-needed stop!"

"I reckon I just wanna git over those dad-burned mountains before the snow flies. I'm gitten a little concerned that we ain't gonna' make it to Oregon before winter sets in."

"This is the last supply stop until we get to Fort Hall," said Eldene. "We're going to need to stock up as well as we can. Romy was telling me that we are more than halfway to Oregon. He said that the trail gets a little easier on the other side of the Rocky Mountains."

"Mom, what's going on over there, where that crowd of people are gathering?" asked Patty as she pointed toward the crowd.

"I'm not quite sure, but it looks like they are gathering around a gallows," commented Eldene.

Just then a stranger shouted, "Hey, come on, folks, they're getting ready to hang Ole Jeb Weatherly!"

"Hang him?" yelled Taylor. "What did he do?"

"He got drunk and shot two fellers over a card game!"

"I certainly don't want to see anyone hanged," said Eldene as she shuddered. "Let's get our supplies and get back to the wagons."

"Oh my goodness, I reckon I've seen enough of Fort John after all," commented Mary. "I'm going to get our supplies as fast as I can and get back to the wagon too!"

"I'm right on your heels, let's git our dad-burned stuff and git out of here!" Harold said emphatically.

After they got their supplies, on the way out of the fort, Taylor and Randy couldn't keep from looking at the old man hanging from the gallows.

"I sure wouldn't want to leave this world like that." Shuddered Randy. "That has to be a horrible way to die."

"Right," said Taylor, "I reckon I'd rather die in my sleep of natural causes!"

Patty and Carrie were holding their heads down as they left the fort. "C'mon, Carrie, let's get away from this place," said Patty as she walked as fast as she could.

Everyone was loaded down with bags of goods. "I sure am glad that's over and done with." Sighed Eldene as she set her bags down on the back of the Bounder. "I don't like having an image of that man hanging and all of those people running to see it happen! It seemed as if it was some sort of entertainment to them. What kind of world are we moving in to? Buffalo hunters taking advantage of innocent girls. I'm hoping and praying that Oregon is at least a little more civilized."

"I reckon things will be what we make them to be." Shrugged Taylor. "We'll just have to keep on believing in God and let him make our own world around us."

"Wowie, just listen to Mr. Philosopher over there!" exclaimed Patty.

"That's some pretty good advice there, young man," said Eldene, raising her eyebrows. "I reckon we'll have to do just that! Let's get things put away and get some rest while we wait for the rest of the people to get their supplies."

Romy rode up. "Since we'll be camping here tonight, and it's been kinda a hectic day, I got some rabbits here for supper. If y'all want to fry 'em up. I've already gutted them and all," He held up three cottontails.

"Sure thing." Smiled Eldene. "I need something to occupy my mind so I can get rid of the image of that man hanging on the gallows inside the fort."

"I'm downright sorry you had to see that. That's the way of the West, though you will probably see a lot worse things."

"Oh, good Lord, I hope not, I can't imagine anything worse than what we've already seen. I'll get busy on these little guys." She held up the rabbits.

"All righty then, I'll be back for supper. Hyah, boy, let's git movin'," said Romy.

"I'll milk the goats so we can have some biscuits and gravy." Offered Taylor as he picked up the milk bucket.

"Yum, yum," Patty interjected, smacking her lips. "I love fried rabbit!"

"Yep, me too, it tastes like chicken," joked Taylor.

"Hahaha!" laughed Eldene. "Kind of like rattlesnake does, right, Patty?"

"Eeyuck!" Cried Patty. "No rabbit for me tonight!"

"That's okay, little sister, I'll eat your share." Laughed Taylor!

The next morning, the wagon train was strung out in a single line that seemed endless. The terrain was flat, and the sagebrush stretched for miles. You could see the majestic Rocky Mountains in the distance, standing tall with their snowcapped peaks, looming as if they were the guardians of the earth.

What a beautiful sight, thought Eldene. *The sky is so blue, the air is so pure. How in the world could things be bad?*

"Hey, Mom!" yelled Taylor. "Do you see the mountains?"

"Yes, they sure are beautiful!"

"I wonder how long it will take us to get to them?"

"I think, probably two or three days at least."

"Wow! Do you really think we're really that far away? They must be pretty dang big mountains!"

"Romy says they are huge! He says they are so big that it takes four or five days to get over them."

Suddenly Eldene stood up in her stirrups and looked into the distance to the north side of the train. "Look at that huge dust cloud over yonder, I sure hope we aren't in for another dust storm."

"I think that's something else!" yelled Taylor. "I hear a roaring sound!"

Just then, Romy rode up and yelled, "Stop the wagons, folks! There's a herd of buffalo stampeding over yonder. We don't want to get in their way!"

Taylor reined in the mules. They balked and stamped. "Whoa! Whoa! You floppy-eared jackasses!"

The buffalo herd turned and stampeded toward the wagon train. The thundering of their hooves hitting the ground was deafening. The dust cloud that they kicked up darkened the sky behind them. The rising sun looked like a giant orange hanging in the sky. The roaring kept getting louder and louder.

"Looks like they are going to run over us!" yelled Taylor as he held tight to the reins.

Barney was getting restless and began whinnying and stomping. "Whoa, boy, settle down, they won't hurt you," said Eldene as she reached down and rubbed his neck.

"Where's Patty and Randy?" she yelled.

"They were riding ahead of us!" yelled Taylor. "They must be right in the path of the herd!"

"Oh, dear god, we have to do something! They'll be trampled to death!" screamed Eldene.

"Hold on, Deeny, I see them!" hollered Romy.

"Yeah, there they come, riding like the dickins! Look at them go!" yelled Carrie

Patty was at a full gallop with Randy right behind her. They galloped past the tack wagon toward the chuck wagon, yelling.

"There must have been a million buffalo running toward us!" yelled Patty as they reined in at the Bounder.

The herd stampeded across the path of the halted wagon train and within two hundred feet of the tack wagon. The horses, mules, and other animals were so excited they were almost making as much noise as the buffalo.

"Everybody, rein in tight! That's a mighty big herd, and it's going to take a while for them to get past us!" yelled Romy.

Harold came running up to the Bounder. "Tarnation! There must be five thousand of them critters in that dad-burned stampede!"

"Yep, and it looks like they are being chased by a bunch of buffalo skinners," yelled Romy.

A gunshot rang out, and a buffalo went crashing down. Another shot and another buffalo fell. By now there were several people gathered around, watching as the skinners slaughtered the buffalo. In just a few minutes, the herd disappeared out of sight, and the dust began to settle. There were dead buffalo everywhere. The skinners were working on the carcasses, taking the hides, and leaving the remains to be scavenged by wolves, coyotes, and buzzards.

"That is an awfully gruesome sight! That can't be right," commented Eldene. "No wonder the Indians don't like them!"

"They just seem to be heartless greedy men, and they need to be stopped before there's no more buffalo left," murmured Mary.

"I think they oughta be skinned alive. They're just dadburned killers, plain and simple. They oughta be strung up and skinned!" said Harold.

"Look over there, there's a bunch of Indians riding full speed toward the skinners!"

"Good grief," said Eldene. "There sure is, and they don't look happy!"

Everyone watched in astonishment as the buffalo hunters mounted their horses and fled for their lives. The Indians were whooping and hollering and shooting arrows and throwing spears at them. Two skinners fell to the ground, and two Indians jumped from their horses and finished them off.

"Oh, dear god, they are scalping those two skinners!" yelled Mary.

"I reckon those two varmints won't be doing any more buffalo massacres. Looks like they got their what fors, dad-burn it!" remarked Harold.

The Indians stopped chasing the hunters and began salvaging whatever they could from the downed buffalo. They worked frantically, gutting the animals so the meat could be saved. They all watched as the Indians systematically loaded whatever they could onto pack animals that the buffalo hunters had left behind. In just a short period of time, the Indians had everything loaded and headed out.

"Look, one of the Indians is waving to us!" said Patty.

"Hey, I recognize him, that's my friend Running Wolf," said Taylor as he stood up in the wagon and waved back!

"They sure don't like skinners much," said Romy.

"Here comes Cap'n Tripper," said Eldene as she pointed. "He looks pretty serious."

"Yep, he'll be wanting a couple of volunteers to bury those two skinners."

"I'll help!" said Harold.

"Me too!" yelled Taylor, Randy, and Axel simultaneously!

"Wait just a minute, young man. I don't think it's a good idea for you youngsters to get involved in this. That's not going to be a very pretty sight over there, and I don't think it would be any good for you to see it," said Eldene.

"Me neither," stated Mary. "There are plenty of older men around here to do it."

"Mom, this is the real West we are moving to, and this is part of it. I want to be a part of it and not be afraid of what's ahead of us," said Taylor.

"The boy's got a good point there, Eldene," Harold argued. "Dad-burn it, it'll help tuffen' 'em up."

"Well…okay, but I'm still not sure it's a good idea."

"Me neither," said Mary. "I'm against it."

"I'll be okay, Mom."

"Me too," said Randy.

"I'll grab shovels off the wagons," said Axel

"Axel, are you sure you want to do this?" asked Penny.

"Yep, I'm sure, I'll be just fine!"

"That was some sight y'all took in. I guess y'all don't look to haggled over it," said the cap'n as he rode up.

"Nope, we're all okay here," commented Harold. "We're ready to help out so we can git back on the dad-burned trail."

"I told them you would be needing some volunteers to help bury those two skinners," said Romy.

"All righty then, let's git to it."

Other people from the train were headed toward the carcasses to see if they could salvage any of the buffalo meat.

"Whatever is left over there is still fresh enough to get a few steaks. We might as well get some of it!" said Romy.

"Well, I guess you're right," said Eldene as she grabbed a butcher knife. "Come on, Mary, grab a knife and some cheesecloth and lets' go shopping for some buffalo meat!"

"I'm right behind you, let's hurry before it's all gone!"

The men approached the dead skinners. The sight was horrifying!

"Dear God in heaven." Sighed Taylor. "This is one heck of a bloody mess."

"I… I… I reckon it sure is." Gulped Randy. I… I don't much like this."

"They sure did mess these two fellers up," commented Axel. "I'm not likely to forget this for a while."

"Yep, I reckon these two won't be massacrin' anymore dad-burned buffalo," said Harold. "Let's git 'em buried and git out of here!"

"I reckon we oughta move them over there," said the cap'n as he pointed toward a patch of brush. "It's out of the buffalo run, and they won't get stomped on, not that they don't deserve it!"

Several of the men carried the bodies, while the others dug the graves. Later back at the wagons, everyone was cleaning up and taking care of the meat.

"It would be a good idea to make pemmican out of the meat you won't be eating tonight," commented Romy. "That way it'll last longer."

'Yep, that would be a dad-burned good idea, quipped Harold. How dad-burned long do you reckon we'll be a stayin' in this here spot?"

"Well, Cap'n Tripper wants to move on and camp a far piece away so we won't be smellin' dead buffalo remains. We'll be circling up in about five more miles."

"Just give us a few dad-burned minutes to salt down our meat and wrap it up so we can keep it as cool as possible, and we'll be ready to git goin'."

"All righty then, I have to go inform the rest of the train, and we'll be headin' out in about thirty minutes. I'll see y'all later!"

The rest of the day went by without incident. The sky was a clear blue again, and the sun was now starting to lower over the snowcapped mountaintops.

Chapter 12

The Proposal

The wagons were circled, and you could smell the aroma of buffalo meat being fried, baked, or boiled. Every wagon in the train had buffalo meat cooking in one fashion or another.

"These are some good-smelling steaks we've got going here," said Eldene.

"I can hardly wait to sink my teeth into one of them," said Patty. "We haven't had a good beef steak since the day before we took the paddle wheeler down the Ohio River."

"Yep," added Taylor, "I reckon I'll never forget how much fun that boat ride was. It's one of the best parts of this whole adventure so far."

"I agree with that. That's where we met our new best friends." Sighed Patty as she rolled her eyes.

"You mean your new best boyfriend," said Taylor as he grinned mischievously, "don't you, little sister?"

"Maybe so, brother dear, maybe so." She looked over her shoulder toward the Thompsons' wagon. "I think maybe you like Carrie a whole bunch more than you let on. We all saw that big kiss she gave you back there when you talked to the Indian chief. I saw the way you looked at her," teased Patty. "I think you are in *love,* brother dear."

Taylor blushed a little. "I… I can't say I didn't like it. In fact, I liked it a lot."

"All right you two smitten ones, the steaks are ready, let's eat up."

The next morning, the wagon train got started just before dawn. The air was cool and still. The sun was beginning to peek up over the horizon from the east, and the snowcapped peaks of the giant mountains were glistening like crystal wine glasses. The foothills were becoming more and more visible as the sun rose higher in the vast blue sky. The long morning shadows lay motionless across the terrain. Dogs were barking, chickens were squawking, and goats were bleating.

Taylor was seated on the Bounder while Eldene and Patty were riding the horses. Harold was handling the reins as he and Mary walked beside their wagon.

Randy and Carrie were riding their horses toward the Bounder.

Romy rode up beside Eldene. "Hey there, pretty lady, how about a nice moonlight walk after supper tonight?" he said as he slightly tipped his hat. "This may be our last one until we get over those mountains yonder."

"I don't think I would mind that at all." Smiled Eldene. "I'll see you after supper."

"You like Romy a lot, don't you, Mommy?" asked Patty.

"Yep, I reckon I do." She watched Romy ride away. "I reckon I do. What do you two think of him?"

"Well, I can't speak for baby sister there, but I for one think he is a real good person, and I like him a lot."

"Yep, me too," said Patty, "I think he's really, really nice. I love the way he says y'all in his deep Southern drawl. Also doesn't hurt that he's tall, well built, good-looking, clean, mannerly, and hardworking. In fact, he is also just downright handsome. Oh, did I mention that he's dreamy, brave, funny, cheerful, smart, and he has this really *cute…* Southern *drawl…and—*"

"Okay, okay, smarty-pants," interrupted Taylor, "we get the picture."

"Oh yeah, did I mention that he has this really cute Southern *drawl…*" said Patty, giggling.

"Okay, y'all…let's change the subject," said Eldene, smiling and trying to mimic a Southern drawl. "I reckon y'all like him."

Everyone laughed.

"Hahahaha, that's got to be the worst Southern drawl I've ever heard." Taylor laughed.

"Hey, everybody, look at that herd of antelope over yonder!" yelled Randy as he rode up beside Patty. "There must be three or four hundred of them!"

"Wow!" exclaimed Taylor. "They're just standing there, looking at us."

"Look at the big one standing there, all alone," said Eldene as she pointed it out. "He's only two or three hundred feet from us."

"He sure is beautiful," said Carrie. "He must be the leader or something."

"Yeah," said Patty, "he's standing there like he's king of the world."

The sunny weather was warm, and the vast terrain burst with browns, greens, and reds. Sage hens darting here and there, quail scurrying across the ground from thickets of sagebrush, clucking and crowing. Startled rabbits would jump from bushes along the trail and scamper away. In the far distance, you could just barely see a large herd of buffalo grazing.

"This a sight to behold." Sighed Eldene. "There are so many things to be thankful for. It's so beautiful and peaceful. Life is good," she said as she soaked up the immense happiness that she was feeling. She had drifted off into deep thought when suddenly, she was flying over Barney's head and landed on the ground in front of the stumbling horse.

"Good grief, Mom!" yelled Taylor. "Are you okay?"

Patty and Carrie dismounted and ran to help Eldene. Randy grabbed Barney's reins and calmed him down.

"Yeah, I'm okay," said Eldene as she jumped to her feet. "What in the world happened to Barney?"

"He stepped in a rabbit hole and stumbled," said Randy. "He's lucky he didn't break his leg." Randy got off his horse and checked Barney's leg. "He looks okay, there doesn't seem to be any broken bones."

Eldene brushed the dirt from her clothes. "Wow, I sure wasn't ready for that."

"You're lucky you didn't get hurt," said Taylor. "That was a heck of a tumble."

"Yeah, Mommy, are you sure you're okay?" asked Patty.

"Yep, I'm just fine," she said as she checked Barney's leg. "Let's get going, we're holding up the train."

Romy came galloping in. "What's the hold up?" he inquired.

"Barney stumbled in a rabbit hole," Taylor answered. "Mom took a tumble, but she's okay. We're ready to get things moving again."

"Well, okay then. I reckon I'll be seeing y'all later on." And he spurred his horse. "C'mon, boy, let's go."

Later on after supper, Eldene and Romy were taking their moonlight walk. Romy stopped suddenly and put his hands on Eldene's shoulders. Looking in her beautiful sparkling green eyes, he stammered, "I... I... I have something to say to you."

"Well, then go ahead and say it," said Eldene curiously, not noticing Romy's nervousness.

"Damn...it, I've been practicing all blasted day, and now I can't seem to say anything."

Cocking her head to one side, Eldene wrinkled her nose and raised her eyebrows. "I haven't seen this side of you, Romy, you're not the nervous type."

"Yeah, well... I never been in this position before."

Eldene just looked at him with her head to one side and smirked.

"Dad blast it anyway. I... I am head over heels in love with you, Deeny. I think about you all day long. We've been taking moonlight walks for several months now, and I... I... I..." He hesitated. Kneeling down and holding her hand, he looked up. "Deeny, I love you more than life. Will you marry me?"

"I have fallen in love with you too, and I will marry you but—"

"Yahoo!" yelled Romy as he jumped to his feet. "You have just made me the happiest man alive."

"You didn't let me finish," said Eldene firmly. "I'll marry you, but you will have to quit taking wagon trains across the country and agree to help me start up a sawmill somewhere in the Willamette Valley."

Romy looked at Eldene and slipped a ring (that he had woven out of wild timothy stems) on her finger. "I think that building a sawmill with you would be a great and wonderful experience. I have saved most of my money for the last six or seven years, and I think I've got enough to build a good life together. I was saving it up to start a cattle ranch, but I reckon a sawmill will be a lotta fun, even though it sounds like a heck of a lotta work."

"Well, there isn't any law against doing them both," said Eldene. "I've saved quite a bit of money too, and I have enough with me to start the mill and build a nice log home on as much land as we can get."

"Oh, wow, I'm getting excited about our future together," said Romy. He put his arms around Eldene and passionately kissed her. "When do you want to have the wedding? The reverend that has been doing the Sunday services could marry us tomorrow or the cap'n could do it!" he rambled in his excitement!

"I don't think we should move that fast," answered Eldene, I would rather wait until we get over the mountains and the kids have had time to get used to the idea."

"Well, if that's what you really want. I would rather do it now and let them get used to it that way. The Rockies aren't the only mountains we have to cross!"

"What I meant was," said Eldene as she pushed Romy back a little, "I would rather wait until we get to the

Willamette Valley, and we have a real threshold for you to carry me over."

"Deeny, you're talking about two or three months from now! I don't want to wait that long."

"I understand," said Eldene. "I'll tell you what. I'll think about it and see what the kids say, and maybe we can move it up some." She put her arms around Romy's neck and kissed him with a long loving kiss. "I must say, you make me want to give into you right here and now, but I wouldn't be able to live with the guilt, so I want to wait until after we are married."

"What would you be guilty of?" asked Romy. "We're two people in love, so where's the wrong in that?"

"I grew up in a Christian family, and I can't go against my faith. I believe I have to be married in the eyes of God, and we must set an example for our children and our family and friends. I can't say one thing and then do another, it just wouldn't be right."

"*Well,* when you put it that way, it does make sense. I… I reckon I'll just have to keep myself extra busy until we figure out a date for the wedding," groaned Romy. "I hope the cap'n has plenty of stuff for me to do." He chuckled. "Or I'll never make it. I seem to think about you all the cotton-pickin' time."

"We've been gone a long time," said Eldene. "We should get on back." She kissed him again, took his hand, and started toward the Bounder.

"Hold up there, pretty lady," said Romy, pulling her back into his arms. He gently leaned her back and kissed her with a long tender passionate kiss.

Eldene melted into his strong muscular arms and put her arms around his neck. Shivers of excitement ran through her body as she got lost in the moment.

Suddenly she realized what was happening and gently pushed Romy back. "Whew," she said, wiping her brow, "I wasn't ready for that one." Breathlessly she turned and took his hand. "C'mon, big fella, before I do something I'll regret."

"I reckon that ought to make you want to speed things up a bit. I know it made me want to." He chuckled.

Back at the Bounder

"You've been gone awhile, Mom," said Taylor. "We we're beginning to worry."

"No need to worry yourselves," Romy commented, "I ain't gonna let anything happen to your mom. Good night y'all." He tipped his hat, untied his horse, took the reins in his hand, and strolled away, whistling.

"It's late, let's turn in," said Eldene. I have something to discuss with you two tomorrow."

Eldene drifted off to sleep with thoughts of a good future for her and Romy, Taylor and Patty.

Everyone was up early the next morning, anxious to get on the road toward the Rocky Mountains.

Eldene had a peaceful feeling and felt completely at ease for the first time since Jake was killed. They were cleaning up after breakfast when Eldene piped up. "What would you kids think if I told you I was going to marry Romy?"

"What!" exclaimed Taylor and Patty simultaneously.

"I think it would be wonderful!" exclaimed Patty as she hugged Eldene. "I'm so excited, when's it going to happen?"

Taylor was a little more reserved. "I think Romy is really a great guy and a good friend, I… I just want you to be sure that you are ready for this big a step."

"You mean so soon after your dad's death?"

"*Well, yeah*, Mom, I reckon that's what I mean," answered Taylor.

"I will never forget your father and the years we had together. No one will ever be able to make me forget all the good times we had or take those cherished memories away. I'll always remember your dad. I know that he would want me to move on with my life. I love Romy and I know we can build a good life together. I am sure that it's the right thing to do."

"*Well*, since you put it that way, then I reckon I'm ready too. Congratulations, I hope Romy asks me to be his best man."

"I'll put in a good word for you." Laughed Eldene.

"What about me?" asked Patty. "What will I be? When are we getting married?" Giggled Patty.

"You, my sweet child, will be my maid of honor, and Mary, Carrie, and Penny will be my bridesmaids."

"I am getting married when we get over those mountains and on our way to Oregon. Romy wants to get married now, but I want to wait until we get on the other side of the mountains."

"Oh my gosh, Mommy, I'm so excited. This is the best news ever! I can hardly wait to tell Carrie and Penny," said Patty.

The wagon train was circled for the night, and the animals were all fed and hobbled. The trail was easy that day except for a few deep-rutted areas, so they were able to make it to the base of the mountains. They would be making the long assent up South Pass.

After supper, everyone was sitting around the campfire. The sun was about halfway down behind the mountain peaks. Everything was peaceful and serene. The shadows were stretching along the terrain, changing shape as they followed the ups and downs of the gullies and ridges. A couple of sage hens were calling back and forth to one another. The sparrows were fluttering around from bush to bush, and the rabbits were hopping around, feeding on the grass and sage flowers.

The women were chattering about what they were going to wear at the wedding. And the men were drinking coffee and playing cards.

"I'm going to wear the dress that I packed in the bottom of my trunk," said Patty. "I hope it will still fit me. I have a pair of pumps and some silk stockings. I can hardly wait to put them on."

"Me too," said Carrie excitedly. "I sometimes wonder if I'll even feel comfortable in a dress, it's been so long, and I'm sort of used to wearing pants!"

"I think I'll wear my Sunday go-to meetin' suit," joked Taylor. "The only problem is it looks pretty much like what I've got on."

"Yep, dad-burn it." Laughed Harold. I'll have to dig out a brand-spankin'-new pair of dad-blamed overalls."

"Well, as long as none of you wear your birthday suit," said Mary.

Laughing, Harold said, "I reckon my birthday suit would have to be ironed!"

Everyone began laughing.

"Well, we won't have to worry about what we are going to wear for a while," said Eldene. "I want us to be over these mountains and away from buffalo skinners. I want to start our new lives with a better environment and nothing but good thoughts for our future together. I know that Romy will understand when I explain."

Early the next morning, the wagons were hitched up and ready to begin the journey up South Pass. Romy rode up to the Bounder. "Good morning, y'all. Are y'all ready to start out?"

"Yep, we're ready and anxious to see what's on the other side," answered Taylor.

"I want to ride along with you for a while so we can talk a little," said Eldene.

"Well, okay then, pretty lady, let's go."

Eldene mounted Barney, and they rode off together.

"Well, Deeny, what do you want to talk about?" asked Romy. "Are you going to tell me that you want to get married tonight?" he inquired with a grin.

Eldene smiled and said, "*Well*, I talked to the kids, and they are okay with us getting married, but I want to wait for a while."

"Whoa, boy," said Romy as he reined up. "That's not what I wanted to hear. If we are going to get married, why can't we do it now?"

"I just want to wait for the time to feel right. I love you, and I know I want to marry you and build our future together. Oh, I don't know quite how to explain it, but I know that I want to feel like it's the right time and place."

"Well, I reckon you're worth the wait. I can't say I like it, but of course, I'll honor your wishes and fill my days with chores and thoughts of our future together. I reckon we can still take a few moonlight walks, and I promise I'll behave myself." He leaned over and kissed her and said, I love you, Deeny, and we'll make things work. You can relax and not worry your pretty little head. I'll see y'all after a while." Romy rode off at a gallop!

Chapter 13

The Long Haul

Evening of the first day of the assent to the summit of South Pass, the sunset was a mixture of reds and oranges as the sun sank over the horizon. Everyone was relaxing around the campfire.

"Tarnation," blurted Harold, "I reckoned that goin' over these dad-burned mountains would be a lot tougher than this. So far, it's not much different than what we done already been through, haven't seen a single dad-burned tree all day. I'm downright glad that it's easygoing, but I... I reckon I was expecting it to be different."

"Yep." Piped Romy. "I reckon it's going to be like this all the way to Fort Bridger. And then we start across a desert that goes on for days. Y'all are going to be mighty glad when we get through it."

"I can hardly wait for that one," joked Taylor. "I've been dreaming about going through a long hot dusty desert."

"Not me." Laughed Patty. "I'm already beginning to look like a prune."

"Yep," joked Taylor, "you are getting kinda wrinkled. Maybe you could put some of that axle grease on it! I reckon we're going to have to iron you out when we get to Oregon."

"Hahaha!" Laughed Patty. "You'll probably just go poof since you're just hot air and dust."

Everyone laughed and yelled, "Yay, Patty, that's a good one!"

"Touché, little sister." Laughed Taylor. "I'll get you back."

"I'll be waiting and watching," commented Patty as she wrinkled her nose.

The following morning, there was a heavy moist fog covering the valley floor. The air was wet and cold enough for you to see your breath. Taylor had moved the animals to the outside of the wagon circle so they could eat some of the tall grass while he was getting them ready for the day ahead. The harnesses were damp from condensation and had to be wiped before they could be put on the animals. Patty milked the goats and fed the chickens, while Taylor dried the harnesses. Eldene was cooking breakfast and getting the Bounder ready for the daily trip.

"Hold still, you flop-eared jackass," yelped Taylor as he tried to put the harness on Jack. Jack was going around in a circle, snorting and being unruly as Taylor tried to harness him. "Whoa, I said. What in the heck is wrong with you, Jack?"

"I'm having a problem with the goats too." Gasped Patty. "They're acting really strange."

"The horses are acting mighty strange too," said Eldene. "Something seems to be spooking them. It sounds like the Thompsons are having problems too. The fog is so thick I can't really tell what's going on, but something is happening."

Suddenly Taylor said in a loud whisper, "Hey, do you hear the distant snarling and growling?" There's something out there."

"Yep, I hear it too," whispered Patty. "What is it?"

"I don't know," said Eldene, "but there is more than one of whatever it is, and they seem to be getting closer. Make sure the animals are tied down and let's stick close together."

Eldene removed the gravy from the fire and grabbed the shotgun and several shells.

"What do you think it is, Mom?" asked Taylor as he grabbed his revolver.

"I'm not sure, but I'll bet it's a pack of wolves, looking for something to eat. Whatever they are, they're keeping their distance and being cautious."

"Yep, they're acting like wolves. I'm going to load up the rifles, just in case we need them," said Taylor."

Harold hollered, "Do y'all hear that ruckus in the distance?" I think we've got some dad-burned wolves stalking us."

"I hear it too!" yelled Axel. "I've got my gun ready. I ain't sure what's going on out there. Do you reckon it could be Indians?

"Naw, I don't reckon it's Indians," answered Harold. "I'm bettin' on a pack of hungry wolves."

"Yep, it's wolves all right!" yelled Taylor. About fifteen feet out, he saw a large figure standing there, snarling and baring his sharp teeth. "They're moving in, there's one of them right there," he said as he aimed his gun and pulled the trigger. There was a loud yelp and a howling commotion like nothing they had ever heard before. "I just got one of them!" yelled Taylor. "He was after one of the goats. They're everywhere!" he yelled as he shot again.

"I… I see them," stammered Eldene as she blasted one with the shotgun. "Hey, I got one!"

Harold and Randy began shooting from their location, and Axel began shooting from his.

"There are wolves everywhere!" yelled Axel. "They're hard to see in this damn fog."

Mary and Carrie were loading muskets for Harold and Randy, and Penny was in her wagon with the baby.

Romy and Captain Tripper rode up to the chuck wagon and began warding off the wolves. "Make sure that your animals are inside the circle and tied down!" Captain Tripper yelled. "They're after the smaller animals."

"They sure are persistent!" yelled Eldene as she blasted another wolf.

"Hey, folks!" hollered Harold. "The dad-burned fog is starting to lift. I can see them, there must be twenty dad-blasted wolves out there."

"There they are, Mom!" screamed Patty as she pointed. "Over there!"

"They're moving farther away. I think maybe we are scaring them off."

"They're staying farther away now that the fog is lifting!" yelled Romy. "They're a pretty smart bunch of critters, they'll be waiting in the distance until we are gone so they can feed on the dead wolves."

As the fog lifted, they could see the carcasses of at least six dead, a couple of them as close as ten feet.

"Looks like we downed a couple of critters over here!" yelled Harold.

"I got a couple of them!" hollered Axel. "That was pretty damned scary. There was shooting going on a couple of wagons down from us. They probably got a couple of them too."

"Looks like they're keeping their distance!" yelled Captain Tripper. "Keep a watch on them and let's get the train moving. I don't think they will attack again."

The last wagon was barely past the dead wolves when the pack moved in for their feast. They began tearing at the dead carcasses and attacking one another, trying to get their share of the bounty.

"Boy, howdy," commented Taylor, "those critters sure are a vicious bunch, I wouldn't want to meet up with a pack of them alone."

"Me neither!" exclaimed Patty as she shook her head and shuddered. "I wouldn't even want to run into *one* of them!"

The long monotonous trip to Fort Hall was boring at times. If not for the periodic stops so wheel bearings could be repacked and spooked cattle could be rounded up by the drovers, they'd all fall asleep in the saddle. The repair stops allowed everyone to visit and check up on one another.

"This dad-burned country is pretty much the same thing over and over," complained Harold as they all sat around the campfire one night. "We've seen a few dad-burned deer and a couple herds of antelope, oh yeah and some jackrabbits, but it sure ain't changed much for the last few days!"

"That sure is a lot better than having to fight off a pack of hungry snarling wolves," said Mary.

"That's for sure!" exclaimed Carrie. "I don't ever have to do that again!"

"I have a feeling that things are going to change pretty soon," blurted Randy. "This can't go on forever!"

Taylor piped up. "Don't you remember the country we left behind us? I remember week after week of nothing but flat country and tumbleweeds and sagebrush. I was thinking that was as bad as it gets. At least we can see some mountains in the distance. Making it to Fort Hall means we are that much closer to Oregon!"

"I can hardly wait to see a bathtub that I can fit my whole body in," said Patty, wrinkling her face. "I'm getting kind of tired of cold creeks and that tiny little bathtub that I have to stand up in."

"Well, at least your smelly feet are clean!" Laughed Taylor.

"You, dear brother, should get in it upside down so you can soak your head!" Smirked Patty. Everyone laughed!

"You two kids have made this trip a lot less monotonous with your bantering back and forth. I hope you'll always love each other enough to have that sort of humor," Eldene said. "You make me very proud to be your mother."

"I can't help it, Mom, she is like a little kitty cat just asking to be teased!"

"Oh yeah!" Piped Patty. "You're kinda like a donkey, hee, hee, hee!"

"Heehaw, heehaw." Barked Taylor, acting like a donkey. "Yep that's me all right, just a little ole donkey!" Everyone was guffawing and laughing as Taylor did his antics and fooled around.

Romy rode up. "I reckon we can head on out again. They got the herd back together. We can't afford to lose any more cattle. We still have to go around eight hundred miles to go before we reach the Willamette Valley. We're gonna' need that beef to help feed us and help people get started with their new lives. I reckon I'm getting a little anxious to get there!"

"I'm ready to get there too," said Eldene, smiling at Romy. "I'm ready to get that new life we talked about, started!"

Axel approached Eldene. "Would you come to my wagon and have a look at Penny? She seems to be coming down with something."

"Let's go see what's going on." She followed Axel to his wagon.

"She started feeling badly this morning, and she had night sweats last night, so bad that she soaked the bedcovers. She seems worse today, and she says even the smell of food nauseates her. I'm really worried about her!"

After Eldene examined Penny, she came out of the wagon and told Axel, "I've seen this before, Penny needs medical attention as soon as possible. I'm pretty sure she has pneumonia, and it could be in both her lungs. If she doesn't get the proper care, she could be in serious trouble. I suggest that we get Romy over here and see if we can get her to Fort Hall, fast!"

"I'll go get Romy, will you stay and watch Penny and the baby?"

"Of course I will, go ahead and get Romy while I see what I can do."

In just a few minutes, Axel and Romy rode up at a gallop. "Axel says that Penny is real sick! What's the trouble, and what can I do to help?"

"I think she has pneumonia, and it's settled in both sides of her lungs. Is there any way we can get her to Fort Hall quick?"

"Well, let me go talk to Cap'n. Bill Winters and Many Moons came in yesterday, and maybe they can take Axel and Penny on ahead. If they can go right through without stopping. They can probably make it in two days. Back a few wagons, there is a family that is pulling a small buckboard filled with extra stuff. They are willing to loan it. If we can put the stuff in Axel's wagon, we can make room for Penny to lie down, and Axel can drive it. We can hook up a couple of the extra horses on Axel's wagon, and Taylor and Randy can drive it on to Fort Hall."

"I knew you would think of a way," said Eldene as she kissed him. "You are amazing!"

"Well, shucks, thank ya, Deeny." He chuckled. "I'll go fetch the buckboard."

"What about the baby?" asked Axel. "Penny can't feed her. She is too sick!"

"Well, it may be best to leave her with us. Among Patty, Carrie, and Mary, we should be able to look after one little baby!" Smiled Eldene. "There are quite a few nursing mothers in the train who I'm sure will help."

No more than thirty minutes had passed when Romy pulled up with the buckboard. Bill and Many Moons were riding with him.

"Ma'am," said Bill as he nodded.

"Howdy, boys, how are you two doing? We haven't seen you for a while," said Eldene.

"Yeah, I reckon it's been a spell, we got supplies at Fort Hall, that way we needn't come all the way back to the train unless we had some dire reason to. The cap'n knows if we ain't reported in for more than a couple of weeks that something is wrong out thar."

"I reckon we'll see you boys at Fort Hall, looks like they have Penny ready to go."

"Little Deeny's blankets and diapers and all are on your wagon seat, I sure do appreciate y'all doin' this for us."

"Just don't you worry none about the baby, she's going to be okay. You take care of Penny, and we'll see you at the Fort."

Eldene walked over to the buckboard to say goodbye to Penny. "Don't you worry none about the baby. You just get yourself taken care of. We all love you, and we'll be prayin' for your recovery."

Penny looked up at Eldene with tears in her eyes and said, "I... I love all of you too!" Eldene can see she is so weak she can barely speak. Everyone watched and waved as they rolled out ahead of the wagon train.

"Dear God, that sweet girl is very, very sick." Sighed Eldene. "I sure hope she is going to be okay."

"Me too," said Mary, "I don't think I have ever seen anyone that sick before."

"I saw my Aunt Mildred that sick a couple of years ago." Eldene hesitated and with a sad look, said poor Aunt Mildred didn't make it. "She passed on after a few days."

"Here, Patty, will you hold little Deeny so I can put her stuff away?" She climbed up into the wagon and made a special place of the baby's things to keep them clean and dry. "Okay, honey, hand me the baby and let's get going!"

"I'll see y'all later," said Romy as he mounted up. "I need to make sure the rest of the train is ready to move on and mention the baby's feeding problem to the other mothers." Then the wagons were rolling again.

Eldene barely heard Romy. Her mind was on Penny. She bowed her head and began to pray. "Lord, I pray that Penny will make it through this terrible sickness. She didn't look well at all, Lord, and she needs your help to get her strength back to fight it off. I ask your help in the name of our precious Lord, Jesus Christ, amen."

Patty was riding close enough to notice her mom was praying for Penny. "Mommy, she is going to be all right. Carrie and Taylor are riding to each wagon, asking people to pray for her."

"That's wonderful, there are a lot of good people on this train."

The next few days were a little hard on Eldene and the other women. Little Deeny seemed to miss her mommy and would not stop crying. She won't eat or drink. There were a couple of other new mothers on the train. They tried to breastfeed her, but she wouldn't do it. She just kept pulling away and crying. They tried a few more times and decided that it wasn't going to work.

"If this baby doesn't eat, she is going to be mighty sick!" Mary exclaimed!

"She hasn't eaten hardly at all in the last three days, and frankly, her constant crying is about to drive me crazy."

"I can understand why," said Eldene as she stoked the campfire. "We need to get her to settle down and eat. She is used to breastfeeding and that awkward nipple on the bottle isn't the same thing to her, I reckon."

"Here, let me try for a while," said Carrie as she took the baby from her mom.

"Okay, she's all yours," said Mary as she sighed with relief. "I've tried everything that I can think of."

Carrie took the baby and the bottle of goat's milk and began walking and singing to little Deeny. Within a few minutes, the baby was sucking on the bottle. "I think she is going to be okay," said Eldene to Mary.

Carrie whispered loudly, "She is eating, and I think she is going to sleep."

"Well, now I reckon you are going to make a very good mommy," said Eldene as she winked at Taylor. Taylor blushed and pulled his hat down as he lowered his head and sipped his coffee.

"Y'all and the next nine wagons are the first to get supplies at Fort Hall for the next leg of the journey. We are going to be there for about two days. We've got to get over that mountain range before snowfall!" exclaimed Romy. "Cap'n Tripper wants to head out each day at daybreak and move on till the sun sets every evening till we get over that mountain range yonder." He pointed to the mountain range in the distance.

"Good grief!" exclaimed Harold. I can barely see that dad-burned far. I reckon we're in for some hard days ahead!"

"Yep, I reckon so," commented Romy, "I sure do reckon so. We'll be coming up on Fort Hall late tomorrow. All y'all will have to be ready early the next morning to get in there and get your supplies so we can get back on the road."

"I reckon we'll be ready," said Harold. I'm getting purty dad-burned tired of looking at these smelly dad-burned mule's butts!" Everyone laughed!

"Yeah, me too." Laughed Taylor. "Especially when they're all gassed up!"

Everyone was guffawing!

"Ew! I always thought that was just your bad breath, Taylor." And she doubled over, laughing!

"Ho, ho, ho, dear little sister, unable to think of anything clever to say, I'll get you for that one when you least expect it," quipped Taylor.

Fort Hall was sitting in a strategic spot on the Snake River. A windy river that meanders through the valleys and canyons and confluences with the Columbia River near a place known as Wallula, meaning "place of many waters" in the Nez Perce language. All were glad to finally reach the fort. Darkness was settling in by the time everyone had finished taking care of the animals and getting camps set up.

"Fort Hall is bigger than I thought it would be," Taylor commented. "I'm anxious to see what it's like on the inside?"

"Me too!" yelled Patty excitedly. "I'm gonna find me a bathtub and take a nice *long* hot bath!"

"I'm sure glad to hear that," said Taylor, "you smell worse than my mule butt breath!" Everyone was laughing at the two of them, knowing a hassle was going to take place.

"*Ooh!*" yelled Patty as she ran toward Taylor and tossed a wet dishrag at him. Taylor ducked and fell over backward and spilled his coffee all over Carrie.

"Ow! That's hot!" screamed Carrie.

"Oops, I'm sorry. Are you okay?"

"I guess I'll live," she said as she burst out laughing.

"I guess we're even now, little sister."

"We'll see about that," quipped Patty! Everyone was laughing at the chain of events!

"Well, folks." Chuckled Harold. "I reckon we'd better turn in for the night afore somebody gets drowned in coffee."

"Yep, I reckon so," said Romy as he walked toward his horse. He was becoming a regular at the Bounder's evening camp. "I'll see y'all bright and early!"

It was still dark when Taylor put the coffeepot on the fire the next morning. You could hear frogs croaking and crickets chirping in the distance.

"This sure is some serious dark around here this morning," he said to himself as he looked at his pocket watch. "Four thirty is just too danged early." He looked up and whispered, "Wow, look at them stars. They look close enough to touch. Maybe I can get one and wrap it up for Carrie." With the mention of her name, he drifted off into deep thought.

Eldene shuffled up to the fire. "It sure enough is dark," she said as she stretched her arms and yawned.

"Whoa, you scared me," said Taylor as he came back to reality.

Patty came over to the fire, rubbing her eyes and yawning. "I hope that coffee is ready and hot, I'm freezing!"

"I'll whip up some biscuits and gravy while you tend to the animals," Eldene told Taylor. "Patty can put on some water for the dishes."

"Okey dokey," said Taylor as he walked toward the mules. "Are you floppy-eared jackasses ready for some eats?"

Dawn was beginning to light up the sky. You could see the hoar frost glistening on the grass blades. The Thompsons came walking up, and Harold asked, "Are y'all about ready to head on over to that dad-burned fort yonder and load up with supplies?"

Chapter 14

On to the Willamette

Fort Hall was bustling with fur traders trading their furs and getting supplies for their departure into the wilderness to get more pelts before winter sets in. The Shoshone-Bannock tribes were trading moccasins made from buffalo hides, artifacts, and other items of use to the trappers and pioneers traveling through.

"The first thing we need to do is find where Penny and Axel are and see how she is doing," said Eldene. "There must be an infirmary here some place."

"Over there, next to the sign that says 'Captains Quarters,'" said Patty, "there is a hospital sign with one of those squiggly things above it. Dr. Bernard had one of them over his door back home in Baltimore."

"Well, I reckon that's it then," said Eldene. "I'll bet Penny is going to be glad to see little Deeny."

"While y'all are checking on Penny, we're going to mosey on over to the supply house and start a loaden' the dad-burned buckboard," said Harold.

Patty and Carrie followed along behind Eldene, saying, "We're comin' with you to see Penny!"

"Me too," said Mary, "we'll catch up to you when we see how she is doin'."

"I reckon I'll go on with Harold," said Taylor.

"I'm a coming with ya," said Randy. "I ain't getting caught between four women."

"I'll swear, youngin'," said Mary with her hands on her hips, "you are soundin' more and more like your dad every day!"

"I reckon I'll take that as a compliment," said Randy, patting Harold on the back.

"We'll catch up with you after we see about Penny," called Eldene.

"Well, all righty then," said Harold. "Let's go, boys."

Eldene, Mary, Patty, and Carrie walked into the hospital.

"We are looking for Penny and Axel Ward," said Eldene to an elderly nurse sitting behind the desk.

"Wait here for just a minute," the nurse said. "I'll fetch the doctor."

In a few minutes, a gentleman appeared in a white jacket and introduced himself. "Hello, I'm Dr. Baxter. The nurse said you are inquiring about Mrs. Ward."

"Yes, we are," said Eldene. "She was traveling with us, and this is her baby girl. Is she well enough to join the wagon train again? I know that she is anxious to see little Deeny."

"I... I'm afraid I have some bad news for you," said Dr. Baxter. "Mrs. Ward passed on about two days ago. She was very sick when she arrived here. We did everything we could, but I'm afraid the pneumonia was too far advanced."

"Oh dear god in heaven," murmured Eldene with tears welling up in her eyes. Sh-she was only eighteen years old. This is just awful."

They were all distraught over the news about Penny.

Eldene turned to Dr. Baxter and asked, "Do you know where her husband, Axel, is?"

"W-well, yes, ma'am. He was so torn up over his wife's passing that he joined the cavalry. There was a troop here for a couple of days. They pulled out yesterday at daybreak."

"Do you know where they are headed?"

"No, ma'am, I don't. The man that runs the fort could probably tell you, though."

"What arrangements have been made for Penny?" asked Eldene, trying to keep calm.

"Mr. Ward said to ask you to take care of the burial. He bought a casket over at the mortuary and paid for everything. They always have a couple made up in advance. You never know when you're going to need one around here. Mrs. Ward's body is being prepared for burial."

"Oh dear god, this is not good at all. Poor Penny," said Patty, not able to hold back her tears. The four women hugged one another and sobbed.

"What about the baby?" Cried Patty. "What's going to happen to her?"

"Well, I reckon we'll just have to take her along with us and make sure she has a good home to grow up in."

"I reckon that's what we are gonna have to do." Sighed Patty, trying to be strong while holding back her tears. Come on, little one," she said as she took the baby from Eldene. "Looks like you are going to be my baby sister now. Let's go get some vittles."

Carrie followed Patty toward the door. "I'll help you with the baby," she said as she wiped the tears from her face.

"I...think... I'll go with the girls," said Mary sadly. "Can you take care of things okay?"

"Sure, go with the girls and help with the baby. I'll catch up with you as soon as I get this taken care of."

Patty saw Taylor and the others over at the mercantile.

"Hey, there you are. Where's Mom?" asked Taylor as he looked around. "How come you still have the baby?"

"Well... Pen... Penny," Patty stammered and began to cry, unable to finish.

Mary put her arms around Patty and told them what had happened to Penny.

"Oh dear god, how's Axel," asked Harold. "We've been keepin' an eye out for him."

"I reckon he was so grieved he couldn't face anyone, so he up and joined the cavalry. They left yesterday at daybreak."

"I guess we must have a baby sister now," said Patty as she cuddled the baby.

Carrie walked over to Taylor. She was obviously shaken. Taylor put his arms around her. "Things are going to be all right. We'll get through this, and God will take care of everything."

The next morning, everyone gathered at the fort cemetery in a fenced area, a short distance from the fort. Reverend Freedman, from the wagon train, was presiding over the ceremony. Most of the people in the first several wagons knew Axel and Penny, so they wanted to be at the funeral.

"Thank you, Reverend Freedman," said Eldene, "for making this a memorable service today. I don't think I would have gotten through it without your words of faith. Penny was like a daughter to me, and it's not easy to lose someone so young and full of life. She was such a good little mother, and we will miss her more than words can say. Thank you again."

"You are very welcome, and if there is anything else I can do to ease your burden, please let me know. You and your family will be in my prayers."

Early next morning, before the sun came up, the wagon train was on the move. They had left the Wards' wagon at the fort. Harold and Mary took their cow, and their mules were put with the wagon train extras.

"It's a bit frosty this morning," said Eldene as she watched Patty taking care of little Deeny. You are going to be a good mother to my grandchildren someday, young lady."

"Not anytime soon, Mommy dear!" said Patty. "I'm thinking ten or twelve years down the road, maybe! I have a lot of things I want to do before I start raising a family. I'm thinking that I might become a nun." She chuckled. "Babies are hard work!"

"I'm thinking that you had better rethink that one, daughter dear," said Eldene, wrinkling her face!

"Just funning with you, Mommy, just funning!"

"Whew," said Eldene as she wiped her brow and laughed. "Are you trying to give your ole mother a heart attack!"

Romy rode up on his paint and yelled, "Cap'n Tripper wants to have a meetin' and some vittles for everyone! We butchered a beef, and he wants y'all to come over to his camp for some relaxation and mountain music! Also he wants to talk to everyone about the trip from here to the Willamette. We are gettin' close to the home stretch!"

"Yahoo, yippee kay yo!" yelled Harold. "That there is some dad-burned good news!"

"We'll be there with bells on," hollered Taylor!

"Oh, I almost forgot," added Romy, "bring whatever you want to have with your steak and a plate and utensils. I'll see y'all in about two hours. I have to let everyone know what's going on!"

"We've got time to bake up some of those potatoes that we picked up at the fort, does that sound okay?"

"Durned tooten' it does," said Randy. "I'll be right back with ours to put in the coals. Yum, yum, yum."

Everyone was eating, dancing, chatting, and having a good time when Captain Tripper stopped the music and announced that he wanted to say something about the rest of the journey West. "All y'all are probably gettin' kinda anxious to see the Willamette Valley by now. We've been on the trail for about five months and have made some good time by having some dang good weather conditions and being able to travel long hours. Y'all know we lost poor little Penny Ward to pneumonia, and her young husband, Axel, joined the cavalry at Fort Hall. Eldene McGrady and her family took on their baby to raise as their own, and I for one think it's very good of them to do that. I know little Deeny will have a right nice upbringing filled with love.

"I have decided to cross the Snake River above where it dumps into the Columbia and travel the south side of the Columbia. This saves us from having to cross the Columbia and could save us a few days. We will be climbing out of the basin before we get to the rapids. When we reach the top, y'all are gonna see somethin' that y'all have never seen before, except maybe in pictures. Y'all are gonna see four of the biggest volcanos in the whole cotton-pickin' world!"

Everyone was yelling and clapping!

"We will be going right around the bottom of one of them. It leads into the Willamette Valley. Oregon City is about three hundred miles from where we are now, so I reckon that puts us there in about twenty more days! We may hit some snow around the big mountain, so y'all be prepared for some cold weather. It rains a lot in the Willamette Valley, so it's always green and beautiful over there. Any questions?"

"Yeah, Cap'n Tripper," called one of the men from the crowd. "Are there any more big rivers to cross afore we git there?"

"We will have to cross the Willamette River and ford the Wy'east and White Rivers and some small tributaries along the way. Once we hit Barlow Road, we'll be okay. Y'all go ahead and finish up y'all's vitals and let's turn in so we can get an early start in the morning. Romy will answer any more questions y'all have. I'll see y'all tomorrow, bright and early!"

"Okay, listen up y'all. Let's burn all the trash and bury the garbage away from the camp a ways so the varmints can't feast on it unless they dig it up. I'll answer y'all's questions while we clean up."

"Only about twenty more days until we can start our new lives! I'm so excited I'm about to burst into a fireworks of happiness!" said Eldene.

"Me too!" yelled Patty excitedly.

"Well, little sister dear, don't pee your pants!"

"Ha, ha, ha! Smarty-pants…oops, I think I just did! Bye, everyone, I'll see you later as she ran toward the wagon. I'll get even with you later, smarty-pants!"

"Don't count on it!" yelled Taylor, laughing!

Everyone was laughing and joking as they cleaned up the camp mess. Romy rode passed and checked each campsite the next morning, as everyone was loading up for the last leg of their journey.

The wagon train moved on at a good pace the next few days. They were at a place where the Snake River and the mighty Columbia collide and caused a lakelike confluence. They had crossed the Snake at the ford near the fort and traveled on the south side of the river. Having traveled this route before, Captain Tripper, being a smart man, knew that although crossing the Columbia was no easy task, by traveling the south side of the Snake and bypassing Hells Canyon, the deepest gorge in the Pacific Northwest, they would save several days of travel time.

Taylor was the first one up the next morning. He did the chores and harnessed the team. He was saddling the horses when he saw a bright flash and heard a clap of thunder. The flash was blinding, and the thunder was deafening!

"Whoa, Barney! Whoa, boy!" said Taylor as he tried to calm Barney.

Eldene and Patty came running to help calm the animals. Socks was having a fit and trying to break loose from her tether. Another blinding flash and loud clap of thunder, and the animals were getting hard to handle.

"Good grief!" yelled Taylor. What in the world is going on? That was almost as close as the last one!"

Another flash and clap of thunder. "That one was a little bit further away. I reckon it's moving on!" yelled Eldene.

"Oh, dear Lord, it's startin' to hail. Just look at the size of them hailstones! They're as big as cherries!" yelled Patty!

"Tie down the animals and get under the wagon before we get stoned to death. These things are beginning to hurt!" hollered Eldene!

Just as they made a beeline for the wagon, the hailstones began coming down so hard that the ground began turning white as the hail got worse. After what seemed like forever, the hail stopped, and the storm began moving on.

"Look at how deep the hail is. I've never seen anything like this. There must be drifts two feet deep out there!" yelped Taylor!

"I reckon I haven't either," said Eldene. "Taylor, honey, you go see if people need help while Patty and I check on our animals and get things together."

"Yes'm," he said as he took off toward the Thompsons' wagon.

"Look over there!" hollered Taylor. "Yesterday that tree was a tall oak, it's been blown apart by that lightning strike, I thought it was awful close. That can't be more than a hundred feet away."

"Oh, heavens," commented Eldene, that's unbelievable!"

"How is that even possible?" said Patty. "That tree was huge, and it is split right down the middle and splintered into a million pieces!" Again in an astonished manner, she said, "How in the world is that even possible?"

"I've seen a dad-burned windmill blown clean out of the ground, and the metal parts were all melted!" yelled Harold as he came walking up to the camp. Confounded lighting can be mighty dad-burned powerful."

"I'll never forget the smell of cow hair burning," said Carrie, "it was sickening!"

"We had to drag them out to the back pasture and let the buzzards and coyotes have them," said Randy.

"Wow, losing three cows at once, that's a lot of beef!" said Eldene.

"A little too well done, though." Laughed Mary.

Romy rode up and told everyone that the wagon train would have to wait for the hail to melt down before they could get started. "Some of those drifts are three or four feet deep, and the ground is covered for a good mile or two."

"I have never seen a storm like that before," said Eldene, "it was pretty crazy."

"As soon as we can head out, we will be running into Barlow Road pretty soon. It's pretty good going after that. There is a toll fee of five dollars for the wagons and ten cents for each animal, but it saves us a week or so in travel time."

Eldene said, "Fine, anything that will get us to our valley faster!"

The wagon train climbed out of the gorge and onto the flats above the Columbia River. The air was crisp and fresh after the big storm, and the sky was cloud-free and blue. "Man alive, you can see forever from up here!" yelled Taylor. "Look at those huge mountains over yonder!"

In the distance, they were able to see four huge mountains, each one like a king overlooking his kingdom and guarding it with his snowcapped knights all around his own forest; each one trying to majestically stand taller than the other. In the distance, there was one taller than all the other mountains that seemed to be claiming his place in the sun, above all the others, as the majestic ruler of all kingdoms.

"It kinda takes your breath away," said Romy. "Those huge mountains are the Lewis and Clark volcanoes. The one we will be goin' around is called Wy'East by the Indians. We know it as Mount Hood, as Lewis and Clark named it. The one to the north of Hood is called Louwala Clough. It means 'smoking mountain.' That one over there is called Klickitat."

"We studied a little about Lewis and Clark in school," said Patty.

"We'll be passing Mount Hood over yonder to the west, right at the base of it. Y'all will be able to tell how big it is. It'll make y'all feel purty danged humble."

"Well, I can hardly wait till we'all get there," said Eldene, mocking Romy's Southern accent. "I jest love the way y'all talk with thet Texican accent." She kissed him on the cheek and hugged him. "I shorely do!"

"Well… I reckon I'm downright happy about that. And that's Texan, not Texican, pretty lady!"

"I reckon I'm happy too." Smiled Eldene!

The Barlow trail was a wide well-traveled road and well worth the toll.

"Look at that funny-looking cloud over Mount Hood!" exclaimed Patty. "It looks like a big hat with no crown, only the brim!"

"There sure is a lot of different kinds of things to see in this country. Everything is so different than Maryland. It's so beautiful and exciting. I can hardly wait to get settled and begin building our new life!"

"Me too, Mom, I'm ready to live in a real house again. My butt is getting pretty darned tired of bouncing around in this saddle and especially on that hard wagon seat!"

"Yeah, the wagon seat is beginning to take the shape of your butt." Chuckled Taylor.

"Ha, ha!" yelled Patty. "Your butt is beginning to make my butt tired, Mr. Smarty-pants!"

"All right, you two, settle down." Laughed Eldene!

Even though the Barlow Road is a good passage over the Cascade, it is a difficult trail. The wagon train wasn't able to circle to corral the animals, so the wagons pulled in close to one another and tethered the animals on rope lines between the trees.

"I reckon this is a better way than having to float down that big river on rafts. I wasn't looking forward to that at all," said Taylor.

"Yeah, I reckon this is a better way. I didn't like that idea either. Look at all this beautiful timber. We will be able to build a good sawmill in this country," said Eldene.

"I'm thinking it might be a pretty good place to raise cattle," stated Romy. "I'm likin' that idea more every day!"

"I reckon I'm gonna like whatever dad-burned heck we do," said Harold. "I'm ready to git off this confounded trail and settle down!"

The next morning was colder than usual, and there was a skiff of snow on the ground. "Brrr," said Taylor as he harnessed up the mules. I... I... I reckon it's time to put on some long johns or something. It's pretty danged chilly this morning."

"Yep, it sure is. I reckon we are getting a taste of mountain air," remarked Eldene.

Romy rode up to the Bounder. "Let's get hooked up and head on out. We want to put as many miles on today as possible. I'm thinkin' we are gonna see more of this white stuff, and we want to get to the valley before that happens!"

"We're almost ready, about ten more minutes," said Taylor.

*****

After a few days of difficult traveling, the wagon train camped in an open meadow, about ten miles to the southwest of Mount Hood. The Willamette Valley and Oregon City were visible from the campsite. Everyone was excited about what they saw.

Romy rode up to the Bounder and yelled, "Yahoo, there it is, folks! What do you think of your new home?"

"That must be Oregon City on that big river down yonder!" exclaimed Eldene.

"Yup, I reckon it is, pretty lady. We'll be pulling in there in two more days!"

"Isn't that the most beautiful sight you have ever seen in your life?" asked Eldene. "We are going to be starting our new adventure in just two more days!"

"The first thing I'm going to do," yelled Patty, "is take a long hot bath!"

"Me too!" yelled Mary and Carrie simultaneously.

"After we get settled in some place, I reckon I will be looking for a land office. I have never seen so much timber. I can hardly wait to get started!"

"Well, I reckon I'll be lookin' for a chapel so we can plan a wedding." Sighed Romy as he winked at Eldene.

Eldene looked at Romy with her big hazel eyes and smiled. "I'm ready for that new life we have been talking about." She put her arm around him and said, "I'm ready to be Mrs. Eldene Ana Childs."

Character Bios

Eldene Ana McGrady: Born April 2, 1813. She is the owner of a dress/fabric shop in Baltimore, Maryland. She is 5'6" tall, nice figure, reddish-auburn silky hair flowing down over her shoulders, hazel-green eyes with a sparkle of life, and a radiant smile with perfectly lined white teeth. She is beautiful, feisty, sassy, and has an Irish temper that flares when provoked. She has an outgoing positive attitude and loves life. She loves adventure and the outdoors. She likes to explore and relishes a good challenge. She has two teen-aged children: Taylor, fifteen, and Patty, fourteen.

Jacob Allen McGrady: Husband, born June 1, 1812. He is 6'2" tall, reddish-brown hair, blue eyes. He is muscular, rugged, and handsome. He is ambitious and active. He owns a company that furnished labor and equipment to load and unload ships. He and Eldene were married when he was twenty years old, and she was seventeen.

Taylor James McGrady: Son, born July 10, 1832. Tall and muscular like his father. He is six feet tall at fifteen years old and still growing. He has features of both parents. He has blue-green eyes, reddish-brown hair. He is good-looking, muscular, happy, funny, rugged, and confident. He has a positive outgoing personality and a good attitude. He has a good relationship with his parents and sister.

Patricia Ana McGrady: Daughter, born June 6, 1833. She was born just eleven months after Taylor. She is pretty and feisty, like her mother. She has auburn hair, hazel eyes. Patty is excited about life and has an outgoing personality. She has a great sense of humor. She is a shapely beautiful young lady and is just beginning to notice boys. She likes school. She is popular and has many friends. She likes being a girl and loves her mother's dress shop. She has a good relationship with her parents and her brother.

James Thomas Sweeny: Father, born September 1, 1793 to immigrant parents from Ireland. He is known as Big Jim, 6'4" tall, with reddish-brown wavy hair, a mustache, and blue eyes. He is in remarkable physical shape and a hard worker. He owns a sawmill and lumber distribution business that he inherited from his parents.

Patricia Ana Sweeny: Mother, born in 1793. She was born to immigrant parents from Ireland. Her parents are still in Ireland. She is devoted to Big Jim and his dreams. She is a very pretty woman in good shape, and she loves to cook.

Catherine Jane O'Leary: Sister, born May 3, 1811. Everyone calls her C J. She has three children and is married to Tom O'Leary, an investment banker. She and Eldene are best friends. She is happy and content to be a wealthy housewife. She's 5'5" tall and has reddish hair and a good shape. She is a pretty proper lady.

John "Tripper" Gerard: Wagon master, born March 8, 1799. He is a rough-looking man, 5'10" tall. He is lean and loud. He chews tobacco and smokes a pipe. He's balding a little and has graying hair. He has a mustache, and his eyebrows stick up like horns. He has a great sense of humor and is strict and decisive. He carries a pistol on his side and a musket across his saddle. His hands are rough, and his legs are bowed slightly from riding a horse for so many years. He is forty-nine years old, and you can tell that he lived every minute of them. He is well liked and trusted to do the right thing by everyone.

Jeromy Childs: Assistant wagon master, born August 12, 1810. He is 6'1" tall. He is thirty-eight years old, lean and strong. He is in excellent physical shape and as tough as they come. He has brown hair, brown eyes, and is very quick-witted. He is fast with a knife and quick with his hands. He carries a pistol on his right hip and a knife on his left. He knows how to fight and is challenged by no one who knows him. He wears a neatly trimmed beard and mustache, and he likes to be clean. He doesn't use tobacco and doesn't like being around smokers and chewers. He is polite to women and is liked by everyone.

Bill Winters: Number 1 scout, born November 5, 1806. He is forty-two years old, six feet tall. He wears his blond-ish-brown hair shoulder-length. He has blue eyes and slightly bucked teeth. He is rugged and tough. He has a leathery type complexion. When he smiles or laughs (which is often), he has vertical lines down his face. He is always joking and friendly in camp. He carries a pistol and a knife and knows how to use both of them. He has a musket in a sheath tied to his saddle. He rides a beautiful well-trained sorrel that he calls Friend. He is a former army scout.

Many Moons: Number 2 scout. He is a full-blooded Navajo Indian from Arizona. He goes by the name Many Moons because he is not sure of his age. He's somewhere around forty. He is six feet tall with long black hair, that he keeps braided, and dark-brown eyes. He and Bill were scouts in the army together and are best friends. He wears buckskin clothes and has a knife strapped to his side and carries a musket. He also carries a bow with a quiver of arrows. He is very crafty and quick. He takes care of his piebald paint with pride.

The Thompson Family: Descendants of Norwegian immigrants, are traveling from Kentucky to Oregon to start a new life as farmers. Harold, the father, born May 1, 1814, is a good-looking man, is 5'10" tall, and tough as they come. Mary, the mother, was born October 12, 1814. 5'3". She has rough skin from being in the sun, working with the soil, but she is a pretty woman. Randal Lee (Randy), the son, was born May 20, 1833. He is tall, 5'10" and still growing. He has dark-brown hair and deep-blue eyes that sparkle with life. He is lean and muscular and full of vim and vigor. Carrie Lou, the daughter, was born July 18, 1832. She is 5'5" with long dark-auburn hair, big brown eyes, and long lashes. Carrie is very intelligent, witty, and has a lot of common sense. She is a very attractive young lady.

Axel and Penny (Penelope) Ward: Axel was born February 27, 1828, and Penny was born March 3, 1829. Penny is three months pregnant and just beginning to show. Axel is 5'9" tall, blond hair, blue eyes. He is lean and strong. He is strong-willed and independent. Penny is 5'1", brown hair, blue eyes. She has a thin shapely frame and is full of life and sass. Their parents were killed in an uprising, and they were rescued by the army and fell in love. They have been married about two years.

There are fifty-six wagons in the train, not including the chuck wagon for the employees, the tack wagon, and the supply wagon. There is a wagon set up with blacksmith tools, horseshoeing, and harness repair, etc.; sixty wagons in all.

Note: Please be advised that the characters and events in this story are strictly from the imagination of the author. They have no historical value, and although some of the events may seem to be authentic, and some of the place names may be real, they did not happen according to historical events.

The End

About the Author

Melvin "Vern" Edwards is a guy who is always ready for a new adventure himself. In this book, he has embarked on many new challenges with unending pragmatic optimism. He's a man who not only loves his family (wife of sixty-two years and five children, grown and multiplyin') but has a great love for the outdoors and life in general.

He joined the navy at the young age of seventeen and married at twenty-one and then spent the next ten-plus years in the Forest Service as a fire control officer and recreation manager. They were glorious years of family camping and skiing. As the forest administration changed, and he would have had to take an office position to stay in the Forest Service, he decided to change his career.

He has lived in or traveled through most of the country he has written about. This story has been with him for a long time. He wishes you as much joy reading this adventure as he has had writing it.